RECKONING OF THE MOUNTAIN MAN

RECKONING OF THE MOUNTAIN MAN

WILLIAM W. JOHNSTONE
AND J.A. JOHNSTONE

PINNACLE BOOKS
Kensington Publishing Corp.
kensingtonbooks.com

PINNACLE BOOKS are published by

Kensington Publishing Corp.
900 Third Avenue
New York, NY 10022

PUBLISHER'S NOTE: Following the death of William W. Johnstone, the Johnstone family is working with a carefully selected writer to organize and complete Mr. Johnstone's outlines and many unfinished manuscripts to create additional novels in all of his series, like The Last Gunfighter, Mountain Man, and Eagles, among others. This novel was inspired by Mr. Johnstone's superb storytelling.

First Pinnacle Books Trade Paperback Printing: November 2026

ISBN: 978-0-7860-5174-8

ISBN: 978-0-7860-5175-5 (ebook)

10 9 8 7 6 5 4 3 2 1

Printed in the United States of America

The authorized representative in the EU for product safety and compliance
is eucomply OU, Parnu mnt 139b-14, Apt 123
Tallinn, Berlin 11317, hello@eucompliancepartner.com.

RECKONING OF THE MOUNTAIN MAN

Chapter 1

The tunes coming from the town hall in Big Rock, Colorado, on this late spring evening were sprightly. What the musicians might lack in talent, they made up for with sheer gusto. The couples swirling around the floor inside the hall, which had been cleared for dancing, seemed to be enjoying themselves.

Smoke Jensen definitely enjoyed having his beautiful wife, Sally, in his arms as they went through the steps of a waltz.

"You're doing very well," she told him. "You must have been practicing."

"You mean I haven't stepped on your feet any, so far," Smoke said.

Sally laughed. "Honestly, Smoke, I don't recall that you've ever stepped on my feet. You've always been a fine dancer. I was just teasing you."

"I guess I'm just naturally graceful," he said with a smile directed down at her lovely face, which was surrounded by waves of thick, lustrous dark hair.

They made an attractive couple, that was for sure. Smoke wasn't classically handsome. His features were too rugged for that. But his face had a clean-cut appeal under his ash-blond hair, and his muscular shoulders were unusually wide. His body had an undeniable aura of tautly leashed power and speed, like that of a mountain lion.

Or like that of a man known to be one of the fastest, deadliest gunfighters west of the Mississippi, which was exactly what Smoke Jensen was.

Most of the time, though, including tonight, he was mighty happy to put aside that reputation and just be a successful rancher and the husband of the former Sally Reynolds.

The daughter of a wealthy family from New England, she had been trying to contribute something to the world by serving as the schoolteacher in the rough frontier town of Bury, Idaho, when they met.

She hadn't known it at the time, but he was there to rain down Colt-flame and death on the men responsible for the killings of several of his loved ones: his father, his brother, his first wife, and their infant son. Those tragedies seemed to have burned the goodness and mercy out of Smoke Jensen, leaving only the need for revenge.

That was what he'd believed at the time, anyway. Over the years since they'd gotten married and established the Sugarloaf ranch, west of Big Rock, Sally had taught him different, taught him that a core of decency, courage, and loyalty remained inside him, and together they had nurtured that core and made him into the kind, decent man he was today.

Kind and decent, but still faster on the draw and more accurate with his guns than just about anybody who had ever ridden down a Western trail.

Smoke wasn't thinking about that tonight. He was just enjoying dancing with his wife and looking forward to visiting with his many friends, most of whom were here in attendance at the town social.

He was even looking forward to drinking some of the punch that was being guarded by several ladies to make sure no mischief-making cowboy tried to spike it.

As the group of guitar-strumming musicians at the front of the room continued playing, someone tapped Smoke on the shoulder. He and Sally paused, and Smoke looked over at a well-dressed, sleekly handsome man somewhat older than him.

"May I cut in?" Louis Longmont inquired.

"I don't know," Smoke said. "Are you planning on stealing my woman away from me?"

Longmont chuckled. "I doubt if the 7th Cavalry could succeed in stealing Sally away from you, Smoke. All I have in mind is a dance."

"Well, if the lady doesn't object, I don't."

"The lady doesn't object," Sally said with a smile of her own.

Smoke handed her over to Longmont, who swept her away with the other dancers. Still smiling, Smoke walked toward the wall on one side of the room where a number of men who weren't dancing were standing around talking to one another.

One of them, also older than Smoke but considerably more weathered than Louis Longmont, grinned and greeted him by saying, "How'd you manage to get away?"

"I wasn't trying to," Smoke told him. "Louis cut in."

Sheriff Monte Carson nodded sagely. "He always did have an eye for the pretty ladies."

Monte and Louis were two of Smoke's staunchest friends. Before Monte had pinned on a star, he had been mostly on the other side of the law, working as a hired gun. In fact, it was one of Smoke's enemies who had brought him to the area before Big Rock even existed. Monte had soon realized that he was on the wrong side of that conflict, however, and had backed Smoke's play instead.

Louis was also noted as a fast gun, but he was a gambler, first and foremost, and had lived a wandering, dangerous life before settling down in Big Rock and opening the town's finest restaurant and saloon.

Both men had fought side by side with Smoke many times. He would trust them with his life, without hesitation. Even more importantly, he would trust them with Sally's life.

"I saw Cal earlier," Monte went on. "He looked mighty down in the mouth."

"That girl he was sweet on wrote to him from back East. I think she must have found another beau and was letting him know. He's been moping around ever since he got that letter from her."

"That Bolton girl? What was her name? Hannah?"

"Susannah," Smoke said.

"That's a shame. Cal hasn't had much luck where gals are concerned, has he? I'd almost say the boy's hoodooed."

"He's young. He'll get over it."

Calvin Woods was one of the hands who worked for Smoke on the Sugarloaf, but he wasn't just one of the crew. He had become almost like a member of the family, along with Smoke's foreman, Pearlie Fontaine. Pearlie regarded Cal sort of like a little brother, and Cal certainly looked up to Pearlie. They were good friends as well as top hands. Smoke figured he couldn't get along without them.

He looked along the wall and spotted both men sipping from cups of punch. Cal looked just as disconsolate as he had been for the past few days, and it appeared that Pearlie was trying to cheer him up without having much luck at it.

Maybe Cal shouldn't have come to town, Smoke mused. Seeing those happy couples swooping around the dance floor might just remind him of the girl he'd lost.

Smoke hoped he wouldn't start any trouble before the night was over, just to let off some steam.

"Dang it, Cal, you've had your heart broke before," Pearlie said as he clapped a hand on his young friend's shoulder. "It stings pretty bad for a spell, but you'll get over it. I'm speakin' from experience, you know."

"Yeah, you're right, I know that," Cal managed to say. "At least Susannah's doing fine, even if she did decide to stay back there where her father's sending her to school. She didn't die or anything. As big a Jonah as I am when it comes to romance, she ought to consider herself lucky she didn't get hit by a bolt of lightning."

"You ain't a Jonah in romance nor nothin' else. It's like breakin' ornery horses. You're gonna get throwed from time to time, and that's just the way it is. And what's the best thing to do when you get throwed?"

"Get right back on the horse," Cal muttered.

"That's right." Pearlie cast a speculative eye across the big room toward the unattached ladies sitting in chairs along the wall on the far side. "And I spy a couple o' likely lookin' fillies right over yonder."

Cal followed Pearlie's gaze and saw two young women sitting by themselves. Both had blond hair, and they looked enough alike that Cal figured they must be sisters. There wasn't enough difference in their ages for them to be mother and daughter. They were both in their twenties, he estimated.

"You're talking about those two blondes?" he asked Pearlie.

"Yep. They're mighty pretty, ain't they?"

"Well, a fella would have to be blind not to see that," Cal grumbled.

"I reckon they must be new in town, too," Pearlie went on. "I don't recollect ever seein' 'em before, do you?"

Cal thought about it and then shook his head.

"We don't know everybody in Big Rock, though. The town's growing all the time."

"Sure it is, but answer me this: If you'd laid eyes on a pair of gals as good-lookin' as those two, you'd remember it, wouldn't you?"

Despite his determination to continue moping, Cal felt his interest perking up.

"I suppose I would," he admitted.

"Well, then, let's go ask 'em to dance."

"I don't know if that's a good idea."

"I ain't suggestin' we ask 'em," Pearlie said as he took hold of Cal's arm in a firm grip. "I'm tellin' you, and I'm your boss, remember?"

"Smoke's my boss," Cal objected, "and anyway, we're not on the ranch right now."

"Maybe not, but I'm still older an' wiser than you, no matter where we are. Come on."

Cal gave up and allowed Pearlie to steer him around the crowd of dancers in the middle of the room. They had to go almost all the way to the entrance to find enough empty space to cross over to the other side.

While they were doing that, the musicians, four guitarists and a chubby man with a big bass fiddle, reached the end of a song. As the dancers paused, the leader of the group stepped up and announced in a loud voice, "We've got a real treat for you folks tonight. You all know Len, here."

He waved at another of the guitar players, a handsome, curly-haired young man who gave the crowd a shy smile.

"He's a good cowhand, but what you might not know is that he's a mighty fine singer, too. Len, step up here and give these folks a song!"

The young man called Len seemed a little reluctant, but he moved up in front of the other musicians and said, "Evenin', folks. If you don't like this, feel free to chuck rocks at me and I'll hush up."

With another shy smile, he strummed the guitar he still held and broke into a lively song about a cowboy from Texas and a beautiful señorita with a red, red rose in her hair. The other musicians briskly accompanied him, and people began dancing again.

Pearlie and Cal reached the far wall and started along it toward the spot where the two attractive blondes were sitting.

"Uh-oh," Pearlie suddenly said. "Looks like a couple other rannies got their sights set on those pretty little mavericks. Hurry up, Cal. We don't want those boys slappin' their brands on 'em before we get a chance to."

Cal saw what had caught his friend's attention. Two men were walking from the back of the hall toward the blondes, and judging by the intent expressions on their faces, they had the same objective as him and Pearlie.

"I know those hombres," Cal said. "They ride for the Three Sevens, don't they?"

"Yeah, maybe, but it don't matter. They ain't cuttin' in ahead of us."

Pearlie tightened his grip on Cal's arm and urged him along at a faster pace. The two cowboys coming from the other direction must have noticed that because they quickened their steps as well. All of them were almost running now.

At that moment, several older ladies inadvertently blocked the path of the pair from the Three Sevens ranch. They had to stop or run into the women, and they were chivalrous enough to throw on the brakes. Both men scowled darkly at the delay, but there was nothing they could do.

That gave Cal and Pearlie time to reach the young women first.

Pearlie put his right arm across his stomach and his left arm behind his back and bowed. Cal thought he looked ridiculous.

"Howdy, ladies," Pearlie greeted the young women. "Or maybe

I ought to say good evenin', since we ain't out on the range. Ain't this just the finest town social you ever did see?"

The older blonde smiled up at him and said, "It's very nice, Mister . . . ?"

"Fontaine, ma'am. Pearlie Fontaine." He put a hand on Cal's shoulder. "And this here is my good friend, Calvin Woods."

"Just Cal is fine," the younger man said with a nod.

"My name is Violet Caldwell," the woman said. "And this is my sister, Daisy."

Violet's hair was shorter and curved fetchingly around her face. Daisy's blond curls tumbled freely around her shoulders. Both wore simple but elegant dresses that displayed their equally elegant figures to fine effect.

"It's a plumb pleasure and an honor to meet you ladies, Miss Caldwell," Pearlie said. "Cal and me, we was hopin' you'd do us the even greater honor of consentin' to have a dance with us—"

Before he could go on, the two cowboys from the Three Sevens spread finally reached the spot, and they definitely didn't look happy.

"You and Woods just mosey along now, Fontaine," one of them said with a scowl. "These ladies are fixin' to dance with Jasper and me."

"Chuck's right," the man called Jasper said. "You two are hornin' in on our range."

Violet Caldwell arched an eyebrow and said in a chilly voice, "Excuse me?"

"Don't pay any attention to him, ma'am," the first cowboy said. He glared at his companion. "A mule kicked him in the head when he was young and he ain't been quite right since."

"Oh, no!" Daisy Caldwell said. "How terrible." She leaned forward and spoke to Jasper slowly and clearly, as if she were talking to a five-year-old, and not a particularly bright one at that. "I'm sure it must have hurt."

Jasper flung out a hand dismissively and said, “Oh, he’s lyin’! I never got kicked in the head by a mule or nothin’ else.” He attempted a smile that probably was supposed to be charming but actually looked a little grotesque. “But I reckon seein’ how pretty you are felt a little like bein’ kicked in the head, ma’am.”

Pearlie said, “You boys might as well just trail your twine, Hendryx. Miss Caldwell and the other Miss Caldwell are gonna dance with me and Cal.”

“We haven’t heard them say that,” the first Three Sevens cowboy responded hotly.

“Well, we got to ’em first.” Pearlie nudged Cal. “Tell these varmints that, Cal.”

Cal ignored the urging and instead said to Daisy, as he held out his hand, “Would you like to have this dance with me, Miss Caldwell?”

As the younger of the sisters, she was only two or three years older than him, Cal thought, close enough to his age so as not to matter.

She laughed and said, “It’s nice to finally be asked politely. Of course I’ll dance with you, Mr. Woods.”

She started to reach up and take Cal’s hand.

Before Daisy could complete the gesture, the first rival cowboy, whose name was Chuck Dade, Cal recalled now, moved in quickly. He grabbed Cal’s shoulder, jerked him around, and threw a punch that crashed solidly against Cal’s jaw.

Chapter 2

During the short break in which the leader of the musicians introduced the young singer to the crowd, Louis Longmont escorted Sally over to where Smoke and Monte Carson stood. The gambler was holding Sally's hand, but it was a friendly gesture, nothing more.

"Thank you for the dance," he told her as they stopped next to Smoke and Monte. He let go of her hand.

"I enjoyed it," Sally said. "You're a very good dancer, Louis."

"I enjoyed it as well."

Sally put her hand on Smoke's arm. "Are you ready to go again?"

"I think I've just about caught my breath," he said. "What about you, though? You didn't get a break."

She laughed. "Oh, don't worry about me. I can dance all night. I grew up attending fancy balls back home. We didn't have cotillions like they do down south, but there was plenty of dancing going on, I assure you."

Smoke linked his arm with hers and said, "Well, in that case, I suppose we should get back out there. The music's already started again."

As they moved onto the dance floor, Smoke overheard Louis ask Monte, "Any trouble tonight?"

"Nope, everything's been peaceful so far. Hope it stays that way."

So did Smoke. He liked to believe that he was a peaceable man, but somehow ruckuses seemed to have a habit of breaking out where he was. Not all the time, of course, but enough so that he had noticed the tendency.

Some men, maybe, were magnets for trouble.

That thought had just gone through his head as he and Sally began to dance again, when a sudden commotion erupted along the wall on the other side of the room. A man yelled and a woman screamed, and as Smoke glanced in that direction, he spotted a knot of men struggling with one another.

And two of them, he realized, were Pearlie and Cal.

The Sugarloaf hands were trading punches with two men who also looked like cowhands. They had slicked themselves up to attend the town social, but they still had the distinctive appearance of men who rode for the brand.

Nor was the fracas confined to those four. As the battle surged back and forth, the battlers bumped into other men, who stumbled and bumped into still other men and, inevitably, offense was taken and fists began to fly. More shouting welled up, drowning out the musicians and young Len, who stubbornly continued playing and singing, anyway.

The ladies who had been sitting near the spot where the brawl broke out scattered like a flock of spooked hens, except for two fair-haired young women in their twenties who hovered near Pearlie and Cal and the two men they were battling.

Smoke and Sally had stopped dancing without hardly getting

started good. Sally clutched Smoke's arm and said, "Oh, my goodness! What have Pearlie and Cal gotten into now?"

"All sorts of trouble, from the looks of it," Smoke replied. He had to make an effort not to smile. Fights often took place at these dances. Cowboys had plenty of rough edges that couldn't help but scrape against one another, especially in a setting where pretty girls and emotions were involved.

"Shouldn't you put a stop to it?"

"It looks like Monte is going to try," Smoke said, "but I'm not sure he'll be able to tamp down this blaze much. There are already too many hombres involved."

The sheriff was wading through the crowd, making his way toward the combatants. Monte yelled for people to get out of his way. The fight was spreading too much, too fast, though. It had almost reached the point where the only thing to do was let the men mixed up in it pound on one another until they ran out of steam.

Smoke watched as Monte, his progress blocked, stopped and drew his gun. He pointed it at the ceiling, but he didn't pull the trigger. A shot might have shocked the brawlers enough to make them stop swinging, but it would put a hole in the ceiling of the town hall, and the members of the Big Rock town council might not look kindly on that.

Smoke chuckled as his old friend, radiating exasperation, pouched the iron and resumed trying to push and shove his way through the crowd.

"It's not funny, Smoke," Sally scolded him. "Somebody could get hurt. It might even be Pearlie or Cal."

"Those two can handle themselves pretty well," Smoke said, "but I suppose you're right. I'll give Monte a hand."

He followed in the lawman's wake. Monte Carson was well-liked and respected in Big Rock, and most folks probably wanted to cooperate with him and get out of the way. It was just that the stampede from the fight had thrown too many people into close proximity and they were jammed up with nowhere to go.

Smoke figured there was one good way to break up that human logjam. He came up behind Leroy Butler, who clerked in Goldstein's Mercantile, and took hold of Leroy under the arms.

"Sorry, Leroy," Smoke said as he picked up the smaller man and turned to set him aside, out of the way. Butler was an inch or two shorter than Smoke and probably weighed thirty pounds less, but Smoke handled him effortlessly, as if he were no more than a child.

The next person blocking Smoke's path was Miss Mary Lou Pendleton. The fortyish spinster let out a high-pitched squeal of surprise when Smoke picked her up and set her aside.

Short, square Mrs. Beulah Stevens was next, but she faced Smoke and pounded pudgy fists against his chest as he moved in on her.

"Don't do it, you brute!" she cried. "Leave me alone!"

Smoke backed up a step and lifted his hands.

"Sorry, Mrs. Stevens," he told her, then turned to take a different route. He had to work hard not to laugh at the sudden look of utter disappointment on the woman's face.

A few moments later, Smoke had cleared a path to Monte's side. Monte had made more progress and had almost reached the knot of fighters. He looked annoyed as he glanced over at Smoke and said, "Wouldn't be a dance if there wasn't a fight or two, I suppose."

"It's pretty common," Smoke agreed.

"I may have to lock up Pearlie and Cal. It looks like they're in the thick of it."

"If they started it, do your duty, Monte. I'll even give you a hand. A night in jail won't hurt those two, and I'll pay their fines in the morning."

"And then take it out of their wages, I hope."

Smoke just grinned. Whether or not he docked the boys' pay would depend on the circumstances. If they hadn't started the ruckus but were only defending themselves, he probably wouldn't worry about it.

Side by side, Smoke and Monte plowed ahead. Smoke had moved the bystanders aside as gently as he could under the circumstances, but he didn't worry about that as he grabbed the collar of a man who was standing toe-to-toe with another fellow as the two of them slugged away at each other. Smoke hauled him backward and slung him to the floor.

Momentum made the second man in that ruckus stumble forward. He sent a looping punch at Smoke's head, probably not even noticing who he was swinging on.

Smoke ducked under the slow, clumsy blow, caught hold of the man around the waist, and lifted him. The man howled in surprise as Smoke dumped him over his shoulder. He hit the floor hard enough to knock the wind out of him and leave him lying there, stunned.

Monte forcibly broke up several fights while Smoke did likewise. The crowd of combatants began to thin out. Smoke saw Pearlie and put a hand on his shoulder.

Pearlie whirled around and started to throw a punch without realizing who had grabbed him. He saw Smoke and stopped short before his fist could land.

"Aw, dang it, Smoke, I'm sorry!" he yelped. "I didn't know it was you."

"Look out!" a man yelled.

Somebody had gotten hold of the punch bowl. Pearlie looked around just in time to get a face full of the bright red stuff as the bowl was dumped over his head. He staggered, sputtering and pawing at his face.

The man who had dumped the punch raised the empty bowl,

evidently intending to bring it crashing down on Pearlie's skull. Smoke stepped forward, said, "Not so fast, mister," and snapped a short punch to the man's jaw.

Smoke's fist didn't travel much more than a foot, but it landed with so much power that the man's feet went out from under him and he flew backward. The punch bowl slipped from his hands and fell to the floor, where it shattered into a million pieces. The sudden crash, plus the threat of broken glass everywhere, made all the men who were still fighting freeze right where they were.

"Nobody move!" Monte Carson bellowed into the shocked silence. "You're all under arrest!"

Pearlie wiped punch out of his eyes and shook it off his fingers. Cal asked him, "Are you all right?"

"Yeah, I reckon. Nobody had gotten around to slippin' any who-hit-John into the punch bowl yet, I reckon. It would've stung a lot more if they had." Pearlie stuck out his tongue and tasted a few drops of the red stiff that trickled down his cheek. "Yep, just pure town social punch."

Monte put his hand on the butt of his gun but didn't draw the revolver as he asked, "Who started this?"

Both cowboys who had been fighting with Pearlie and Cal pointed at the Sugarloaf hands and declared loudly in unison, "They did!"

The older of the two attractive blondes stepped forward and said, "That's not true. It was that man right there who threw the first punch."

She pointed at the stocky, redheaded member of the pair from the Three Sevens.

"Chuck Dade," Monte said ominously. "Is the lady telling the truth?"

Dade glowered but said, "You don't expect me to call a lady a liar, do you, Sheriff? Especially one as pretty as Miss Caldwell here."

"What I expect is the truth," Monte snapped.

Dade scuffed a boot on the floor. Broken glass grated under the sole. He sighed and said with a note of defiance in his voice, "Yeah, I took a swing at Woods. He had it comin', though, hornin' in like him and Fontaine did when they knew good an' well Jasper and me were fixin' to ask these ladies to dance."

Pearlie said, "We got there first and had every right to ask 'em."

Dade and Hendryx jutted out their jaws and clenched their fists. Pearlie and Cal stiffened and returned the angry looks.

"Blast it, settle down," Monte ordered. "If you start that fight up again, I'll see to it that the judge gives you all thirty days in jail!"

The four cowboys relaxed slightly but continued glaring at one another.

Monte turned to look at the crowd and asked, "Is anybody hurt?"

It didn't take long to determine that no serious injuries had resulted from the brawl, only assorted scrapes and bruises.

"Are you really going to arrest all of us, Sheriff?" a townsman asked. "We just got kind of carried away when all the punching and shoving started."

Monte shook his head disgustedly. "I don't have room in my jail for all of you." He turned to look at Pearlie, Cal, Chuck Dade, and Jasper Hendryx. "You four, though, march."

He jerked a thumb over his shoulder toward the door.

Pearlie looked at Smoke and appealed to him. "Smoke, this ain't fair."

"Sorry, boys, it's Monte's decision," Smoke said. "I'm not going to interfere."

Cal said, "That's all right. I didn't much want to come tonight, anyway."

"Speak for yourself," Pearlie said with a snort.

"I am."

Before Monte could march the prisoners out of the town hall, the younger blonde stepped up beside Cal and touched his arm lightly.

"I'm sorry we didn't get to have that dance," she told him. "If we had, I would have cheered you up and made you not regret coming tonight, after all."

The young cowboy looked a little flustered. "Why, thank you, ma'am. I reckon I feel better already."

"Oh, stop with that ma'am business," she said as she gave him a dazzling smile. "My name is Daisy. And you're Cal, you said. I hope we'll see each other again, Cal. My sister and I have just opened a dress shop here in Big Rock."

Pearlie snorted again. "We ain't got much call for visitin' dress shops."

Cal ignored that comment and said, "I'll try to stop by and say hello the next time I'm in town, Miss Caldwell. I mean, Daisy."

She squeezed his arm. "I hope you do."

Daisy's sister said to Pearlie, "You'll be welcome, too, Mr. Fontaine, even though you're not exactly the sort of clientele we expect to do business with in Big Rock."

Pearlie suddenly seemed a little flustered, and that wasn't a common sight. He wiped some hair, wet from the punch dumped on him, away from his forehead and said, "Thank you, ma'am. Miss Violet, I mean. Maybe, uh, next time Cal and me come to town, you and your sister would like to have a piece of pie with us at Lambert's Restaurant. They bake some mighty good pies there."

"Blast it, Sheriff!" Dade exclaimed. "You said they were under arrest like Jasper and me, and you're lettin' 'em stand there and pitch woo at these ladies!"

"Nobody's pitching woo," Monte said. "Come on, let's go, let's go."

A lane opened up in the crowd so he could usher the four

cowboys out of the town hall. He added over his shoulder to Smoke, "Keep an eye on things until I get back from the jail, would you?"

"Sure," Smoke agreed. He didn't know where Monte's deputies were tonight, but he was happy to fill in.

Sally had joined him by now. She smiled at the two blondes and said, "Hello, ladies. Let me introduce myself and welcome you to Big Rock. I'm Sally Jensen. This is my husband, Smoke. Did I hear you say you'd just opened a new dress shop?"

"That's right, Mrs. Jensen," the older one said. "I'm Violet Caldwell. This is my sister, Daisy."

Sally guided the blondes away from the scene of battle and began introducing them to some of the other women in the crowd. Soon there was a whole group of them chattering happily among themselves.

While Sally was doing that, Smoke told a couple of the other Sugarloaf hands who were in attendance at the social to find some brooms and mops and start cleaning up the mess left behind by the spilled punch and broken bowl. As the cowboys got busy with that chore, Smoke and Louis Longmont righted the chairs that had been overturned in the scuffle and lined them up again.

"With Sally taking them under her wing, the Caldwell sisters will be respected members of the community in no time," Louis commented. "They seem to have almost reached that point already."

"She's good at making folks feel welcome," Smoke agreed.

"I suspect the young ladies will be quite popular among the unattached young men in these parts."

Smoke laughed and said, "That's a sure bet."

A short time later, things had been cleaned up and put back in order. Monte Carson returned from locking up the four cowboys, and the dance resumed. Instead of another song from Len, the group of musicians played a fast number that had couples moving around the floor in brisk fashion. Everybody wanted to put the trouble behind them and concentrate on enjoying the rest of the evening.

That wasn't the case everywhere in the vicinity of Big Rock on this evening, however.

Chapter 3

Twenty miles east of the settlement, a round water tank stood on sturdy legs next to the railroad tracks, looming in the moonlight. It looked like some sort of monster that might start stomping around and crushing anything unlucky enough to get in its way, including fellows who might have had just a wee bit too much to drink, such as Hobie Del Mar.

Hobie was sitting on the eight-by-ten-covered platform in front of the little flag-stop shack across the tracks from the water tank. He had his back propped against the building wall and a half-empty bottle of whiskey cradled in his lap. An empty bottle lay on its side not far from him.

Hobie squinted up at the large, round tank and tried to decide if it had moved. He didn't think it had, but you never could tell. More than once in his life, he had known supposedly inanimate objects to scurry around and wind up in places that weren't right. He tripped over pieces of furniture all the time, in fact. If an overstuffed davenport could move by itself, then so could a water tank.

The whiskey in the bottle gurgled as Hobie took another long swallow from it. The night was quiet and peaceful. A breeze with a welcome hint of coolness to it swept across the prairie and rippled the grass.

The swaybacked horse tied to the post next to the platform nickered and shifted restlessly. At the top of that post was the arm-and-flag arrangement that could be raised to let train engineers know a passenger was waiting to board.

The flag was down now. Hobie had no interest in getting on a train. He was fine right where he was. The building, which held only a desk, a chair, and a telegraph key, was dark and empty at the moment. Hobie could sit here and drink in peace. Unless, of course, that dang water tank started walking around.

The elderly nag tied to the post was the most valuable thing Hobie owned, or was likely to ever own. In recent weeks, he had been working as the cook's helper on the Flying M spread, south of here, until the stove-up old cowboy who handled the cooking chores had gotten fed up with his drinking and run him off earlier that evening.

Hobie had thrown his well-worn saddle on the horse, grabbed the two bottles he had stashed in a hole under the bunkhouse, and rode off with the old-timer yelling curses after him.

It wasn't like he'd never been fired before, he consoled himself. He'd had plenty of jobs and could always get another one.

But that was a problem for tomorrow's Hobie. Tonight's Hobie was going to finish off the second bottle and then maybe doze for a spell, although he couldn't allow himself to sleep too soundly because he had to keep an eye on that water tank.

He was about to lift the bottle to his mouth again when he heard the hoofbeats.

In Hobie's muddled state, he couldn't tell where the sounds were coming from at first, but as they grew louder he figured out that they originated north of the tracks, the side the water tank was on. The riders were coming closer.

Maybe they planned to flag down the train. Was there a train coming through tonight? Hobie asked himself that question but didn't know the answer. Train schedules were a challenge for him, even when he hadn't been drinking.

Or maybe those horsebackers were just headed south for some reason and would ride right on past the tank and the shack when they got here.

Alarm jolted through Hobie as a terrible thought occurred to him. Maybe they were coming to steal his whiskey!

He had to prevent that at all costs, and he knew of one surefire way to do it.

He tilted the bottle to his lips, swallowed enthusiastically, and didn't stop until the last drop of the fiery stuff had trickled down his throat.

Then he lowered the bottle to the platform and let out a long "Ahhhh" of satisfaction, followed immediately by the realization that he didn't have any more booze. It was a situation sad enough to bring tears to his eyes.

He didn't cry for long because a few moments later, a dozen men on horseback swept up to the flag stop. The cloud of dust kicked up by their horses' hooves swirled across the tracks, stung Hobie's eyes, and tickled his nose. He struggled not to sneeze because even in his inebriated state, he sensed it was best not to announce his presence to a bunch of hombres he didn't know. At least, not until he figured out what they were doing here.

Unmoving, blending into the shadows cast by the awning over the platform, he watched as the men dismounted. Some of them began moving around the thick wooden legs holding up the water tank. Others, carrying rifles, walked up and down the tracks in both directions, appearing to be looking around.

One man stood off to the side. A sudden flash of orange lit up his face under the brim of his hat. He had struck a match, Hobie realized, and was using it to light a long, thin cigar clenched between his teeth. He was only about thirty feet from where Hobie sat. The hard, smooth-shaven planes of his face were clearly visible to the man on the platform.

The dying match traced a little arc in the air as the man flipped it away.

"Hey, Linc," one of the other men called to him. "Somebody left a horse tied here."

Hobie bit back a groan. These odd circumstances were struggling to dispel the whiskey fumes cloaking his brain, making it hard for him to think straight. He had forgotten all about his horse standing there in the open. He should have gotten it and taken it around back of the building.

Even better, he should have climbed into the saddle and lit a shuck out of here. But it was too late for that now.

"Maybe somebody left the nag here for somebody else to pick up."

The man called Linc took a deep drag on the cigar, causing the tip to glow brightly enough to illuminate his face again for a second. Then he said, "That's not very likely. Whoever tied it to that post is probably still around here somewhere. Find him."

A couple of the riflemen crossed the tracks and walked toward the shack.

Hobie heard a low rumble in the distance. That was a train approaching from the east, he realized. So one was coming through tonight, after all. Was it going to stop to take on water? Sometimes they did, sometimes they didn't. It all depended on how much they had in their boiler, and Hobie had no way of knowing that. The train might just roll on west to Big Rock.

Linc turned his head to look at the men now working at something under the tank and called to them, "Get those charges set. The train'll be here in a few minutes."

Charges? *Charges?* As in dynamite charges?

Hobie heard a throbbing, booming noise, but it wasn't explosives going off. No, that rhythmic racket was his own pulse hammering inside his head. These men were going to blow up the water tank, and the only reason for them to do that would be to stop the train, and the only reason to stop the train was to rob it. They were outlaws, plain and simple, and they wouldn't want any witnesses around, not even harmless drunks.

He had to get out of there.

His only chance was to make a dash for his horse, leap into the saddle, and gallop off before they could stop him. Maybe they wouldn't come after him since the train was almost here. They might not have time for pursuit. He steeled himself, tensing his muscles in preparation to make his move.

He'd have to jerk the reins loose from the post, too, he reminded himself. If he didn't do that, he wasn't going anywhere.

The riflemen were almost there. No more time.

In his mind, Hobie sprang gracefully to his feet. In reality, he hoisted himself slowly and clumsily and fell back against the wall behind him.

Hearing that thud, Linc pivoted toward him. The man's hand dropped to his hip, came up with a gun in it. Flame lanced from the muzzle, an orange gash in the darkness.

A sledgehammer slammed into Hobie's midsection, doubled him over, and knocked him backward. He hit the wall again and slid down it until he was in almost exactly the same position he'd been in before the men rode up. His foot struck one of the empty bottles and sent it spinning away until it reached the end of the platform and fell off, landing on the ground with a soft plop.

Hobie had never hurt this bad in his whole life, not even when he fell off his horse and landed in a clump of cactus. The pain filled him from head to toe.

The two riflemen jumped onto the platform. One of them snapped a lucifer to life and held it so the glare spilled over Hobie.

"You got him, Linc! Right in the belly!"

Linc slid his gun back in its holster and asked, "Who is it?"

"No idea. Looks like some saddle tramp. There's an empty whiskey bottle beside him. Must've been just sittin' here drinkin'."

"Does he have a gun on him?"

"Don't see one. Wait a minute. Cover him, Tupelo."

Hands patted at Hobie's body. He barely felt them. Sour bitterness consumed him. Even when he'd been young and sober, he never would have been able to pull off something like the getaway he had just tried.

He'd been a dead man as soon as those hombres rode up.

Then again, maybe he'd been a dead man for a long time.

"No gun on him, Linc. Not even a knife. He's harmless, and he ain't long for this world. Should we go ahead and finish him off?"

An icy chuckle came from Linc. "No, let him be. No need to waste a bullet. Maybe he'll live long enough to see a spectacular finish."

The two men left Hobie sitting there with blood filling his lap. It was a fitting end, he supposed. He wasn't even worth a few ounces of owlhoot lead to finish him off.

A locomotive whistle shrilled. The rumble along the tracks was louder now. The train was bearing down on the flag stop, and it didn't seem to be slowing any. It wasn't going to be stopping to take on water.

Men and horses drew back from the tank. They untied Hobie's mount and took it with them. No point in wasting a horse, even a sorry one, on a dead man.

One outlaw remained behind. He bent over, another match flared, sparks flew and danced in the shadows. The man turned and ran as hard as he could.

The night came apart in flame and noise. The wave of force from the explosion slammed across the tracks and into the building. It felt like a giant hand crashing into Hobie and pressing him back against the wall. His eyes and mouth opened wide of their own accord. The blast seemed to have knocked the pain out of him. He didn't feel it anymore, didn't feel much of anything, although he was still conscious.

The outlaws had blown the two legs closest to the tracks. Without their support, the tank shuddered and leaned and tipped forward. It was *moving*! The son of a gun was moving, just as Hobie had feared it would.

The whole thing toppled across the tracks and burst open, sending water flooding everywhere. The beam from the locomotive's headlight lanced across the torrent. The engineer saw what was happening and threw on the brakes. They screamed like banshees, and the train shuddered all along its length, from the cowcatcher to the caboose.

But it was too late for the train, just like it was too late for Hobie Del Mar. The locomotive struck the wreckage of the water tank and jumped the tracks, and the other cars followed suit. Twisting, turning, buckling, the coal tender swept over the spot where the shack had stood a second earlier, crushing it to splinters and wiping out all but faint traces of it.

Just like it did to Hobie.

Chapter 4

Monte Carson was at his desk in the sheriff's office, idly going through a new stack of wanted posters he'd picked up at the post office a short time earlier. If he didn't come across anything interesting, he would add them to the multitude of such notices already stuffed in a desk drawer.

Earlier, Smoke had stopped by and paid the ten-dollar fines that the justice of the peace had assessed on Pearlie and Cal. Chuck Dade and Jasper Hendryx had ponied up their own fines. All of the prisoners had had to spend the night behind bars and wait for court to convene this morning before their fines were set.

The cell block was empty now, Big Rock was quiet, and Monte didn't have anything else to do except look through the reward dodgers. So the distraction was a welcome one when a young man opened the door and hurried into the office.

Monte recognized the bow-tie-wearing youngster and said, "Morning, Eddie. Something wrong? You seem to be in kind of a rush."

"Mr. Williams sent me to fetch you, Sheriff," replied Eddie, who worked as a messenger for Western Union. He delivered telegrams to folks in Big Rock and sometimes on the surrounding ranches, and he was also a telegrapher-in-training.

Monte set the wanted posters aside and stood up. "Is it something urgent?" he asked.

"I don't know, sir. Mr. Williams didn't tell me. He seemed worried about something, though, and sent me to come and get you."

Monte came out from behind the desk. Coe Williams was the current manager of the Western Union office inside the railroad depot. Monte didn't know him all that well, but he seemed like a sensible enough fellow, not given to getting spooked easily. If he was worried about something, it would probably be worthwhile to check it out.

"Let's go see about it," he said to Eddie as he snagged his hat from a hook beside the door.

Big Rock's main street was busy this morning. Women doing their shopping strolled along the boardwalks. Horses and wagons were tied at the hitch rails. A buggy rolled down the street, carrying the local sawbones, Dr. Colton Spaulding, on a call.

The town was bustling but peaceful, and that was the way Monte liked to see it. While he wasn't an old man, he had enough hard years behind him that he didn't mind taking it easy some of the time.

As that thought went through his mind, something stirred inside him. An instinctive warning, maybe, not to get too accustomed to peace and quiet?

Coe Williams was a slender man around forty, with thinning brown hair and a pair of rimless spectacles perched on his nose. He wore a bow tie, which was probably why young Eddie had begun sporting one. When Monte came into the office, he looked up and said, "Sheriff, I'm glad to see you. I hated to bother you."

"Don't worry about that," Monte told him. "If something's wrong, I want to know about it."

"That's just it, I don't know what's wrong. But the westbound train that was supposed to come through last night never arrived. I had inquiries about it from the station at Red Cliff waiting on my desk when I came in this morning. Lester, the overnight man here, took them. He tried to wire the next station to the east but couldn't get a message through."

Monte thumbed back his hat and frowned. "Does that mean the line's down somewhere between here and there?"

"That's the most likely explanation. As for the westbound not showing up, there are all sorts of things that could have happened to delay it. Mechanical breakdowns, damaged tracks, that kind of problem."

"But the train being late and the telegraph line being out are bound to be connected, aren't they?"

"They certainly could be, but coincidences do happen, I suppose."

"Why am I just hearing about this now?" Monte asked.

"No one wanted to get ahead of themselves, Sheriff. If it was five years ago, I might have thought that Indians pulled down the wire and stopped the train, but from what I've heard, there hasn't been any trouble like that around here lately. I'm new to the area myself, you know."

Monte rubbed his chin, still frowning in thought. "Maybe I'll take a ride out the tracks a ways and see what I can see," he said.

Williams nodded and looked relieved. "I hoped you'd say that, Sheriff. But I don't know what to hope you'll find. If it's just some minor problem, I'll feel like I shouldn't have bothered the law with it. But I wouldn't want to wish serious trouble on the railroad, or on Western Union, just to justify my concern."

"It's better to find out and know for sure," Monte told him.

The sheriff headed for Patterson's Livery Stable, where he told the hostler who was working to saddle his buckskin, the horse Monte considered his most dependable mount. Monte would have thrown the hull on the horse himself, but while the stableman was doing that, he returned to his office to get his Winchester and a pocketful of cartridges.

He didn't know exactly what he was going to find out there, so he wanted to be prepared for trouble if that was what he ran into.

He thought about stopping at Longmont's on his way out of town to see if Louis would like to go with him, but he discarded that idea. Whatever was out there, Monte was confident he could handle it.

The railroad tracks ran mostly east from Big Rock but curved a little to the south as they went along. Thickly wooded hills stretched to the north and south, with broad, grassy valleys between them. Those hills rolled eastward toward the snowcapped peaks of the Front Range, beyond which lay Denver and the seemingly endless plains. In the clear, high country air, Pikes Peak was often visible to the southeast as Monte rode alongside the tracks winding through the hills.

Everything seemed fine as the miles fell behind him. The tracks and roadbed were in good shape, and the telegraph poles and wire appeared perfectly normal. He began debating with himself as to how far he should go before turning around and heading back to the settlement.

Then he followed the tracks between two hills and had a good view out into the next broad valley. Monte caught his breath and drew back on the reins in surprise at what he saw.

A couple of miles away, a locomotive sat with smoke and steam puffing from its diamond-shaped stack. A number of boxcars and flatcars, as well as a coal tender, were attached behind it, but no passenger cars. This wasn't a regular train but more likely a work train.

Scattered along the ruined tracks in front of that locomotive were more than a dozen train cars, all of them derailed, most of them toppled completely onto their sides. Others leaned crazily. Some had burned.

At the front of that swath of destruction lay the locomotive that had pulled the wrecked cars, twisted and distorted by the metal-buckling crash of its derailment.

Monte now knew why the westbound had never reached Big Rock.

Although he was still too far away to make out the details, he knew a wreck like that would have taken out some of the telegraph poles and snapped the lines, too. That was why no messages were getting through.

Men scurried everywhere around the devastation. At this distance, they looked like little more than ants, but Monte knew that would be a work crew, probably sent out from Denver or Leadville. They would have to clear away the debris from the catastrophe and repair the rails before traffic could resume along the line.

Monte sat there for a moment, hands crossed on the saddle horn, pondering whether to turn around and head back to Big Rock with the bad news or ride down there and see if he could find out more about what had happened. He knew he couldn't help repair the damage, but he wanted to know what caused it.

Reaching a decision, he nudged his horse into motion and rode toward the scene of the awful wreck.

When he was within a couple of hundred yards, someone saw him coming and spread the word. Several men carrying rifles walked out to meet him.

Monte slowed his horse as he spotted several blanket-covered shapes lying on the ground, off to one side. Grim lines appeared on his face. He had seen too many shrouded corpses not to recognize what he was looking at.

The men with rifles stopped and waited for him to come closer. When twenty feet separated them, Monte reined in.

"Sheriff Carson, I didn't expect to see you out here," the man who was slightly in the lead called to him. He was a burly, barrel-chested man of middle age, with gray hair and shaggy eyebrows and a mustache of the same shade.

Monte recognized the man as Ward Calhoun, the superintendent in charge of this district of the railroad. His office was in Denver, and he was usually dressed in fine suits, which looked slightly out of place on him because he'd started as a section hand and worked his way up to a position where he ran a good chunk of the rail line.

Today he wore rough workingman's clothes like the others and seemed more at home in them, although the marks of his reaction to this tragedy were stamped on his face.

Monte nodded and said, "Howdy, Mr. Calhoun. Folks in Big Rock were worried because the westbound never made it through last night and the telegraph line is dead. I can see why, now."

Calhoun lowered his rifle, sighed, and motioned to the men who had come with him.

"You fellas go on back to work," he told them. "I'll talk to the sheriff."

The men returned to their duties as Monte swung down from the saddle. He stood there holding the buckskin's reins as Calhoun walked up to him.

Monte asked the most important question first. "How many people were killed?"

"Only four."

Monte raised an eyebrow in surprise.

"I know," Calhoun said. "From the way it looks, you'd think it would be a lot worse than that, wouldn't you? But we were really lucky. There were only a few passengers. One of them died of a broken neck, and some others are hurt pretty bad, but we could have lost more of them. We still might, if some of the injured don't pull through."

"Who else didn't make it?"

"The engineer and the fireman never had a chance. You know them. *Knew* them. Dig Webster and Ben Coates."

Monte made a face. He knew the two men, all right. They were regular members of the crew on this run.

"And the express messenger was killed," Calhoun went on. "But here's the thing: He didn't die in the wreck. He was shot."

Monte stiffened and repeated, "Shot!"

"Yeah. Two bullets in the chest. You know what that means."

Monte surveyed the destruction with a look on his face that blended sickness and anger.

"This wasn't an accident," he said.

Calhoun shook his head. "Nope, it sure wasn't. There used to be a flag stop and a water tank here, although you can't really tell that now."

"What happened?"

"The best I can figure it, somebody blew up the legs of the water tank and toppled it over on the tracks." Calhoun tugged on one end of his mustache, a habit he had when he was thinking, Monte knew. "I'm just guessing, mind you, but I don't figure whoever did this intended for the train to derail. It seems more likely to me they tried to block the tracks with the water tank to make the train stop, and then they'd take over the cab and go after the safe in the express car."

"Was there much in the safe?"

Calhoun was the one who made a face now. "Fifteen thousand dollars."

Monte let out a low, impressed whistle and then said, "This was a flag stop. Why didn't they just raise the flag, stop the train that way, and then move in?"

"I couldn't tell you," Calhoun replied with a shake of his head. "Maybe they just wanted to do something big and dramatic. Some outlaws like to put on a show."

"That's true. If they blew up the water tank, you think they mistimed the charges so that Webster didn't have enough room to stop?"

Calhoun shrugged. "It could have happened that way, or there might have been some other reason the train couldn't stop in time. If Webster and Coates had survived, I would have asked them. But as it is . . ."

His voice trailed off and he shook his head again.

"Well, this is just terrible," Monte said. "Is there anything I can do to help, Ward?"

"No, the injured folks have already been taken back to St. Vincent's Hospital in Leadville. If need be, some of them can be sent on to Denver. I'm sorry, but it's going to take at least a couple of days for us to clean things up enough to repair the tracks. Until then, there won't be any trains getting through either way. The same thing's true about the telegraph. I've been told Western Union has a crew on the way to put up new poles and string more wire, but it'll be a day or two before it's working again." Calhoun pointed over his shoulder with his thumb. "We tied in to the line where it's still standing about a quarter of a mile that way. If anybody in Big Rock has an urgent message that has to get through, they can ride out here and we'll send it, but it had better be important."

"I imagine most folks can wait for regular service to start up again. Probably all of them, actually." Monte pounded his right fist into his left palm and went on, "Blast it, Ward, I sure hate to see this. Maybe the owlhoots responsible for it didn't mean for it to be this bad, but innocent people died, anyway. Did you see any tracks they might have left?"

"No, but I wasn't looking for them," Calhoun said. "I'm no tracker, and anyway, I've had my hands pretty full with other things."

"Of course you did. I didn't mean any offense. Do you mind if I take a look around?"

Calhoun waved a hand at the devastation. "Help yourself; just be careful. We don't need anybody else getting hurt. Do you think you can follow the varmints who did this?"

"I don't know, but it won't hurt to scout around some."

Monte climbed back into the saddle and set out to ride a wide circle around the scene of the derailment and crash. Any bunch of owlhoots that would set out to stop and hold up a train had to be pretty good-sized. Half a dozen men, anyway, more likely a dozen or more. It hadn't rained since last night, so he hoped he would be able to find their tracks.

Even if he couldn't, he knew somebody who was better at such things than he was who wouldn't mind lending a hand.

Chapter 5

Pearlie and Cal didn't have much to say for themselves during the ride from Big Rock back to the Sugarloaf.

At one point, Pearlie announced, "I'm gonna pay you back what you had to give the justice o' the peace for my fine, Smoke. You won't even have to take it outta my wages. I got that much dinero stashed in my war bag."

"I'm afraid I don't have it," Cal said. "I'll work off the debt, though, Smoke, you can count on that."

"I'm not worried about it, either one of you," Smoke assured them. "I know you're both good for it. I'd tell you just to forget about it, but—"

"Not hardly," Pearlie broke in, his back and his voice both stiff. "We pay our debts, don't we, Cal?"

"We sure do," the young cowboy agreed.

"And I know that," Smoke said, "so as I was about to say, I won't even suggest it." He chuckled. "Although, to be honest, it's almost worth it for the example you've set."

"Example?" Pearlie repeated in surprise. "What in blazes are you talkin' about?"

"I like knowing that I'm an old married man and don't have to worry about fighting over pretty girls anymore."

"I'm older than you are, dadgum it," Pearlie muttered. "Anyway, I still say it ain't no ways fair the judge fined us all the same. Chuck Wade and Jasper Hendryx are the ones who horned in where they didn't belong, and it was Wade who threw the first punch. Ever'-body knows that."

"Judge Buchanan was just trying to be fair and not favor one spread over another. I can understand why he did that. Jack Brodie over at the Three Sevens wouldn't by happy about it if his men were fined and you weren't."

"Yeah, I reckon. That don't mean I have to like it, though, and I don't give a hoot whether Jack Brodie's happy or not. I s'pose it's a good thing to get along with your neighbors, though."

"I've always thought so," Smoke said.

The three of them fell silent again, and that quiet lasted until they reached the ranch. As soon as the horses were put up, the members of the crew who were on hand and not out on the range promptly began hoorawing Pearlie and Cal about spending the night in the calaboose.

They all went into the bunkhouse while Smoke headed for the main house. He found Sally in the kitchen preparing the midday meal.

"Did you liberate our wayward lambs from their captivity?" she asked when Smoke came up behind her and slipped his arms around her waist.

"Yep, they're home, although I'm not sure it would be a good idea to let Pearlie hear you refer to him as a lamb. He's in a surly mood. More like a bear."

"What about Cal?"

"He didn't have much to say. I don't know if he's still thinking about Susannah Bolton or if his mind is focused more on that younger Caldwell sister."

"Violet and Daisy are both very sweet," Sally said as she leaned back in Smoke's embrace, clearly enjoying having his arms around her. "I'm going to have to pay a visit to their shop very soon and see just how good they are at dressmaking."

"Are you planning on buying a few new dresses?"

"I just might," she said. "Do you have any objection to that?"

"Nope," Smoke said. "I'm sure they'll look mighty good on you, and they'll look good coming off of you, too."

Sally laughed. "Smoke, you're incorrigible."

"Me? No, you've got that wrong. I'm an old married man, all settled down."

She turned her head to look at him from the corner of her eye. "Are you sure you want to make that statement?" she asked. "Because if you're an old married man, that would make me an old married woman, and I don't think I'd appreciate being referred to that way."

"Oh, no, that's not necessarily the case. Just because I'm old and you're married to me, that doesn't make you old, too." He cocked his head to the side. "I'm not likely to win this argument, am I?"

"We're not arguing, we're just talking. And no, you're not likely to."

"We'll leave it at this, then. You should pay a visit to the Caldwell sisters' shop real soon and buy whatever you want, and I'll love it."

"That's better," she said. She turned in his arms to face him, rested a flour-dusted hand on his cheek for a second, and went on, "Now, let me finish this if you want fresh biscuits with dinner."

Smoke bent his head and gave her a quick kiss. "Sounds good to me."

* * *

Late that afternoon, Monte Carson rode out to the Sugarloaf. Smoke warmly welcomed his old friend, even though he had seen Monte in Big Rock less than twenty-four hours earlier.

Smoke could tell right away that something was wrong. Monte greeted them pleasantly enough as Sally brought lemonade and the three of them sat in wicker chairs on the ranch house's front porch, but Smoke saw the troubled look in the lawman's eyes.

"Did something happen in Big Rock?" he asked.

Monte shook his head and said, "Not in town, but something did happen. You know that flag stop on the railroad about twenty miles east?"

"Sure. I haven't been over that way in a while, but I recall seeing it."

"Well, last night somebody blew up the water tank there and caused the westbound train to derail and crash."

"Oh, no!" Sally said. "Were many people hurt?"

"Four killed, and more than a dozen folks injured, some of them seriously," Monte said. "I rode out there today and had a look. It was mighty bad."

Smoke leaned forward, the glass of lemonade on the little table beside him forgotten for the moment.

"You said somebody blew up the water tank. You mean outlaws, don't you?"

"That's right. They gunned down the express messenger and looted fifteen thousand dollars from the safe in the express car."

"That's terrible," Sally murmured. "The whole thing, not just the robbery."

Monte nodded. "I knew what you meant, and I agree with you. Ward Calhoun, the district superintendent, was out there at the scene, and I talked to him. He's not convinced that whoever did it actually intended to wreck the train. He thinks they just meant to stop it and hold it up, but that's not what happened."

"Were you able to pick up their trail?" Smoke asked.

Monte chuckled, but the sound held no genuine humor.

"I tried," he said, "but I didn't have much luck. I found some tracks that might belong to them, but they petered out after I followed them north a ways." He paused. "You know what I'm hoping, Smoke, what I've come to ask you."

"Sure," Smoke said, nodding. "I'll ride out there with you tomorrow, and we'll take a look. Meet you in Big Rock at first light?"

"That'll be fine. You might want to bring along Pearlie and Cal and a few more of your crew, too."

"So if we run those varmints to ground, we'd have a chance to round them up?"

"That's what I'm thinking," Monte said. "Although after the stunt they pulled, I don't care as much as I usually would about bringing them in alive. They could have killed a dozen people, easy. Maybe more."

"Whatever happens," Smoke said, "it sounds like they'll have it coming to them."

Sally invited Monte to stay for supper, but he graciously declined and headed back to Big Rock.

"Monte looked tired," she commented to Smoke after the sheriff was gone.

"He's lived through a lot of violence in his life," Smoke said, "but it never gets much easier to deal with, especially when innocent people were killed."

"The gang that wrecked that train sounds particularly vicious. You'll be careful going after them, won't you, Smoke?"

"I'm always careful," he assured her with a grin, which didn't seem to comfort her much at all. She had known him long enough to be well aware that when it came to the pursuit of evildoers, not much slowed him down.

And to be honest, she wouldn't have really wanted it any other way.

After supper, Smoke went out to the bunkhouse and told the hands about the news Monte had brought. All of them were quick to volunteer to go along the next day and help track down the outlaws responsible for the atrocity. Smoke picked out half a dozen men along with Pearlie and Cal, and told them to be ready to ride to Big Rock before dawn the next morning.

Sometime after midnight, however, as Smoke slept peacefully next to Sally in their room on the second floor of the ranch house, a huge boom jolted him out of his slumber. He sat up, his hand reaching automatically for the Colt .45 lying on the small table beside the bed. He had no idea what had blown up, but all his instincts were kicking in, preparing him to fight back.

The next instant, a bright flash lit up the room and another loud crash shook the house a little. Smoke heard a loud rushing noise and realized what was going on.

Sally was awake, too. She sat up in bed and said, "Was that thunder?"

"Yeah," Smoke said, "and it sounds like it's pouring down rain outside, too."

Lightning flashed again, close enough that Smoke could hear it sizzle and crackle, and thunder rolled over the valley once more. When the fingers of electricity clawing across the nighttime sky lit up the bedroom windows, he saw the sheets of rain lashing against the glass.

"If it's pouring down rain like this where that trainwreck happened, it'll wash away all the tracks the outlaws left, won't it?" Sally asked.

"Yeah, it'll ruin any chance of following their trail, that's for sure. But that's more than twenty-five miles from here. Just because it's storming like this on the Sugarloaf doesn't mean it's raining there, too."

Smoke knew he was right about that, so there was some hope left to cling to. They probably wouldn't know for sure until they rode out there, though.

The fierce storm continued through the night, not stopping until the gray of impending dawn crept across the landscape. Smoke was restless after being jolted out of sleep like that. He had dozed a little now and then but never really settled down again, so he was tired when he got up and started coffee brewing in the kitchen. Sally was still asleep, and he was thankful she was getting more rest.

The rain had stopped, but thunder still rumbled in the distance as the storm moved on. Smoke looked out the front window and saw that a lamp was burning in the bunkhouse. The men were awake and preparing for the day, too.

Pearlie knocked on the front door a short time later. "We're still ridin' out with Monte to try to pick up the trail o' them owlhoots, ain't we?"

"That's right. We won't know whether the storm washed out the trail without going and taking a look at it."

Pearlie nodded. "That's what I told the boys. We'll be ready to ride in a few minutes, Smoke."

Sally came downstairs in time to kiss Smoke goodbye before he rode out with the other men. "You should have gotten me up," she said. "You didn't have any breakfast."

"We've had coffee and we have biscuits left over from yesterday and some jerky we can eat on the way into town. We'll be fine."

"Has the rain stopped?"

"Yeah, it seems like the storm is over."

That was true, but the road was a sodden, sloppy mess, anyway.

That slowed the seven riders as they headed for Big Rock. When they got to town, the main street was just as bad.

Monte was waiting for them on the boardwalk in front of his office. His horse was tied at the hitch rail.

"I don't have high hopes of finding that trail," he said to Smoke, "but we have to try. Maybe the rain missed that part of the railroad line."

That turned out not to be the case. The overcast was breaking as the sun came up, and by the time Smoke, Monte, and the other men reached the site of the trainwreck, the clouds were gone and the sun was shining brightly, reflecting on the large puddles of water that dotted the ground everywhere.

The bodies of the people killed in the crash were gone this morning, having been taken back to Leadville or Denver, and some of the debris had been cleaned up, but the scene was still one of appalling devastation.

Smoke and the other men rode past the wreckage to the work train parked half a mile away, where the railroad tracks were still intact. Ward Calhoun stood on the platform at the rear of the caboose, sipping from a cup of coffee.

Calhoun nodded as the riders reined in. "I appreciate the gesture, fellas, but you wasted your time riding out here," he told them. "After that downpour last night, you won't be able to locate any tracks left by those killers. It rained hard enough to wipe them all out."

Monte said, "We were hoping that storm might've missed you out here, but no such luck, I see."

"No luck at all," the railroad superintendent said. "I sent a telegram to my boss, Jaggers Dunn, the president of the line, who's down in Texas right now supervising the construction of a new spur line. His reply was so blistering I'm surprised it didn't short out the wires. Ol' Jaggers doesn't take kindly to anybody messing with his railroad."

"I've met Mr. Dunn," Smoke said. "He's the sort who's liable to come up here and try to track down those outlaws himself. Maybe we can find them before he feels like he has to do that."

Calhoun shook his head. "Not today, you won't. And if you get another chance at them, you know what that'll mean."

Monte nodded and said grimly, "It'll mean they've pulled another job. And there'll be a good chance more people will have died."

Chapter 6

At midmorning, wearing a gray skirt and jacket and a matching hat, Sally walked out to the barn, picking her way carefully between the diminishing puddles. She asked the wrangler to hitch a team of horses to the ranch buckboard.

"Ma'am, the road's a mess," the man told her. "You're liable to get stuck."

"The sun's already drying out the ground," Sally said. "I think I can handle it all right."

"Yes, ma'am, if that's what you want, I'll sure do it."

The man still didn't sound like he thought it was a good idea, though.

Sally could have waited to go into Big Rock and pay a visit to the Caldwell sisters' dress shop, but she wanted to make sure Violet and Daisy weren't upset about the part they had played in the uproar at the town social. The brawl had been in no way their fault, of course, but they might blame themselves for it, anyway. Sally wanted to make sure the recent arrivals knew they were welcome in the settlement.

When the buckboard was ready to roll, the wrangler helped her climb to the seat and then said, "A few of the hands are around right now, Miss Sally. Do you want one of them to ride into town with you?"

"No, I'll be all right," Sally said. She smiled and touched a pocket in her skirt, where she carried a .38 caliber Smith & Wesson Model 2 revolver with a three-and-a-half-inch barrel. She was a crack shot and had no compunction about using the gun when she needed to.

In fact, when Calvin Woods had first come to the ranch, he had found himself staring down the barrel of Sally's revolver because, hungry and desperate, he'd made the mistake of trying to hold her up while she was on the road between the Sugarloaf and Big Rock.

Fortunately for everyone concerned, she had taken pity on the youngster, and Cal wound up not only joining the ranch crew but becoming a vital part of it, and pretty much a member of the family. Sally would always be grateful she hadn't been forced to shoot him.

But she would have if she'd had to.

Not only did Sally have the .38 in her pocket but a fully loaded Winchester carbine was also kept in the buckboard, and she could handle it in expert fashion, as well. She didn't expect to run into any trouble, but if she did, she was confident in her ability to take care of it.

Now all she had to do was drive the buckboard to Big Rock without getting it stuck in the mud. If that happened, it would be very embarrassing, especially after the wrangler had warned her about it.

Fortunately, she was also skilled at handling a team of horses and had no problem staying out of the worst of the mud. She had to go slower than usual in order to do so, but she wasn't in any hurry. With Smoke probably being gone most of the day, if not longer, she didn't have to be anywhere at any particular time.

As she had mentioned to the wrangler, the sun was drying up

the puddles, and a brisk breeze helped with that, too. It took a little longer than usual to cover the seven miles between Sugarloaf headquarters and Big Rock, but she arrived in the settlement before midday.

The Caldwell sisters' dress shop was on the same block as Earl's Barber Shop, Nancy's Bakery, and Tim Murchison's leather goods and saddle shop. It was a milliner's at one point, before the lady who owned the business moved, so the building had traded one form of ladies' apparel for another, so to speak.

The front window had CALDWELL SISTERS in fine, curlicue gilt lettering arching across the upper half, while smaller letters underneath read FINE LADIES' DRESSES AND ACCESSORIES. Lacy curtains hung inside the window, tied back at each side.

Sally parked the buckboard in front of the building and wrapped the reins around the hitch rail. Two steps led up to the boardwalk. A little bell above the door made a merry tinkling sound as she went inside.

The walls inside were covered with fine wood paneling; the parts of them that were visible, anyway. A number of dresses in various colors and styles hung in an open rack on the left. To the right, a pair of comfortably upholstered benches sat along the wall, with a large full-length mirror between them. Two dressmaker's dummies stood in front of the window, adorned in elegant gowns.

Long curtains hung over a doorway, but they were pushed open far enough to allow a glimpse into a spacious back room with more dressmaker's dummies and several tables, benches, and stools. A cabinet with open doors held numerous bolts of fabric. Two tables had sewing machines on them. Sally assumed the back room was where much of the actual work of designing and sewing the dresses went on.

She didn't see anyone at first, but then Violet Caldwell, wearing a simple but stylish dark green dress, emerged from the back room and smiled as she recognized Sally.

"Mrs. Jensen, how nice to see you again," she said. "I know you said you'd be dropping in on us, but I didn't really expect your visit this soon."

"It's nice to see you again, too," Sally said. "You are open for business, aren't you?"

"We are definitely open for business." Violet gestured toward the dresses on the rack. "As you can see, we have quite a few dresses already made, but we can alter them as the customer sees fit or design a completely new garment to the lady's specifications."

Sally nodded toward the rack. "Do you mind if I look through these?"

"Not at all. Please help yourself."

As Sally began going through the dresses hanging on the rack, she asked, "Is your sister here today?"

"Not right at the moment. Daisy is out running some errands."

"This is beautiful work," Sally murmured as she fingered the delicate stitchery on one of the dresses. "This looks like it was done by someone who's been sewing for many years. You and your sister must be very skilled to turn out work like this at your ages."

Violet smiled. "We started very young. Our mother was one of the best seamstresses in St. Louis, and she had Daisy and me sewing almost before we could walk."

"You must have inherited her natural talent, too."

"I'd like to believe we did." Violet laughed. "I know we inherited her dressmaking dummies. All of these were hers."

"She's passed away, then?"

"Yes, several years ago."

"I'm sorry."

"Thank you. She made sure we were self-sufficient, even as young as we were, so we've been able to manage fairly well."

"What about your father?"

"He died when we were very young."

"What made you decide to come West?" Before Violet could

answer, Sally went on, “I’m sorry, I don’t mean to pry. I don’t know why I’m being so nosy today.”

“Don’t worry about that,” Violet told her with a smile. “You’re not prying at all. You’re just being friendly, and Daisy and I certainly don’t have anything to hide. I suppose we just both have a bit of a restless streak. We wanted to see some new places, and since there was nothing holding us where we were, we set out to make a new start.”

“What made you settle on Big Rock?”

“Honestly, we just liked the name. Now that we’re here, though, I think it must have been fate that brought us here. We love the area, and so far, the people—well, most of the people—have been very nice.”

“Are you getting many customers?”

“Actually, you’re the first.”

Sally looked at her in surprise. “Really? That won’t do at all!” She gestured at the dresses. “I have many friends in Big Rock. I’m sure as soon as I spread the word among them about what fine work you and Daisy do, you’ll have all the business you could ask for.”

“It would be very nice if you did that, Mrs. Jensen, and we’d really appreciate it.”

“Please, call me Sally.”

“Thank you, Sally.”

Sally continued chatting with Violet as she looked through the dresses. She took several of them off the rack and held them up in front of her on their hangers as she studied her image in the big mirror.

Violet suggested that she try them on, but Sally hadn’t made up her mind about that when a door opened and closed somewhere in the back of the shop. A moment later, Daisy Caldwell appeared in the opening between the back room and the front.

“Violet, I’m ba—” she began, then stopped short, both physically and in her greeting, as she caught sight of Sally standing beside the rack.

"Look who's here, Daisy," Violet said. "Mrs. Jensen has come to visit us, just like she said she would."

"So soon," Daisy said. Then she flashed a smile at Sally. "Welcome to our little shop, Mrs. Jensen."

"It's not that little," Sally said. "In fact, it's quite impressive. You two ladies are very well set up here, it appears. And please, call me Sally."

She was trying to keep the surprise from her face at the sight of Daisy's outfit. The younger sister wore boots, a brown, divided riding skirt, a long-sleeved shirt, and a lightweight jacket. In one hand, she held a flat-crowned brown hat with a chin strap.

That was a riding outfit, and one designed to be more functional than stylish, to boot. Since the Caldwell sisters were new to the area, Sally couldn't help but wonder where Daisy had gone this morning. Did they own a horse, or had Daisy rented one at the livery stable?

Even as those questions went through Sally's mind, she reminded herself that the answers to them were none of her business. Daisy could ride wherever she wanted.

Violet must have noticed the curiosity in Sally's eyes, though, because she said, "Daisy was just, ah—"

Sally held up a hand to stop her. "You don't have to explain anything to me," she said. "Like I told you, I'm usually not so nosy."

Daisy laughed and said, "It's no big secret, Mrs. Jensen. I mean, Sally. I like to ride, that's all. I always have. I rented a horse from Mr. Patterson at the livery stable and took a ride around the area, just to get a good look at the place. That's all right, isn't it?"

She caught her breath suddenly, and her eyes widened a little, as if she had just thought of something alarming.

"Oh, my goodness, what I did was safe, isn't it?" Daisy asked.

"There are no savage Indians or anything like that around here, are there?"

"We haven't had any Indian trouble for several years," Sally assured her.

"What about outlaws? Are there desperadoes roaming around? Is it likely I'd be set upon by thieves or . . . or worse?"

Sally thought about the trainwreck and robbery that had taken place a couple of nights earlier. Other outlaws had descended upon Big Rock from time to time. The Indian threat might be over in these parts, but the possibility of lawlessness was not.

On the other hand, she didn't want to scare the Caldwell sisters and make them regret moving here, so she said, "It's not likely you'd encounter any problems. A respectable lady is safe almost anywhere in the West, even traveling alone." She reached into her pocket, closed her hand around the revolver's wooden grips, and lifted it out. "Even so, if you're going to be out riding by yourself, it probably would be wise if you were armed."

Violet and Daisy both stared at the nickel-plated Smith & Wesson. After a moment, Violet said, "You carry a gun?"

"Just as a precaution. I haven't had to use it very often."

Sally didn't say anything about the carbine out in the buckboard.

"But you *have* had to use it," Daisy said.

"Only occasionally."

"Are you a good shot?" Daisy asked.

Sally smiled. "My husband made sure I know how to use a gun. So I had a very good teacher."

"Yes, we've heard about the famous Smoke Jensen," Violet said. As Sally stiffened slightly, Violet hurried on, "I'm sorry. I didn't mean for it to sound that way. I just meant that most people around here seem very proud to have your husband as part of the community. And you, too, of course."

"Smoke is well-known, there's no denying that," Sally allowed. "For several years, right after we came to this valley and started our ranch, no one in the area really knew who he was, and that was just fine with both of us. But then, as more and more people moved in and a town was established, word got around about him." Her smile had a touch of wistfulness about it. "After that, things were never the same."

"That was when Big Rock was founded?" Violet asked. "After you and Mr. Jensen moved here?"

"Actually, the first town was called Fontana. It was located a mile or so away from here. Big Rock came later."

"What happened to Fontana?" Daisy asked curiously.

"Most of the people decided they would rather live here. Eventually Fontana became a ghost town, I suppose you could call it, and now there aren't even any signs of it left."

That was only a small part of the story of how Fontana was an outlaw town and Smoke, along with Monte Carson, Pearlie Fontaine, Louis Longmont, and many of their friends, were responsible for cleaning it out and turning it into a ghost town. Sally had played her part in that time of fire, powdersmoke, and blood, too. She didn't like to dwell on those days.

As if she might have sensed that slight feeling of unease in Sally, Daisy said, "I didn't mean to interrupt what you were doing, Mrs. Jensen. You just go right ahead with your shopping."

Violet asked, "Did you see anything interesting on your ride, Daisy?"

"Oh, a lot of things," the younger woman said. "I'll tell you all about it later." Daisy reached over to the rack and plucked a pink gown from it. She held it out toward Sally and asked, "Have you seen this one yet?"

Sally took the dress and said, "It's lovely. I'm not sure pink is my color, though."

"Pink is every lady's color. Hold it up in front of you and take a look in the mirror. What do you think, Violet?"

"I agree, it's quite beautiful," Violet said. "It might be a bit too extravagant for Big Rock, though. But if you and Smoke ever travel to Denver or San Francisco, it would be a perfect gown for some fine affair there."

Sally cocked her head to the side as she held the dress in front of her and studied her reflection. Behind her, Daisy murmured to her sister, "I'm going to go change clothes."

When Daisy was gone, Violet asked quietly, "Is it really safe for my sister to ride around like that?"

Sally hesitated before answering. "I didn't want to alarm either of you unduly, but there was a train robbery night before last, the same night as the social."

"Right here in town at the station?" Violet sounded shocked.

Sally shook her head. "No, at a flag stop east of here. But there was an explosion and the train derailed. Several people died in the crash, and the outlaws shot and killed the express messenger, probably because he was trying to defend the safe in the express car."

"That's terrible," Violet said in a hushed voice. She seemed genuinely shocked.

"I know."

"The criminals responsible for all that, they got away?"

"For now. Smoke and Sheriff Carson are going to try to track them down."

"Do you think they'll be able to?"

"With the storm last night and all that heavy rain, it's going to be difficult to follow their trail." Sally tried to sound optimistic as she added, "But if anyone can do that, it's Smoke and Monte."

"But right now, the outlaws are somewhere out there, on the loose?"

"For now," Sally agreed.

"Then I'm going to have a talk with Daisy and forbid her to go riding by herself again," Violet declared. "I hate to do that because she enjoys it so much, but her safety is my main concern."

"Of course."

"And I'm wondering, where can we get a pistol like the one you carry?"

Out of habit, Sally touched the familiar, comforting hard weight of the .38.

"Go see Mr. Goldstein at his mercantile store," she said. "He carries a good supply."

"And we'll need someone to show us how to use it."

Sally's first impulse was to say that Smoke could give them some pointers, but then she checked herself. She didn't have a jealous bone in her body, not really, so it wasn't that she was worried about Smoke teaching two young, beautiful blondes how to shoot.

It was just that she suddenly thought of two fellows who might be more suited to the task: Pearlie and Cal.

"I'm sure something can be arranged," she told Violet. "Just let me know when you're ready."

Chapter 7

Sally bought two dresses from the Caldwell sisters. Not the fancy pink gown, although she debated with herself for quite a while about that one. She might come back and get it later, she decided.

She tried on the ones she picked out. Each would require a few alterations.

"We'll have them ready for you by the end of the week," Violet promised.

"That's fine. I'll pick them up on Friday, since I planned to come back to town and do some shopping then, anyway."

Daisy had changed her riding outfit for a simple but stylish light brown dress and traded her boots for a pair of high-button shoes.

Violet didn't mention the robbery to her sister, or the possible presence of an outlaw gang in the area, so Sally didn't bring it up, either. Violet could pick her own time for that.

Sally tried to pay for her purchases, but Violet told her to wait until she picked up the altered dresses and settle the bill then, once she was fully satisfied with the alterations. She left the shop after repeating her promise to spread the word about the Caldwell sisters' skill as seamstresses. Sally was a member of the Ladies' Aid Society in Big Rock, and she would bring up the topic at the group's next meeting.

Since it was the middle of the day, she walked up the street to Delmonico's Restaurant to eat before heading back to the Sugarloaf. It was while she was enjoying her meal that some odd thoughts began to stir inside Sally's brain.

Considering the storm the night before and the muddy ground it had left behind, today might not have been the best one to take a ride in the countryside around Big Rock. A good saddle horse was usually sure-footed, but even an experienced rider might have trouble if the ground was soft enough.

Of course, Sally had seen for herself that the sun and the breeze had done a good job of drying things up. Just in the time she'd been in town, the puddles in the street had gotten much smaller. Daisy hadn't said anything about having any trouble during her ride, but even so, Sally was a little surprised that she had chosen today for her excursion.

Then there was the matter of her boots. It was to be expected that there would be mud on them, even if she hadn't dismounted while she was out. In all likelihood, she would have gotten some on the boots just walking to and from the livery stable, even if she was careful.

Sally looked down at her own feet and saw a few bits of dried mud clinging to her boots. It had gotten on them when she'd climbed down from the buckboard in front of the dress shop.

So the fact that Daisy's boots had mud on them wasn't puzzling. What made Sally frown slightly was the realization that it had been black clay. She hadn't thought anything of it at the time, but she remembered it now. A few clumps of the sticky stuff had fallen off the boots onto the floor around Daisy's feet.

The streets of Big Rock didn't have any black clay in them.

It was unlikely Daisy would have picked it up walking between the shop and the livery stable. So evidently she *had* dismounted somewhere.

Smoke would probably know better, but Sally couldn't recall any areas right around the settlement where black clay was common. Daisy must have gone farther from Big Rock than she had made it sound.

Sally shook her head. She had no reason whatsoever to be suspicious of Daisy Caldwell, or Violet, either, for that matter. They both seemed like sweet, enterprising young women. Daisy hadn't done anything wrong by going for a ride. She was making things up out of thin air, Sally told herself. She tried to put the whole thing out of her head.

Even so, when she left Delmonico's and went back to the buckboard, she turned the vehicle toward Patterson's Livery Stable.

The stocky, red-bearded proprietor was one of Smoke's friends and was happy to answer Sally's questions.

"Sure, I remember the young lady," he said. "She wanted to rent a good saddle mount. I would have given her the gentlest horse I have, but she said she'd ridden quite a bit and didn't need any special consideration. She just wanted a good, strong mount that could cover some ground, she said." He nodded toward one of the stalls. "I gave her that big bay gelding."

Sally took a look at the horse over the stall gate. "It's a fine-looking animal," she said. "Did Miss Caldwell bring it back in good shape?"

"Yeah, she did. It didn't look like she'd run it hard or anything. She said she didn't have any trouble. I'd warned her to stay out of the worst of the mud."

Sally took a guess. "The horse had gotten into some black clay, though, hadn't it?"

"It sure did." Patterson frowned. "Now that you mention it, that kind of surprised me. I wasn't sure where it would have picked up any of that stuff around here. But there was enough I figured I'd better clean it off. Took a while to scrape that sticky muck off its hooves and dig it out of the shoes, too."

"Where's the closest place she could have gotten into mud like that, do you know?"

Patterson scratched his bearded jaw and frowned in thought. After a moment, he said, "You can find it here and there lots of places, but only in little patches. It's pretty common over in the Flat Rock country, that high tableland on the other side of the Armadillo Hills, but that's more than ten miles from here."

"Was Miss Caldwell gone long enough to get there and back?"

Again the liveryman looked puzzled. "I suppose it's possible, especially if she actually is a good rider and wouldn't have to take it easy." He shrugged. "Of course, when I rent out a horse, I don't really care where somebody rides it, as long as they take good care of it."

"I know. I just saw the mud on Miss Caldwell's boots and was curious where she'd gotten it." Sally laughed. "It doesn't matter at all. I guess I'm just being a busybody."

"I don't reckon anybody would ever accuse you of that, Miss Sally."

They might not accuse her of it, Sally thought as she said her goodbyes to Patterson and headed the buggy out of town, but she was acting like one. She was slightly ashamed of herself, and she hoped that word wouldn't get back to Violet and Daisy that she was poking her nose into their affairs. She could trust Mr. Patterson not to say anything. He wasn't the type to gossip.

For now, she would just put it out of her mind, she vowed.

Smoke, Pearlie, Cal, and the other men got back to the Sugarloaf late that afternoon.

When Smoke went into the ranch house, Sally said from the

chair in the parlor where she was doing some needlework, "You didn't find those outlaws, did you?"

Smoke hung his hat on a hook near the door and went into the parlor. He sat down in an armchair near where Sally was sitting and shook his head.

"When we got out to the site of that robbery, we found that the storm had gone through there, too," he said. "I'm stubborn enough that we tried to find the tracks they left, but it was no use. Any sign was long gone, washed out."

"So they're going to get away with killing those people and stealing that money?"

"For now, but in the long run, that depends. If they're satisfied with their loot from this robbery and ride on out of the country, there's not much anybody can do about it other than hope justice catches up to them eventually. But owlhoots like that are hardly ever satisfied. If you're broken enough inside to rob and kill ruthlessly like that, chances are you're going to want more and more."

"So they'll strike again."

"I hate to say it, hate to even think about it, but yeah, I figure that's pretty likely." Smoke paused for a moment and then said, "Let's change the subject to something more pleasant. What did you do today?"

"I took the buckboard into Big Rock and paid a visit to the Caldwell sisters' dress shop. They're very nice, Smoke, and they have an excellent selection."

"You bought some dresses?" he asked.

"Two, as a matter of fact."

He grinned. "Well, let's have a look at them."

"You can't yet," she told him. "Violet and Daisy are going to be altering them so they'll fit even better. They should be ready on Friday."

"You could wear one of them to church on Sunday, then."

She laughed and shook her head. "These aren't exactly church dresses, Smoke. I'm afraid they're not sober enough for that. They're bright and colorful, more suited to having dinner at Louis's, for example."

"Well, then, we'll have to do that."

"There was one other thing that came up while I was there. Evidently Daisy is quite a horsewoman. She rented a saddle mount from Mr. Patterson and went for a ride today."

A slight frown creased Smoke's forehead. "I'm not sure that's a good idea, what with a band of outlaws roaming around the area. They haven't hit close to town yet, but you can't ever be certain what hombres like that will do."

"I know. That's why I showed them my gun and suggested that they might want to be armed if they were going to be traveling by themselves."

Smoke's frown disappeared. "What did they say to that?"

"They seemed to be quite impressed and in total agreement with the idea. Violet wanted to know where they can get a pistol like mine. I suggested Goldstein's Mercantile."

Smoke nodded and said, "He'll give them a good deal. They'll need to practice some, too. I can show them a few things, if you'd like."

"I thought about that," Sally said, "but then I had a better idea."

Smoke looked at her and cocked an eyebrow as he waited for her to continue.

"I thought perhaps Pearlie and Cal would like to give the young ladies some shooting lessons," she said.

Smoke didn't respond for a few seconds. Then he chuckled and nodded. "That's a mighty fine idea," he said, "and I have a hunch those two cowboys will think so, too!"

Chapter 8

Two days of fine, clear weather allowed the last puddles of the big rainstorm to dry up and go away. The moisture that soaked into the ground caused the grass in the valley's pastures to take on an even deeper green hue. The cattle grazing on that grass enjoyed it, too, spending hours cropping at the tender shoots as they slowly drifted across the range.

As the sun was setting, Tom Maulden and Jim Evans sat on their horses and gazed across a broad pasture that dipped down slightly between their position and a line of trees almost a mile away. The terrain gave the two cowboys a good view of the grazing cattle.

Maulden and Evans rode for old Ezra Martell's Slash Diamond M spread. It wasn't one of the bigger ranches in the valley. Ezra had only five men in his crew. The old-timer was still whang leather tough and could spend more hours in the saddle than men thirty years younger than him, so with himself included, the small crew was plenty to handle his herd.

And it was a mighty fine herd, too, rivalling in quality if not numbers the cattle raised on the Sugarloaf, the Three Sevens, the

Double B, and the other top spreads in the area. Ezra was proud of his cows, and so were the hands who rode for him and took care of them.

Maulden and Evans would nighthawk the herd until they were relieved after midnight. Things had been peaceful in recent months, but there was always the chance a grizzly bear or a mountain lion might come along and decide to help itself to some fresh beef on the hoof. Maulden and Evans would ride a slow, looping course in opposite directions around the herd to make sure that didn't happen.

Evans thumbed back his hat on his sandy red hair and said, "I reckon we'd better go ahead and split up, Tom. You know how fast night comes crashin' down in this part of the country once the sun sets."

Maulden nodded and lifted a hand in farewell as he nudged his horse into motion.

"See you in a bit," he called as he rode off. The two cowboys would meet every half hour or so as they made their rounds.

Maulden cut straight across the pasture toward the trees. The thick growth ran up a long hillside, and if there were any grizzlies or catamounts around tonight, he would be more likely to run into them over there. As he rode, he made sure the Winchester saddle gun would pull easily from its scabbard if he needed it.

He also had an old .44 Remington holstered on his hip, but he freely admitted he wasn't the best shot in the world with it. Nor would the revolver be likely to bring down a bear unless he hit it just right. But with fifteen rounds in the Winchester, he wasn't worried.

When he got close to the trees, he turned his horse before entering the dark shadows underneath them and rode north over the open ground between the pines and the herd.

He began singing softly, starting with "In the Sweet By and By." The soft strains of the hymn floated across the pasture. Singing while riding nighthawk was a habit with Maulden, as it was with a lot of cowboys. The low, pleasant sound kept the cattle soothed and complacent.

Of course, it wasn't the same when the cows were here on their home ranch, on their accustomed bed-ground. Out on the trail, during a drive to the railhead, they were a lot more likely to spook and stampede. It was on such drives that Maulden had gotten into the habit of singing, and it had never left him, even though these days, the railroad had reached the area and actual cattle drives were mostly a thing of the past.

A lot of ranchers didn't even have their crews guard the herds at night. It just wasn't necessary anymore. However, Ezra Martell was old enough that he had spent long years defending his cattle from Indians, rustlers, and other sorts of predators, and he claimed he slept better when he knew somebody was keeping an eye on the critters. His men didn't mind; they were all veteran hands who had been through the same sort of experiences.

By the time the two riders had circled the herd and met twice, full darkness had settled over the valley. The moon was just a thin crescent, low in the sky, but millions of stars blazed brightly in the black sky overhead. Maulden's eyes were adjusted to the gloom, and he had no trouble seeing where he was going.

He saw the men on horseback who rode out of the trees ahead of him to his left, too. Nobody should have been out here cutting across Slant Diamond M range. Maulden reined in and reached for the carbine snugged in its sheath under his right leg.

He pulled the rifle out and worked its lever, throwing a cartridge into the chamber.

The four riders approaching him must have heard that distinctive metallic sound. They reined in, and one of them called, "Hold your fire, friend! We mean no harm."

"This is Slash Diamond M range," Maulden said as he held the rifle ready for instant use. "You fellas are trespassing."

"We're mighty sorry," the spokesman responded. "We must have gotten turned around in the dark. This isn't the Sugarloaf spread?"

"The Sugarloaf is a good five miles from here."

"Well, blast it to Hades," the man drawled. "Smoke's probably wondering where we are."

Maulden lowered the rifle slightly. "You're looking for Smoke Jensen?"

"That's right."

"Is he a friend of yours, or do you have some other reason for looking him up?" Maulden asked. He knew that Smoke had plenty of enemies, no matter how well-liked he was in these parts.

"Sure, we're old friends of his." The man chuckled. "Knew him in Idaho when he was runnin' wild up there."

Maulden wasn't that well-acquainted with Smoke, although like everyone else around here, he had heard plenty of stories. For a young man, Smoke had gotten around to a lot of places and done a whole heap of things. Maulden knew that Smoke had spent some time in Idaho. In fact, that was where he had started gaining his reputation as one of the fastest men with a gun to ever roam the frontier.

The Winchester's barrel sagged even more as Maulden let go of the weapon with his left hand. He half turned in the saddle and raised that hand to point to the south.

"If you just follow this pasture, you'll hit a trail, and you take it for a couple of miles—"

A faint sound warned him and made him break off in mid-sentence. For a second, he couldn't figure out what he'd heard, but then part of his brain started yelling at him that it was the whisper of metal against leather as guns were drawn. He twisted back toward the shadowy riders and tried to raise the Winchester again.

Four shots crashed out before he could bring the rifle level.

At least two of the bullets slammed into Maulden and drove him backward in the saddle. The shock was so great, he couldn't tell if the other two slugs found their target. But he knew he was hit high on the right side, just under the shoulder, and somewhere in the middle of his body. He had felt those impacts.

He dropped the unfired Winchester without being aware of it. As he began to topple sideways, he tried to make a grab for the saddle horn, but his right arm wouldn't work at all and his left was too weak. His fingers slid off the horn. He fell to the ground, but he was lucky that his feet had come out of the stirrups, so his horse didn't drag him as it bolted off into the darkness.

Yeah, lucky. That was him.

That bitter thought was the last one to go through his mind as the towering shapes of men on horseback surrounded him, blotting out the stars, and more shots thundered.

Close to a mile away, on the other side of the big pasture, Jim Evans was crooning a song about a saloon girl named Esmerelda, a tune normally sung at a fast, foot-stomping tempo. Evans had slowed down the bawdy lyrics, though, as he sang it in his raspy voice. The cattle seemed to like it.

Then shots roared in the distance. The unexpected sound snapped Evans straighter in the saddle and choked off the chorus about Esmerelda and her fellas. He stood up in the stirrups to stare across the pasture, over the backs of the still calmly grazing cows.

Muzzle flashes winked in the darkness like fireflies over there.

Evans came back down hard in the saddle and jabbed his bootheels into his mount's flanks as he jerked the horse's head around. The horse didn't like that rough treatment and reared for a second, but then it leaped forward in a run.

The cattle were spread out enough that Evans figured he could ride straight across the pasture. It wouldn't be like trying to force his way through a densely packed trail herd.

He hadn't gone very far when he heard a sharp crack behind him, followed instantly by something humming past his ear. He whipped his head around to look over his shoulder. A spurt of garish orange flame split the darkness in that direction, then another.

Somebody was back there shooting at him! Probably part of the same bunch causing the ruckus over where Tom Maulden ought to be.

Fear for his friend's safety welled up inside Evans. Fear for his own hide, too, because more bullets sizzled through the air around him, doing their best to ventilate him. He leaned forward in the saddle to make himself a smaller target and urged more speed from his horse.

The fact that he had to veer from side to side to avoid the scattered cattle probably contributed to keeping him alive. He didn't see any more muzzle flashes from the other side of the pasture. Maybe that meant Maulden had run off whoever jumped him.

Evans wanted to believe that, but he couldn't bring himself to do so. He was afraid his old friend might have come to a bad end. The same sort of bad end that kept reaching for him.

As gunfire continued to slam through the night behind him, he reached to his hip and pulled the Colt holstered there. Hitting anything from the back of a running horse was next to impossible, but he wasn't trying for accuracy as he reached behind him with the gun and thumbed off a couple of shots. He just wanted to put up a fight, and maybe cause the men pursuing him to hesitate a little.

He thought about breaking off his desperate ride across the pasture and circling back in an attempt to lose the men trying to kill him. The odds would be against such an effort, but there was a slim chance it might succeed.

But that would mean abandoning Maulden, and he couldn't bring himself to do that. When men rode for the same brand, they had to be loyal to one another as well as to the spread they worked for. That was just the way things were. Maulden never would have abandoned him, Evans knew.

He jammed the Colt back in its holster. He might need the other rounds in it.

Leaning to the left in the saddle, he angled the horse past a clump of grazing cattle when one of the brutes suddenly took a notion to wheel around and get in front of him.

Evans's mount was a lot more nimble than that cow, but they were too close together. The horse couldn't avoid a collision entirely. The horse's shoulder rammed against the cow, and its legs went out from under it.

Evans barely had time to jerk his feet free of the stirrups and throw himself out of the saddle as the running horse fell in a rolling tangle of flailing legs. He managed to avoid having the horse land on him, but he came down hard enough on the ground to knock the breath out of him and leave him stunned.

Bawling in outrage because the horse had run into it, the cow started running. That reaction spread to the other cattle nearby. They lurched into motion as well. As far as stampedes went, it was a very small one.

But it was headed straight for where Jim Evans lay motionless on the ground.

With the rumble of hooves coming at him, pounding and slashing the ground, Evans finally got his muscles working after what seemed like an eternity. He pushed up onto his hands and knees, spotted a shadow on the ground a few yards away that he hoped was a hummock, and scrambled for it as fast as he could. With the panicked cattle almost on top of him, he threw himself forward, pressed himself against the small rise, and tried to flatten his body as much as possible.

If he'd had a few minutes, he would have dug halfway to China with his bare hands. But as it was, all he could do was hope the slight irregularity in the ground would protect him.

He shoved his face into the dirt. Whatever was going to happen, he didn't want to see it coming.

The earth vibrated so much that it shook up his insides. He was convinced that some of the hooves missed him by mere inches. But then the cows were past him, and somehow he was still alive.

"Linc, where'd the other one go?"

The man who shouted that question was close enough for Evans to make out the words. From the other direction, a second man answered, "His horse fell in the middle of that stampede. I saw him go down with it."

"You want us to find the body?"

A harsh laugh came from the man called Linc. "After those cattle trampled over him, there won't be enough left to find. The important thing is that he's dead and there's nobody to stop us from driving off all these cows. Get busy with that."

The grass was fairly long where Jim Evans was lying. He stayed absolutely still, barely breathing, to make sure he didn't disturb it. Movement caught the eye, and if that grass started waving around, the rustlers might notice it.

That was what they were, he thought. Rustlers. No doubt about it now.

Nor was there any doubt that Tom Maulden was dead. That was why the shooting had stopped earlier. Tom had gone under, gunned down by killers who didn't care about anything except getting what they wanted. In this case, somebody else's cattle.

But if he could manage to stay alive, Evans told himself, he could fetch some help once the men were gone. They wouldn't get away with killing Tom and stealing old Ezra's stock. He wouldn't waste the opportunity for revenge that the rustler boss's arrogant overconfidence had given him.

Evans lay there for a long time as the thieves choused the cattle out of the pasture, whistling at the cows and calling to one another. He didn't hear any names other than Linc. But he would remember that, he vowed, and he would recognize the man's cold, callous voice if he ever heard it again.

Finally, the sound of hoofbeats faded into the distance. Evans waited still longer, just in case any of the men had stayed behind to make sure he was dead. At last, he was convinced it was safe to move.

Even so, he unconsciously braced himself for the shock of a bullet as he climbed to his feet and started making his shaky way toward the far side of the pasture. His horse was gone, he didn't know where, so he had to move on foot.

Hoping against hope, as he neared the trees, he called softly, "Tom! Tom, are you anywhere around?"

No answer. Evans hadn't expected one, but the silence put a bitter taste under his tongue, anyway.

A short time later, he found Maulden's bullet-riddled body. Biting back curses, he choked out, "I'm sorry, Tom. I'll settle the score for you, Pard. I give you my word."

Maulden's horse was grazing at the edge of the trees. Evans knew the animal well, and the horse knew him. Speaking to it in a calm, quiet voice, Evans approached and reached for the dangling reins. The horse let him take hold of them.

Evans tied the horse to a sapling and then dragged Maulden's body over to it. The horse didn't like the smell of blood and spooked a little, but Evans was able to get his friend's body draped over the saddle.

He pulled the reins loose, climbed up behind the corpse, and a moment later he was riding hard through the darkness toward Slash Diamond M headquarters.

Chapter 9

Sometime after midnight, the swift rataplan of approaching hoofbeats roused Smoke from sleep, and he was fully awake instantly, gripping the .45, which was never out of reach. When a rider came pounding up to the Sugarloaf ranch house a few minutes later, Smoke greeted him with gun in hand, ready for trouble.

The cowboy brought news of trouble, all right, but nothing that directly threatened the Sugarloaf. He was one of old Ezra Martell's riders, and he brought word of a rustling raid on the Slash Diamond M spread that had left one man dead and seen two hundred head of fine stock disappear.

"Ezra sent me to spread the word around the valley," the puncher explained. "He'll be settin' out from his place first thing in the mornin' to go after the varmints, and he said he'd appreciate help from anybody else who wants to pitch in."

"I'll be there with some of my men at first light," Smoke promised.

The cowboy said, "Much obliged, Mr. Jensen," then waved in

farewell, turned his horse, and galloped off to continue his grim errand.

Sally was on the porch with a dressing gown wrapped tightly around her as Smoke came up the steps from the yard.

"I heard what that man said," she told him. "Smoke, do you think the same gang that held up the train raided Mr. Martell's ranch tonight?"

"I don't know," Smoke replied honestly. "Most of the time, train robbers don't go in for rustling, too. Some of them will hit banks as well as holding up trains, but stealing stock isn't as common for them." He shook his head. "But we're talking about outlaws. Most of them don't have much of a conscience and will do anything if they think it'll give them a good enough pay-off."

"Do you think you can follow their trail?"

"We'll sure give it a good try." Smoke glanced up at the sky and saw millions of stars shining overhead. "Looks like no storms tonight, so there won't be any rain to wash out their tracks. It's hard to move two hundred head of cattle without leaving considerable sign."

When the sun came up the next morning, Smoke, Pearlie, Cal, and several other members of the Sugarloaf's crew arrived at Slash Diamond M headquarters. Volunteers from most of the other ranches in the valley were on hand to help with the search for the rustlers, too.

Monte Carson was also there to give the group legal standing if they needed to dispense some rough justice at the end of a rope. Not that men such as these actually required a lawman's presence to deal with rustlers. They all came from the rugged frontier tradition that called for a man to stomp his own snakes. But nobody objected to having Monte along. He was one of them.

Ezra Martell came out of his ranch house, and the talk quieted. Ezra was an old bachelor, a tall, rawboned man with a shock of rusty, reddish-gray hair and a black patch over his left eye. He raised his voice to say, "I'm obliged to you fellas for comin'. Some of you knew Tom Maulden. He's the man those blasted rustlers killed last night. They durned near did for Jim Evans, too. It was pure luck they didn't murder him, too. So I got a score to settle with those no-good buzzards."

"We'll help you settle it, Ezra," Jack Brodie said. The owner of the Three Sevens was a spare man with a hawk nose and a brush of a mustache, another old-time cattleman whose spread had been one of the first in the valley after the Sugarloaf.

"Appreciate that, Jack. Let's ride!"

The group numbered around thirty men. They swung up into their saddles and rode out following Ezra, who led them several miles to the pasture where the herd had been rustled and Tom Maulden had been killed.

The volunteers from each of the various spreads rode together for the most part, but some mingling inevitably took place. Pearlie and Cal found themselves riding alongside a couple of men from the Three Sevens and stiffened in their saddles as they recognized Chuck Dade and Jasper Hendryx.

Dade and Hendryx had the same reaction at the sight of the Sugarloaf duo. With his lip curling, Dade said, "Maybe we'd better find somewhere else to ride, Jasper. The smell's kinda bad right here."

"Yeah," Hendryx agreed. "Skunk, maybe."

"If you're smellin' polecat, it ain't comin' from our direction," Pearlie snapped. "Best look under your own hats."

Cal said, "Let's all just take it easy. A man died last night. We don't need to waste our time and energy squabbling."

"And I don't need to take advice from no wet-behind-the-ears kid," Dade said, still sneering.

"Cal may be the youngest fella in this bunch," Pearlie said, "but he's done a whole heap in his time. I'd pick him over anybody here to ride the river with. 'Cept maybe Smoke, of course." He glanced over at his friend. "No offense, Pard."

Cal chuckled. "None taken. Smoke would be anybody's choice to ride the river with, I expect."

"Overrated, if you ask me," Hendryx muttered.

Cal's conciliatory attitude vanished in the blink of an eye. "What did you say?" he demanded.

Hendryx glared back at him. "I said Smoke Jensen's overrated, and I don't mind sayin'—"

"That's enough, Jasper." Jack Brodie had ridden up on Hendryx's other side in time to hear the comment, and his reprimand was sharp. "You know good and well that's not true. You're just carrying a grudge against these men."

"Sorry, Boss," Hendryx said in a surly voice. "But if anybody deserves to have a grudge held against 'em, it's these two pelicans. They got a habit of buttin' in where they ain't wanted."

"Settle it later," Brodie ordered. "Right now, we've got something more important to do. We need to track down those rustlers."

"Sure, Boss," Dade said. "We understand. Don't we, Jasper?"

"Yeah," Hendryx allowed through clenched teeth.

Brodie gave them a curt nod and moved on toward the head of the group. Dade and Hendryx nudged their horses to the right, moving away from Cal and Pearlie.

"Good riddance," Pearlie said under his breath.

When they reached the big pasture, even with the thick grass it wasn't difficult to see where the cattle were bunched up and driven to the north. Once out of the pasture, the trail turned east and entered a range of rugged hills. The ground was a lot rockier here, but despite that, the cattle had left signs that experienced trackers such as Smoke and Monte were able to follow.

Late in the morning, Monte reined in abruptly and said, "Smoke, do you see what I see?"

Smoke brought his horse to a stop as well and studied the ground ahead of them. It sloped down to a broad, brush-choked valley that stretched for a couple of miles before slanting back up to a shallow plateau. The ground here at the top of the rise was beaten down and chopped up, indicating that the herd had stopped and milled around for a while before moving again.

The problem was that the tracks led seemingly everywhere from here. Monte said disgustedly, "They split up and took off in all directions into that valley. Must not have been more than ten or twelve head in each bunch. How many outlaws are we dealing with, anyway?"

"Two men could handle each bunch," Smoke said. "There weren't that many in the group we've been following, so they must have rendezvoused here with the main part of the gang."

Monte looked over his shoulder at the posse. "We can split up, too. We have enough men to follow all of them."

Ezra Martell had pushed up his mount alongside Smoke and Monte. He shook his grizzled head and said, "If we did that, those boys would be ridin' into a lion's den, Sheriff. I already lost one good hand. I won't risk the other members of my crew, or anybody from the other spreads. It ain't worth it."

"But you lost nearly all your stock, Ezra," Monte protested.

"Yeah, I know that, but I ain't got a lot of debts pressin' on me right now. Anyway, I'm gettin' old enough that I've started thinkin' it might be time to sell the place and take life easy, what I've got left of it."

Monte frowned. "That doesn't sound like you. You've always been a cattleman."

"Yeah, it's all I knowed, and I liked livin' that life, hard as it was sometimes. But when you get to be my age, you get tired, even when you're doin' something that suits you." Ezra grimaced. "Losin' cattle is bad enough, but what really gnaws at my guts is lettin' those varmints get away with killin' Tom Maulden. He was a good hand. But gettin' another dozen good men killed ain't gonna bring him back."

"No, I suppose it won't," Monte admitted.

Smoke said, "How about this? Pearlie, Cal, and I will track one bunch of the stolen cattle. There's a good chance that sooner or later they'll all head for some spot where the whole herd will be gathered. If we can find the gang's hideout, we can fetch help and go back there to clean it out later."

"You'll still stand a good chance of ridin' into an ambush," Ezra said.

"Well, it won't be the first time," Smoke said with a smile. "And we're pretty good at handling trouble when we have to."

The old cattleman thought it over for a moment and then nodded. "I reckon that would be all right," he said. "If anybody can find where them skunks are holed up, it'd be you, Smoke."

"It's settled, then," Smoke said. "The rest of you can head back while we stay on the hunt. This isn't over, Ezra. One way or another, we'll get your cows back and get justice for Tom."

"That's what I care about more'n anything else." Ezra held out a gnarled, rope-calloused hand. "I'm obliged to you, Smoke, more than I can say."

Smoke clasped the old man's hand, then he and Pearlie and Cal picked out what seemed to be the clearest of the many trails and started following it down into the wasteland of scrub brush and trees.

Smoke had learned how to track from the mountain man called Preacher, and there had never been anyone better at it than that rugged old-timer. Smoke's abilities were nowhere near the level of Preacher's, but he could follow sign better than most men.

Pearlie was good at it, too. He pointed out the tracks left by the cattle they were following, as well as the branches that were broken when the cows pushed past them.

They came to a game trail through the brush that was wide enough for the cattle to have followed it single file. But as the three riders reined in, Smoke and Pearlie frowned in puzzlement.

"What's wrong?" Cal asked. "Didn't they go this way?"

"They must have," Smoke said, "but there aren't any tracks."

Pearlie said, "The ground's been pounded down until it's pretty hard, but there ought to be some sign."

"They've brushed it out," Smoke said, "and this trail is wide enough that the cows didn't leave any hide on the branches. They even picked up any droppings the cattle left."

"But this has to be the way they went," Cal pointed out. "If they'd continued pushing through the brush, we'd be able to see where they went."

"The kid's right," Pearlie said.

"But did they go on toward the plateau, or did they double back?" Smoke said. "We can't tell."

Pearlie took off his hat and scratched his head. His puzzled frown deepened.

"Dang it, that's a good question," he finally muttered. "It don't really make sense they'd double back and head the way they came from, but at the same time, anybody chasin' 'em wouldn't hardly expect that, would they?"

"Maybe we should split up and check both directions," Cal suggested.

Smoke considered the idea but then shook his head.

"We'll stick together," he said. "Come on."

He nudged his horse into motion, heading along the trail toward the plateau. That was the most likely of the two alternatives, he decided.

It didn't take long to reach the far side of the brushy valley. The trail ended at the base of the slope leading up to the shallow plateau. The ground here was a mixture of rock and soil packed so hard it might as well have been rock.

Smoke, Pearlie, and Cal saw no hoofmarks or any other sign that the stolen cattle had been brought this way. They rode half a mile to the left from the spot where the game trail came out, then doubled back and checked half a mile in the other direction.

"Blast it," Pearlie said. "It's like them cows just up and vanished into thin air."

"They can't have done that," Cal said. "They had to go somewhere."

"What do you think, Smoke?"

"They could have covered up their sign along the trail, like we said earlier," Smoke replied. "And then they wrapped the hooves so the cattle wouldn't leave any marks as they were being driven up onto the plateau."

"You reckon that's what they actually did?"

Smoke nodded toward the slope. "Let's go up and have a look around."

The angle was gentle enough that the horses had no trouble handling it. The rustlers and the stolen stock would have been able to do so, as well.

The plateau was mostly level, with only a few dips and swales. It was about two miles across from west to east and ran five miles from north to south. A few clumps of small trees grew here and there, with the ground between them covered by sparse grass. Smoke knew that not much grew up here because the soil wasn't very good, and a huge slab of solid rock underlay most of the plateau. The dirt was only a foot to a foot-and-a-half thick no matter where you went up here.

On the far side was another valley, smaller than the one they had just crossed, that rose into foothills leading to rugged mountains. The plateau wasn't a particularly appealing range for cattle and was no good for farming. Smoke had no idea who owned it. It might even be unclaimed land. Some of the ranchers in the area ran stock on it when they had to have some extra graze, but most of the time it was empty. That appeared to be the case today.

"Spread out," Smoke told Pearlie and Cal. "About two hundred yards apart. We'll have a look around. If you run into trouble, fire a shot."

The three men rode in different directions and headed across the plateau. As Smoke kept his horse moving at a steady walk, he studied the ground ahead of him and to both sides. He didn't spot any telltale signs of cattle crossing the area. If the rustlers had brought that stolen stock over here, they had done a mighty good job of getting rid of any signs of it.

The sun was directly overhead when Smoke called to Pearlie and Cal and waved his hat over his head to call them back in. He could tell by the disappointed looks on their faces that they hadn't had any more luck in their searches than he had, but he asked the question, anyway.

"Find anything?"

"Not a blessed thing," Pearlie replied.

"Same here," Cal said. "Where did they go, Smoke? Cattle can't just up and vanish. They're too big and bulky for that."

"Those rustlers know what they're doing," Smoke said. "They either threw us off the trail completely, or they did a mighty good job of hiding their tracks."

"We ain't givin' up, are we?" Pearlie asked.

"I don't see what else we can do, at least for now."

"Ol' Ezra's gonna be mighty disappointed," Pearlie said, shaking his head regretfully.

"This isn't over," Smoke said as he sat with his hands resting on the saddle horn and gazed across the plateau toward the mountains. "Whoever stole those cattle and wherever they took them, I've got a hunch we haven't seen the last of them."

Chapter 10

A couple of days passed with no further trouble in the valley. Pearlie and Cal rode to Big Rock one morning after talking to Sally and reined their horses to a halt in front of the Caldwell sisters' dress shop.

"I'm not sure about this, Pearlie," Cal said without dismounting.

"Remember, we're doin' this as a favor for Miss Sally," Pearlie reminded him. "After all the bear sign she's fried up for us, I reckon this is just a little start on payin' her back, which I don't reckon we'll ever be able to do in full."

To the cowboys in the Sugarloaf crew, no greater delicacy existed than the bear sign Sally made for them. The doughnuts had gotten that nickname because their distinctive round shape resembled bear tracks. The ranch hands would have gobbled them down every day of the week if they could, but Sally only fried up a batch every now and then so that eating them would remain a special occasion.

"It's not like Sally asks for a lot of favors from us, either, I suppose," Cal said. He took a deep breath and then swung down from the saddle. Pearlie dismounted, as well, and they looped their reins around the hitch rail in front of the store.

"Anyway," Pearlie said as they stepped up onto the boardwalk, "it ain't like you ought to be complainin' about spendin' time with a couple of pretty girls."

"Pretty girls can be trouble," Cal pointed out.

Pearlie snorted. "Durned near anything can be trouble sometimes. As far as I'm concerned, it's worth the risk."

"We'll see," Cal said as he reached for the doorknob.

They went into the shop and found the front room empty.

Both of them had cleaned up a little before riding into town, although they hadn't gone to the lengths they would have for attending a social or something like that. But they had washed and shaved and put on clean duds.

Even so, Cal felt clumsy and dirty and definitely out of place in this neatly furnished room full of beautiful dresses.

Violet Caldwell pushed aside the curtain covering the entrance to the back room and smiled at them as she came in. Both men quickly took off their hats and held the headgear in front of them.

"Mr. Fontaine, Mr. Woods, it's so nice to see you again," Violet said.

"It's Pearlie and Cal," Pearlie said. "No need for that mister business, ma'am."

Violet laughed. "In that case, there's no need for that ma'am business, either. I'm Violet." She turned to call through the opening, "Daisy, we have visitors."

"I know, I'm coming," Daisy replied from the back room. She joined her sister a moment later and smiled a greeting at the two cowboys.

Cal had to admit she looked as fresh as her namesake in a bright blue dress. Violet was wearing a darker maroon outfit. Both dresses were stylish without being fancy.

"It's very nice to see you again," Daisy said. "What brings you to Big Rock?"

Violet laughed. "I doubt if you're in the market for new dresses!"

"No, ma—" Pearlie began, then stopped for a second and went on, "No, we're sure not. Miss Sally said you ladies need somebody to teach you about gun-handlin'. Not to brag, but Cal and me are both tolerable shots and would be mighty happy to show you a few things."

Pearlie was being modest about his own skill. He was good enough with a gun that he had been able to make a living hiring out his Colt for a number of years before meeting Smoke. He didn't possess the same level of speed and accuracy that Smoke and Louis Longmont did, but his abilities were comparable to those of Monte Carson.

"Have you been able to purchase some revolvers?" Cal asked the sisters.

"Yes, we certainly have," Violet replied. "Mr. Goldstein at the mercantile was very helpful. He sold us a pair of . . ." She looked at Daisy. "What are they called?"

"Smith & Wesson Model 2 revolvers," Daisy said. "In .38 caliber. Just like the one Sally carries, in fact, right down to the nickel plating."

"I think my sister may be a more natural shooter than I am, but I'm certainly willing to learn. When would you gentlemen like to conduct this lesson?"

"Why, any time that's convenient for you ladies," Pearlie said. "Right now would be just fine, if you want, or later today, if that would be better. Or just about any other day that would work out for y'all."

Violet and Daisy looked at each other. Daisy said, "I don't see any reason why we can't do it right now, do you?"

"We'd have to close the shop," Violet said with a slight frown. "I'm not sure if that's a good idea."

"No one is scheduled to come in for a fitting or anything like that,"

Daisy said. "We can put a sign in the window saying when we'll be back. I don't think we'll lose a great deal of business, if any."

"You're probably right about that," Violet conceded with a nod. To Pearlie and Cal, she added, "Customers haven't exactly been beating down our door, although a few have stopped in this week. Mrs. Jensen promised she would spread the word about the shop."

"If Miss Sally said it, she'll sure do it, whatever it is," Pearlie declared. "She's a lady of her word, no doubt about it."

Daisy asked, "Where are we going to do this shooting?"

"There's a small area in back of the store," Violet suggested.

Pearlie thought about it and said, "It might be a good idea to get out of town. Otherwise, when guns start goin' off, the sheriff might come a-runnin' to see what's goin' on."

"There's a nice meadow alongside a creek about a mile south of town," Cal put in.

"Oh, I like the sound of that," Daisy said. "We can get in some target practice in a nice, pretty setting."

"We can rent a buggy for you ladies to ride out there."

"That's not necessary. We both have riding outfits. We can just rent a couple of horses from that nice Mr. Patterson at the livery stable."

"You're a better rider than I am, too," Violet said, "but I think I can manage."

Pearlie nodded and said, "All right, why don't Cal and me fetch the saddle mounts, and that'll give you time to change into your ridin' duds?"

Violet smiled, touched his forearm lightly with her fingertips, and said, "That's an excellent plan. We'll be ready to go by the time you get back here with the horses."

Her prediction proved to be true. Both sisters were attired in boots, riding skirts, and long-sleeved shirts when Pearlie and Cal returned leading the saddle mounts they had picked up at the livery stable. Daisy wore a flat-crowned brown hat, while Violet's similar hat was cream-colored.

Pearlie let out a low whistle of admiration, then hastily apologized.

"I didn't mean to be forward, ladies," he said. "It's just that a sight as pretty as the two of you ought to be in a book or somethin'."

"Thank you, Pearlie," Violet said. She looked at the bay and the chestnut the cowboys had brought from the livery stable. "Which one is mine?"

"I rode that bay before," Daisy said. "I claim him."

"All right. I suppose I'll take the other one."

Pearlie said, "Patterson has some sidesaddles, but since you ladies said you already had ridin' skirts, we didn't figure you'd need 'em."

"That's right," Daisy said. She took the reins of the bay Cal was holding, grasped the horn, put her foot in the stirrup, and swung up into the saddle with graceful ease. With a smile, she went on, "I'd rather ride astride any time. In a sidesaddle, I always feel like I might fall off if the pace gets too fast. Sometimes I like a good hard gallop."

Cal looked down at the ground as he felt his face growing warm. He was sure Daisy meant exactly what she said and nothing more, but even so, her words were provocative enough to make him blush.

Violet hesitated next to her horse and said, "I'd appreciate it if you'd give me a hand, Pearlie."

"Why, I'd be happy to," Pearlie said as he moved closer to her. "You just grab hold of the saddle horn and put your foot in the stirrup—"

"I know how to get on a horse, but since this animal is strange to me, I wouldn't mind if you'd hold on to him to make sure he doesn't shy away."

"Why, sure, I can do that." With his left hand, Pearlie took a firm grip on the chestnut's headstall while Violet prepared to mount.

He held up his right arm so that he was in position to steady her if she had any problem getting on the horse.

She climbed onto the chestnut without any trouble and settled herself in the saddle. She looked a little nervous but had a smile on her face as she said, "Thank you, Pearlie."

"You're mighty welcome, ma'am. Are you ready to ride?"

"Yes, indeed."

"Let's go," Daisy urged. "I'm ready to get out there and burn some powder." She looked at Cal. "Did I say that right?"

"Well, it depends," he replied with a faint smile, glad that she had changed the subject. "It sounds a little like something you might read in a dime novel."

"It should. That's where I read it. Is there anything wrong with that?"

"Oh, no, not really. Smoke always says those yarns are written by scribblers who don't know what they're talking about and only care about making money for a bottle of whiskey, or to pay off their gambling debts, but I've read some that were pretty good. You could tell the fellas were trying, anyway, even if they didn't get everything exactly right." Cal cleared his throat. "But burning powder is fine. Let's go do that." He started to turn toward his horse but paused. "You do have your guns, don't you?"

Daisy reached into the pocket of her riding skirt and brought out a Smith & Wesson Model 2, as she had said. Cal recognized it as the same kind of gun Sally usually carried. Daisy lifted it and said, "It's not loaded. Should I go ahead and load it?"

"No, it would be better to wait until we get out of town. You can load it when we get to where we're going to practice."

Violet said, "I have mine, too." She took it from her pocket and showed it to Pearlie.

"Yes'm, that's fine," he said. "Do you ladies have shells for them guns?"

"A whole box of cartridges," Daisy said. She patted her pocket and then slipped the .38 back inside it.

Cal and Pearlie mounted up, and the four of them rode out of Big Rock along a side street that turned into a trail leading south. Violet and Daisy were side by side, Violet on the right and Daisy on the left. Pearlie rode alongside Violet, while Cal flanked Daisy. It was a beautiful day, and they all seemed to enjoy being out in the sunshine and fresh air.

Daisy seemed very much at home in the saddle, Cal noted. Watching her, he had no doubt that she would be fine if her mount broke into a run.

Violet wasn't quite as much at ease, but she had no trouble handling her horse, and the others didn't have to slow down for her. She looked like she would be happy to get where they were going and get her feet back on the ground, though.

A while later, they came to the creek and meadow Cal had mentioned. They rode into the shade of the trees that grew along the bank and dismounted.

Cal and Pearlie tied the horses to a couple of small trees. If they had been going to stay here longer, they would have picketed the animals so they could graze and reach the creek for water, but that didn't seem necessary. They hadn't come that far, and likely they would only be here for an hour or so before heading back to Big Rock.

"All right, ladies," Pearlie said. "Now you can go ahead and load them guns. Just be careful to keep your fingers away from the triggers. You don't want to ever touch those until you're ready to shoot."

Violet took the .38 and the box of cartridges from her pocket. "Mr. Goldstein showed us how to open these guns, but I'm not sure I remember what you're supposed to do."

"Gimme the shells," Pearlie told her. When she had done so, he went on, "Now, hold the gun in your right hand and push up on that little bar right in front of the hammer with your left. That'll open the cylinder."

"Like this, Violet," Daisy said, proceeding to open the cylinder on the revolver she held. She put out her hand and added, "Five rounds, please."

Cal took the cartridges from the box Pearlie held and passed them to Daisy, who thumbed them into the chambers with ease.

"Have you been practicing?" Cal asked her.

"No, some things just come naturally to me. A lot of them do, actually."

Violet loaded her gun and snapped it closed as Pearlie told her.

"Remember, don't touch the trigger until you've lined up your shot," he said. "Cal, you see anything we can use for a good target?"

The creek was only ten or twelve feet wide and flowed leisurely. Cal pointed across the water to a dead tree on the other bank and said, "How about that branch sticking out, five feet up the trunk? It's thick enough to make a decent target."

Pearlie nodded. "And it'll be easy to see where the bullets hit. That'll do. Come on, ladies, right over here. Stand so that you're squared up with what you're gonna be shootin' at. Miss Violet, you go first."

"Age before beauty," Daisy said with a grin.

Pearlie said, "In the case of you gals, I don't reckon that really applies, seein' as how you're both mighty easy on the eyes."

Violet laughed. "Why, Mr. Fontaine, I didn't expect such flattery from you."

"Just statin' a fact, ma'am. I mean, Miss Violet."

"Just Violet is fine," she told him. She raised the Smith & Wesson in her right hand and pointed it across the creek toward the tree branch Cal had suggested. "Like this?"

"Yep. Don't close your left eye, and don't squint your right one. Just look over the top of the barrel and line up the sight with that branch. You got it?"

"I think so," Violet breathed. She was concentrating intently on what she was doing.

"Hold it steady. Use your thumb and pull back the hammer until it locks in place."

Violet cocked the revolver.

"You still got your sight lined up?" Pearlie asked.

"Wait. Yes, now it is."

"Put your finger on the trigger. Now, squeeze it slow and steady."

Violet did so. The sudden blast of the shot, accompanied by a spurt of flame and smoke from the gun's muzzle, made her jump and exclaim, "Oh!" She looked accusingly at Pearlie. "You didn't warn me it was going to be so loud."

"I'm sorry. I reckon it didn't occur to me since I'm used to bein' around guns goin' off."

Violet peered across the creek. "Did I at least hit the target? I don't see any marks on that branch."

"No, I think you shot just a mite high," Pearlie said. "That's easy to do startin' out. Thinkin' about what's gonna happen when the gun goes off makes you pull back just a tad, and that raises the barrel. To be honest, though, you didn't do it as much as some I've seen, Violet. I don't figure you missed by a whole lot."

"Let me try," Daisy said eagerly. She waved her sister back and stepped up to the edge of the bank.

Cal moved forward and took hold of her left arm. "Careful," he told her. "The bank could cave in if you get too close to the edge. It's not enough of a fall to hurt you, but you don't want to get dunked in the water, either."

"Thank you, Cal. I don't mean to be careless. This is just all so new and exciting." She gave him a brilliant smile.

Cal realized after a moment that he still had hold of her arm, and she didn't seem to be in any hurry for him to let go, despite her eagerness to try her hand at shooting. He released her arm and stepped back, and Daisy moved a little farther from the creek.

Facing the dead tree on the other side, she leveled her arm and thrust out the revolver, earing back the hammer as she did so.

"Careful," Cal said. "You just cocked it."

"I know. I want to be ready to fire as soon as I've lined up the shot. I'm being careful not to touch the trigger."

"All right," Cal said warily. "Go ahead and aim."

She settled the sight at the front of the barrel on the target, and without waiting for Cal to tell her to go ahead, she squeezed the trigger. She flinched slightly, but not as much as Violet had, and she didn't gasp or make any other sound.

On the other side of the creek, splinters flew in the air as the slug chewed its way into the dead branch.

"I hit it!" Daisy cried, her voice exultant with triumph. "You saw! I hit it!"

"You sure did," Cal told her. "That was a good shot. You must have fired a gun before."

Daisy shook her head. "No, that was the first time." She laughed. "But don't you dare say it was beginner's luck. I'm just a good shot, that's all."

"Maybe so," Cal said, nodding.

Pearlie said, "Violet, you go ahead and try again. I reckon you'll probably do better this time, since you know what to expect."

"I'm not sure that will help," Violet said, "but I'll certainly give it a try."

She raised the gun, aimed, cocked it, and squeezed the trigger. She still jumped when it fired, but not as much as the first time, and she didn't cry out.

Pearlie grinned and pointed. "See that little notch on top of the branch?" he asked her. "You did that."

"You mean I hit it?" Violet asked, her eyes widening in disbelief.

"Yep. You shot a little high again, but not as much, so you didn't hit the target head-on but grazed it instead. And to be honest, that ain't bad shootin'."

"It was still awfully loud, though."

"Oh, you'll get used to it, Violet," Daisy said. "Let me go again."

For the next half hour, the sisters took turns shooting at the branch. They handled their own reloading when their cylinders were empty. Daisy hit three out of every four shots, Cal estimated, although he didn't keep an exact count. Violet wasn't as accurate, but she hit the branch squarely several times and showed definite improvement as she practiced.

Eventually, Violet flexed her fingers and said, "My hand is starting to get a little sore."

Pearlie nodded. "These .38s don't kick as much as a .44 or .45, but if you ain't used to shootin', they'll make your hand ache after a while. Might be best to call it good for today."

"But we have bullets left," Daisy protested. "And my hand doesn't hurt."

"It probably will in the morning," Cal told her. "You don't want to do too much your first time."

Daisy started to roll her eyes but stopped herself. "I suppose you're right," she said. "Although I'm not sure it's wise to go through life being that cautious about everything."

Cal didn't know what to say to that, so he didn't respond.

"It'd be a good idea to clean them guns once we get back to town," Pearlie said. "Did Goldstein tell you what you'll need to do that?"

"He did," Violet said. "And he told us what to do, but again, I'm not sure I really understood all of it."

Pearlie nodded. "Cleanin' a gun is like most things. You just got to do it to learn what works."

"Now that's wise advice," Daisy said. "What's the old saying? Experience is the best teacher?"

"Stop being so impudent," Violet told her. She turned back to

Pearlie and put her hand on his arm. "Thank you, Pearlie. We really do appreciate you and Cal helping us this way."

"Shucks, we're glad to do it, ain't we, Cal?"

"Sure," Cal said. "This was a lot more pleasant than dealing with cattle all day."

"Well, I should hope so," Daisy said with a touch of indignation in her voice. Then she softened her tone and went on, "You'll come out here with us and help us practice again, won't you?"

"I think we can find the time for that," Cal said.

"And if there's anything Violet and I can do to show our gratitude, anything at all, you just let us know."

Daisy surprised Cal by coming up on her toes, leaning closer to him, and brushing a light kiss across his cheek.

A few feet away, Violet did likewise, pressing her lips to Pearlie's grizzled face for a second.

The kisses were just friendly gestures, but both cowboys were a bit flustered by the unexpectedness of them. Pearlie cleared his throat and said, "I reckon we'd best be gettin' back to Big Rock. Wouldn't want you ladies to miss any important business at your shop."

"Learning how to take care of ourselves out here in the West is important, too," Violet said. "I think with your generous help, we'll be able to get everything we want out of moving to Big Rock."

Chapter 11

The ride back to the settlement was peaceful and uneventful. Once again, Pearlie and Cal enjoyed chatting with the Caldwell sisters. Cal knew they had come from St. Louis, so he tried to draw out a little more information about their background, such as whether they had lived in that city on the Mississippi their whole lives, but Violet and Daisy didn't seem to want to talk much about their past. They were too focused on what the future might hold for them, Violet explained, and Cal couldn't blame them for feeling that way.

It was a little past midday when they reached Big Rock. After dropping off the rented horses at the livery stable, Pearlie suggested that they get something to eat.

"If you ladies haven't been to Lambert's yet, Cal and me would be mighty pleased to treat you," he said. He hadn't checked with Cal before he made that offer, but the younger man had no objection to the idea. "The food's good, and they put on an entertainin' show, too."

"A show?" Violet repeated. "What sort of show?"

"Throwed rolls," Pearlie said.

Both sisters looked confused.

Cal chuckled and said, "The waiters don't bring dinner rolls to your table. They throw them across the room to you. I'm not sure why they started doing that, but folks seem to enjoy it. And the rolls are mighty good, too."

"Well, that sounds interesting," Daisy said. "We've already been away from the shop for a while, Violet. I don't think being gone a little while longer will matter, do you?"

"I suppose not," Violet said, although she didn't sound as eager as her sister. She smiled, though, as she linked arms with Pearlie and told him, "Lead on, sir."

Daisy followed her example and took Cal's arm, and both cowboys had a bit of a strut in their step as they went up the street to Lambert's Restaurant, accompanied by the lovely young blondes.

The meal was very enjoyable. Violet got Pearlie to spin a few yarns about his adventurous life before settling down on the Sugarloaf. The stories were colorful and humorous, but Cal knew Pearlie was cleaning them up considerably as he told them. Pearlie's life had been a lot more rugged and dangerous than he was making it out to be.

"How about you?" Daisy asked Cal. "How did you wind up working for the famous Smoke Jensen?"

"That's easy," Cal said. "I tried to hold up his wife."

Both young women stared at him. Finally, Daisy said, "You were an outlaw?"

"Well, I sort of took it into my head to become a highwayman," Cal said, "because I was hungry and didn't see any other way out. I had an old pistol that didn't even work, but it looked threatening. So I waited for somebody to come by on the road, figuring I could hold them up and get money for food. Lucky for me, that happened to be Miss Sally."

"Lucky she didn't blow a hole clean through you, that's what you mean," Pearlie said. "I've knowed it to happen when folks were foolish enough to point a gun at that lady."

"You're absolutely right. But I guess I looked pretty pitiful, because she didn't shoot me. She took me home with her, gave me a good meal, and told Smoke to give me a job, as long as I swore I'd never do anything so stupid again." Cal grinned. "And so far, I guess I haven't, since I'm still there."

"I'm glad she didn't kill you," Daisy said. "I had a good time this morning."

"So did I," Cal said, and he realized that he meant it. He still had a certain amount of fondness for Susannah Bolton, but if she wanted to stay back East instead of returning to the valley, that was her decision to make. The time had come for him to look ahead again, rather than backward. A part of him still wondered if he was cursed when it came to romance, but he was going to try not to dwell on that.

While they were talking, they ate roast beef, potatoes, gravy, greens, and the rolls that Pearlie and Cal caught when they were tossed toward them by the waiters. Apple pie and cream finished off the meal. All four of them were pleasantly full when they returned to the dress shop.

Violet took the hand-printed card that announced the shop would be open again that afternoon from the window. Daisy said, "Come on into the back room. We can use one of the tables back here to clean the guns."

Once again, the two cowboys felt somewhat out of place. Their world normally didn't include dress dummies, bolts of cloth, sewing machines, and pincushions. But Violet cleared a place for them to work, and it didn't take long for them to demonstrate to the sisters how to clean and maintain the revolvers, using the equipment they had bought at the mercantile.

"You take care o' these guns and they'll take care o' you," Pearlie told the sisters when they were finished. "I'm hopin' you'll never need to use 'em, but if you do, don't hesitate."

Cal said, "Sally told us you like to go riding, Daisy, and after seeing the way you handled your horse today, I can understand why. But if you do, take the gun with you, and make sure it's loaded. Same goes for you, Violet."

"A respectable woman is safe 'most anywhere out here on the frontier," Pearlie added, "but there's a few times when that ain't true, so always keep your eyes open."

Daisy said, "That's good advice. I intend to take it."

No customers had come in while Pearlie and Cal were there. It was time they were getting back to the Sugarloaf, so they went out through the front room and paused on the boardwalk to say their farewells.

Violet took Pearlie's right hand in both of hers and said, "Thank you again."

"You're mighty welcome, ma—" Again, he caught himself before calling her *ma'am* and chuckled. "Hope to see you again soon, Violet."

"That's my hope, as well." She kissed him on the cheek, as she had earlier in the day.

Daisy faced Cal and put both of her hands on his shoulders. "You're going to think I'm a brazen hussy," she said.

He started to shake his head and say, "Why, no, I'd never—"

She stopped him by kissing him on the mouth. It was quick and not really that passionate, but it sent a jolt through Cal, anyway.

"Come see us," Daisy told him with a mischievous smile as she stepped back.

"Uh . . . yeah. We will. We surely will."

The sisters went back into the shop. Violet closed the door.

Cal looked over at Pearlie and asked, "What in blazes just happened?"

"You got smooched by a pretty girl, and so did I." Pearlie

grinned. "I figured you were smart enough to understand that, boy." He clapped a hand on Cal's shoulder. "Come on. We need to get back to the ranch."

They climbed into their saddles and headed west out of Big Rock. After the beautiful, almost cloudless day they had enjoyed, a low line of clouds had appeared on the western horizon. There might be another rainstorm that night, or there might not. It was too soon to tell.

For now, both men felt that it had been a mighty fine day, and they were already looking forward to the next visit they paid to the Caldwell sisters.

Cal said, "I think I'm going to ask Daisy ahead of time to go with me to the next town social, so I won't have to worry about varmints like Dade and Hendryx trying to cut in."

"You reckon she'll say yes?"

"Well, I hope so."

Pearlie looked and sounded dubious as he said, "I don't know. There ain't no doubt that Miss Daisy's right fond of you, Cal, but gals like her tend to enjoy gettin' attention from lots of different fellas."

Cal frowned. "You shouldn't talk about her like she's some sort of shameless flirt."

"That ain't what I'm sayin'. It's just that you can tell she likes havin' gents fuss over her."

"And her sister doesn't?"

"Miss Violet's more . . . restrained," Pearlie said. "Ladylike."

Now Cal was definitely getting a little hot under the collar. He turned in his saddle to glare at Pearlie, who was riding to his left. "You can't say that Daisy's not lady—"

He didn't finish the sentence because at that moment something flicked past his ear. He recognized the sensation as the wind-rip of a bullet coming way too close for comfort. He had experienced that unsettling feeling before, and it was something a fellow never forgot.

A split second later, the whip crack of a rifle shot sounded. Pearlie yelled, "Ambush!" and leaned forward in the saddle, then spurred his horse into a sudden run. "Split up!"

It was a good tactic. They didn't know how many bushwhackers had lain in wait for them. If there was only one, there was no point in giving him two easy targets.

Pearlie went left and Cal headed to the right as they charged ahead. The shot had come from somewhere in front of them. Cal's insides went cold as he realized that if he hadn't turned to glare at Pearlie at that particular instant, the bullet probably would have struck him in the head.

A clump of trees lay ahead on the left of the road, about a hundred yards away. That seemed to be the most likely source of the shot. Cal saw dirt fly in the air near the flashing hooves of Pearlie's horse and knew a second bullet had caused that.

Convinced now that the shots were coming from the trees, Cal pulled his Colt and triggered two rounds toward them. He tugged on the reins and leaned over in the saddle as he began to circle back toward the little grove.

Pearlie had figured that out, too. He charged at the trees with his revolver roaring and bucking in his hand. Cal continued firing as well. Their slugs ripping through the branches might be making it pretty hot for whoever was hidden in there.

Cal spotted movement in the shadows under the spreading branches, and a second later, a muzzle flash erupted. Cal's hat flew off his head and sailed backward.

Cal clenched his jaw and hunched over in the saddle. He fired twice more at the trees, aiming now at the spot where he had seen the muzzle flash. He glanced around, looking for cover. Maybe this frontal assault wasn't such a good idea, after all.

However, Cal didn't see anything except open ground. Turning and fleeing wouldn't do anything except make it easier for whoever was trying to kill him.

Anyway, Cal had learned from Smoke that a man didn't run from his troubles. He tackled them, head-on when he had to. Like now.

Unfortunately, Cal had only one more round in his gun. He wasn't far from the trees now, so he straightened in the saddle and fired that last shot, bracing for the impact of a bullet coming back at him.

Nothing happened. He hauled back on the reins and brought his horse to a skidding halt before it crashed into the trees. Off to his left a ways, Pearlie was reining in as well. The older cowboy dropped to the ground and ran into the grove, his Colt held ready in front of him. Cal stayed in the saddle.

Quickly, he plucked fresh cartridges from the loops in his shell belt and reloaded while he sat there waiting to see what was going to happen with Pearlie. No more shots came from the trees.

Cal lifted his head sharply as he heard the swift rataplan of hoofbeats coming from somewhere on the other side of the grove. The sound steadily diminished as the riders hurried away from there.

A minute or so later, Pearlie emerged from the clump of trees still holding his gun, but his arm was down at his side now.

"Looks like they took off for the tall and uncut," he told Cal. "Ain't nobody in there now."

Cal nodded. "I heard their horses when they rode off. It sounded like two riders, and that matches up with the shots I heard."

As Pearlie began reloading his gun, he asked, "You ain't hit, are you?"

"Nope," Cal replied. "At least I don't think so." He reached up and touched his right ear, then looked at his fingers. "Just checking. No blood, so I guess that first shot missed. I'd hate to ever have one come any closer, though."

"Yeah." Pearlie pouched his iron and went to his horse. He swung up into the saddle. "Who do you reckon was shootin' at us?"

Cal shook his head and said, "I don't know. Riding for the Sugarloaf, we've made some enemies, I suppose. There's been plenty of trouble over the years."

"Most of the hombres causin' that trouble have wound up dead, though. It usually happens that way when Smoke's involved."

"They could have relatives," Cal said with a shrug. "Or it could have been just some thieves out to rob us."

Pearlie scoffed at that. "Who'd figure a couple o' cowhands would have enough dinero to make holdin' 'em up worthwhile?"

"There are folks out there sorry enough to kill a man for a silver dollar."

"Yeah, that's true." Pearlie lifted his reins. "Let's ride around those trees and take a look around. Maybe we can pick up their trail."

They found the tracks left by the fleeing bushwhackers' horses without much trouble, but they weren't very distinctive. It would be hard to identify the hoofprints beyond a doubt if they came across similar tracks in the future. Even so, the prints confirmed that two riflemen had been hidden in the trees. Cal and Pearlie studied the tracks and committed them to memory.

They followed the trail, which led west for a mile or so and then angled sharply north. A short time later, the tracks led into a shallow creek and disappeared.

"I know this creek," Pearlie said with a disgusted note in his voice. "They could ride five miles in either direction in it before comin' out. The chances of us bein' able to pick up the trail again are mighty slim."

Cal nodded slowly and said, "It would probably just be a waste of time to even try. They've given us the slip."

"I hate to say it, but I think you're sight." Pearlie made a face and then jerked his head toward the road. "We might as well head on back to the ranch. Best keep our eyes peeled, though, in case those varmints might've doubled back to take another crack at us."

"How likely do you think that is?"

"Not likely after we put up a good fight like we did, but you can't never tell."

They returned to the road between Big Rock and the Sugarloaf and were jogging along it a short time later when Cal spotted two riders up ahead, coming toward them.

"Pearlie," he said as he drew back on the reins.

"I see 'em," the foreman responded. He also brought his mount to a stop. "And I reckon they see us, so the only thing we can do is sit right here and wait to see what they do about it."

The two men in the distance had reined in, too. This could quickly turn into a standoff if both sides stayed where they were, staring at each other over a distance of three hundred yards.

But after a tense moment, the other pair nudged their horses into motion again and came toward Pearlie and Cal at a steady, deliberate pace.

It wasn't long before Pearlie exclaimed, "Dadgum it! It's those two rannies from the Three Sevens."

"Yeah," Cal said. "It's hard to mistake those two."

The riders were close enough now that Pearlie and Cal were sure of their identities. Stocky, redheaded Chuck Dade and burly, barrel-chested, dark-haired Jasper Hendryx didn't rein in again until they were twenty feet from the Sugarloaf hands.

"Move aside," Hendryx growled. "You're in our way."

"This trail's plenty big enough for you to go around us," Pearlie said. "Anyway, we got more right to be here than you do. We're on our way to the Sugarloaf. The Three Sevens ain't in this direction."

"Where we ride is none of your blasted business," Dade said. "This is a free country, ain't it?"

With a sneer directed at Pearlie and Cal, Hendryx said, "It was, the last time I looked, Chuck."

Pearlie's eyes narrowed as he regarded the two men. He cocked his head a little to the side and said, "Those horses you're ridin' got some dried mud on their legs."

Dade and Hendryx both looked puzzled. "So?" Dade asked.

Cal kept his face impassive, even though he realized what Pearlie was getting at. It came as a bit of a shock to him, but not much.

"Looks to me like you might've been ridin' along a creek bed for a spell," Pearlie went on.

"We crossed a creek a ways back while we were cuttin' across country. I don't see as that's any business of yours."

"You didn't just cross a creek," Pearlie snapped. "You rode along one to throw us off your trail after you bushwhacked us and then took off like a couple o' yellow dogs when we fought back."

"What the devil are you talkin' about?" Hendryx burst out. "Have you gone loco, Fontaine?"

"Not hardly. I reckon I'm just now startin' to figure things out. Two lowdown skunks tried to ventilate me and Cal a little while ago, and I think I'm lookin' at those polecats right now."

An angry look suddenly appeared on Chuck Dade's face. "Watch out, Jasper!" he cried. "This is a gun trap! They aim to murder us!"

Both men clawed at the guns on their hips.

Chapter 12

Pearlie jabbed his spurs into his horse's flanks, and the animal leaped forward. At the same time, Pearlie let out a yell.

Cal knew he did that to urge the horse to greater speed, and also to disorient Dade and Hendryx. He followed his friend's lead, figuring Pearlie didn't want to engage in a shoot-out with the men.

Dade managed to draw his gun, but it had barely cleared leather when Pearlie left his saddle and crashed into the Three Sevens cowboy in a diving tackle. The impact drove Dade off his horse. He and Pearlie fell heavily to the ground with Pearlie landing on top.

At the same time, Cal reached Jasper Hendryx and tried to duplicate Pearlie's maneuver, leaping from the saddle with arms outstretched.

However, since Hendryx hadn't gotten his gun completely out of its holster, he let go of it and allowed it to drop back into leather. That gave him just enough time to jerk up his arms and grab Cal when the young cowboy attempted his tackle.

That took Cal by surprise. Hendryx wrapped his arms around him in a bear hug, leaving Cal's legs waving in space as Hendryx's mount jumped around skittishly, disturbed by the extra weight and the struggle taking place on its back.

The two men wrestled awkwardly for several seconds before Hendryx's horse had had enough. Whinnying shrilly, the horse reared up and pawed at the air with its front hooves.

With his hands full, Hendryx had no hope of holding on. He kicked his feet free of the stirrups as he slid from the saddle. He and Cal fell to the ground.

Both pairs of combatants had to deal not only with each other but also the threat of being stepped on by the spooked horses. Pearlie jabbed a knee into Dade's midsection and then broke free to roll a few feet away. He came up on his knees, grabbed Dade's ankles, and scuttled backward, hauling the Three Sevens rider out of reach of the slashing hooves.

Hendryx was on top of Cal. He hooked a hard left into Cal's belly and then groped for the young man's throat with his right hand.

Gasping for breath from the brutal punch, Cal could still think clearly enough to realize that if he allowed Hendryx to grab him like that, the man might choke him to death. Hendryx's face was brick red, flushed with hot blood from the fighting rage in which he was caught up.

Cal got the heel of his right hand under Hendryx's chin and levered the bigger man's head back as hard as he could. That gave Cal enough room to throw a left of his own.

His fist slammed into Hendryx's solar plexus with enough force to make the man's face turn white. Cal bucked up from the ground and threw Hendryx to the side.

On the other side of the horses, Dade was curled up, gasping from the knee in the stomach Pearlie had given him. The fall from horseback had jolted the gun out of his hand. Spotting the Colt lying on the ground a few feet away, Pearlie started toward it on his hands and knees, intending to grab it so that Dade couldn't go after it.

Dade unwound from his jackknifed position and straightened both legs, driving his bootheels into Pearlie's ribs. The vicious double kick sent Pearlie rolling over the ground again. Dade got his hands and knees under him and crawled toward the gun.

Pearlie flung out a hand and latched on to one of Dade's ankles. Ignoring the pain in his side from the kick, he hauled back as hard as he could on Dade's leg. Dade fell on his belly, and his face smacked hard into the ground.

Cal made it back to his feet just ahead of Hendryx. There was a moment while Hendryx was struggling to get up that Cal could have kicked him in the face, but the young cowboy hesitated. It went against the grain for him to kick a man while he was down.

But as Hendryx got both feet under him and rose from the ground, Cal stepped in and, with no hesitation at all, threw a looping right that smashed into Hendryx's jaw and sent him sprawling again. That was perfectly fair, as far as Cal was concerned.

A few yards away, Pearlie landed on Chuck Dade's back and straddled the man. He grabbed Dade's hair, jerked up his head, and drove his face into the ground again. Then, while Dade was stunned, he looped his arm around Dade's neck and locked it in place by gripping that wrist with his other hand. He shifted, planted a knee in the small of Dade's back, and bent Dade's spine the wrong way.

"I can snap your neck or bust your back, Dade, and I'll do it if you don't holler uncle!" Pearlie told him.

Dade couldn't holler anything with Pearlie's arm clamped across his throat like that. But he could make gurgling noises and slap his open hand against the ground several times, which was what he did.

Pearlie interpreted that as a surrender. He hung on for a few seconds longer just for good measure, and to deny Dade that much more air. Then he let go, pushed upright, and stepped back. Breathing hard, he brushed the back of his hand across his mouth.

Dade stayed where he was, making a rasping sound as he dragged air down his windpipe.

Pearlie picked up the man's gun, opened the cylinder, and dumped the shells into his palm. He threw them one way and the revolver the other, then turned to see how Cal was doing with Hendryx.

Cal was bent over the burly cowboy. He snagged Hendryx's gun from its holster and followed Pearlie's example, throwing the Colt and the cartridges well out of reach in opposite directions.

"What are we going to do with these two?" he asked.

Pearlie reached down to his hip, pushed aside the little strip of rawhide that had kept his gun from falling out of its holster during the ruckus, and drew the iron.

"We're gonna get the answers to a few questions," he said. Holding the gun ready, he prodded Dade in the ribs with a booted toe and ordered, "Get up, you sidewinder."

Dade didn't respond for a moment, but then he groaned and rolled onto his back. The lower half of his face was smeared with blood that had leaked from his nose. He seemed to be having trouble breathing, so he struggled to sit up. When he managed that, he said in a thick voice, "You broke my nose." He added some choice obscenities.

"Shut your filthy mouth or I'll slap this gun across it," Pearlie said. "Cal, is Hendryx awake?"

"Well, sort of, but not really," Cal said. He used his left hand to massage the knuckles on his right. "I hit him pretty hard."

"Good for you. Keep an eye on him and make sure he ain't playin' possum. Dade can tell us what we want to know."

Dade snarled and said, "I'm not gonna tell you anything except to go to blazes!"

Pearlie ignored that and asked, "Why'd you bushwhack us?"

"We never did!"

"You're lyin'," Pearlie said coldly. "Two men tried to kill Cal and me about an hour ago. They lit a shuck when we put up a fight, and we trailed 'em to a creek north of here. We lost their sign there because they rode off along the creek bed, which means their horses are bound to have mud stuck to their legs, like those nags o' yours."

"Don't call 'em nags, blast you! Those are fine horses. And we told you why they've got mud on their legs. We rode across what must be the same creek you're talkin' about, but we didn't bushwhack you or anybody else. Jasper and me wouldn't do a low-down thing like that, even to a couple of dirty dogs like you two."

Dade made a face and probed gently with his fingertips at his injured nose.

"It ain't broke," Pearlie said disgustedly. "It'd be swellin' up more by now if it was. I just bloodied it for you, that's all."

"And you'll be sorry you did," Dade said. "Jasper and me won't forget about this."

"You sure won't, because Cal and me are gonna haul you back to Big Rock and have Monte Carson throw you in jail. You'll answer to the law for tryin' to murder us."

With some puffing and groaning, Dade climbed to his feet. He pulled a bandanna from his pocket, dabbed at his nose, and grimaced again.

Then he said, "How'd we bushwhack you? With rifles?"

"How else?"

Dade pointed at the horses he and Hendryx had been riding. "I don't have a saddle gun with me, and Jasper's Winchester hasn't been fired in a week or more. Check it and see for yourself."

Cal frowned as he looked at the horses. With everything that had been going on, he hadn't noticed until now that no saddle scabbard was strapped to Dade's mount. He stepped over to Hendryx's horse, which had calmed down considerably now that the fight was over, and caught hold of the dangling reins. Talking softly to the animal to keep it calm, he wrapped his hand around the stock of the Winchester sticking up from the saddle boot and pulled the repeater from it.

Cal sniffed the barrel and looked at Pearlie. "It doesn't smell like it's been fired recently."

"Check the chamber," Pearlie said.

Cal worked the lever. No shell flew out, indicating that the rifle hadn't been cocked since it was loaded. Cal lifted it closer and sniffed the open breech.

"No round in the chamber, and no smell of powder here, either."

Pearlie frowned. "They could've cleaned it. And Dade could've stashed his rifle somewhere."

"Why would we do that?" Dade asked. "We didn't know we were gonna run into you two jackasses." He grew more heated as he went on. "And why would we bushwhack you in the first place? Just because of that fracas at the dance? That was almost a week ago!"

"Maybe seein' us with the Caldwell sisters today rubbed some salt in them wounds," Pearlie said. "Especially when those gals up an' kissed us!"

Dade stared at him and then said, "What in the Sam Hill are you talkin' about, Fontaine? I don't know anything about this, and neither does Jasper."

As if he heard his name, Hendryx groaned and stirred a little, but he didn't try to get up yet.

"We haven't been in Big Rock today, or any other time in the past few days," Dade went on. "You can ask the rest of the crew at the Three Sevens about that if you want to."

Pearlie snorted. "Like they wouldn't lie their fool heads off for you two."

"Then ask the boss. You know Jack Brodie's a straight shooter."

Pearlie and Cal exchanged a glance. They both knew the

Three Sevens owner wasn't the sort of man to lie. Dade was right about that.

Cal said, "If you didn't ambush us, who did?"

"How in blazes would we know?"

"Did you see anybody suspicious while you were riding this way? Two men, maybe?"

Dade shook his head. "Look," he said, "I don't give a hoot if you two get shot full of holes, especially after the way you jumped us like this. But Jasper and me didn't have anything to do with it, and we don't know anything about it. So you can just go to blazes, and if you're gonna gun us down, go ahead and do it."

"Nobody said nothin' about gunnin' you down," Pearlie snapped. "I just said we were gonna have you thrown in jail, that's all."

"I don't reckon we can stop you, but you're just gonna look like fools if you do. You can't prove a thing against us, because we ain't guilty."

Cal said, "He might have a point, Pearlie."

"All right, all right," Pearlie groused, frowning darkly. "I ain't sayin' I believe you, you skunk, but I reckon you're right about one thing: We can't prove nothin'. So we're gonna go on our way, and you can get your pard on his horse and go on about your business. But you best not cross our trail again. I might not be so forgivin' next time."

"Yeah, well, we ain't gonna forgive and forget about this, neither," Dade said.

Pearlie and Cal went over to their horses. Pearlie said, "We'll drop this rifle a hundred yards up the road. Don't go after it or your six-shooters until we're out of sight. We'll be keepin' an eye on you."

Dade muttered some more curses but didn't respond otherwise. He started to kneel next to Hendryx, but then stopped to look at the two Sugarloaf punchers.

"Did those gals really kiss you?" he asked.

Pearlie and Cal swung up into their saddles, and then Pearlie said, "Durned right they did."

"Why would they do a loco thing like that?"

Cal said, "They were grateful to us for teaching them to shoot."

"What are you talkin' about?"

"That's right," Pearlie said. "Miss Violet and Miss Daisy are gonna be packin' iron from now on, and let me tell you, they're pretty darned good shots for ladies who never handled guns before now. So you and that big galoot you call a friend better steer clear of 'em. You get outta line and they'll pin your ears back for you."

"We wouldn't never get out of line with ladies," Dade insisted. He shrugged. "I reckon it's a good thing they can take care of themselves, though. You never know what kind of trouble you'll run into out here, especially with that gang of rustlers and train robbers on the loose."

He started trying to help Hendryx to his feet as Pearlie and Cal turned their horses and headed toward the ranch again. Pearlie kept checking over his shoulder to make sure they didn't try to retrieve their Colts. When they had gone a hundred yards or so, Cal paused and lowered the Winchester's stock to the trail, then let it fall sideways.

"Do you believe them?" he asked Pearlie as they rode on.

"I don't want to," Pearlie said. He rubbed his side where Dade had kicked him and winced, knowing he was going to be sore and bruised in the morning. "I don't like them two rannies, not even a little bit." He sighed. "But Dade told a pretty convincin' story. It does seem a mite far-fetched that they'd go to all the trouble o' hidin' Dade's rifle and cleanin' Hendryx's. And if they figured on doublin' back and takin' us by surprise, they wouldn't have been ridin' along the trail bold as brass, out in the open the way they were."

"That's how it seemed to me, too," Cal said. After a moment, he added, "But if they didn't ambush us, then who did, and why?"

Pearlie shook his head. "Right now, I ain't got no earthly idea." Off to the west, a low rumble of thunder sounded from the gathering clouds. Pearlie nodded in that direction and went on, "Maybe if that storm comes through tonight, it'll blow some answers in with it."

Chapter 13

The storm hit Big Rock that night, with frequent flashes of lightning that clawed brilliantly across the sky, rolling peals of thunder loud enough to make the ground shake a little at times, and rain that slanted down in a vicious downpour.

Yellow lamplight shone in the window of the little parlor where Violet and Daisy Caldwell sat quietly in armchairs. In the glow from the lamp, the rain made numerous fast-running streaks on the glass.

The parlor was the front room of a small, neat cottage behind the dress shop, part of the same property the sisters had rented when they came to Big Rock. Having their living quarters so close—only a few steps away—was very handy.

Violet had some needlework in her lap. Her hands moved deftly and efficiently as she wielded the needle and thread.

Daisy held a book, but even though it was open, she wasn't reading. Her attention had drifted, and she was staring at the rain-washed window instead.

Suddenly, she gasped and jumped enough that the book slipped out of her fingers and slid from her lap, landing with a thump on the floor at her feet. She raised a hand to her mouth and let out a muffled cry.

Instantly, Violet set her needlework aside on the small table next to her chair. Her hand dipped into the space between her hip and the arm of the chair and came up with the nickel-plated Smith & Wesson. Retrieving the gun had required little more than the blink of an eye.

"What is it?" she asked tersely. "What's wrong?"

"I saw something at . . . at the window," Daisy said. She pointed. "Something was looking in."

"A man?"

"I don't know. I couldn't tell much. Then the lightning flashed, and I could see something big silhouetted there—"

A sharp knock on the cottage's front door broke into what she was saying.

Violet came to her feet and so did Daisy, who kicked the book aside. She reached to the table beside her chair and picked up the little revolver that lay there.

Both young women seemed much more at ease holding the guns than they had earlier in the day, when they were out at the creek practicing with Pearlie and Cal.

Without saying anything, Violet motioned to her sister. They kept well apart as they approached the door, Violet to the right and Daisy to the left. Another knock sounded, even more peremptory this time.

Outside, thunder boomed again as Violet stepped close to the door. She waited for its echoes to die away and then called, "Who's there?"

As soon as she spoke, she moved quickly to one side as a precaution.

"It's me, blast it," a man's voice replied through the panel. "Let me in, Vi. It's pourin' down hard enough out here to strangle a frog."

Violet looked at Daisy and rolled her eyes. Daisy's tense attitude disappeared as she laughed, shook her head, and went back to her chair. Violet turned the key in the lock and opened the door.

"Lincoln Pollard, don't you have the sense God gave a donkey?" she asked the man who stood there with water running off the brim of his black hat. He wore a dark slicker that made him blend in with the shadows back here behind the dress shop, except when lightning flashed overhead.

Pollard moved into the room as Violet stepped back. She held the Smith & Wesson down at her side now. He heeled the door closed behind him.

"Stay on the rug," Violet told him. "I don't want you dripping all over the floor."

"I'm not gonna just stand here," Pollard said. "I want to get out of this wet slicker. Blasted thing leaks."

"You should have thought of that before you came out on a night like this. You could be back at the hideout, nice and warm and dry."

"Yeah, well, you should have thought of some things, too," he replied with a scowl.

Pollard took off his hat, shook rain from it, and hung it on a hat tree standing to the side of the door. Violet glared at him but didn't say anything as he peeled off the slicker and hung it on one of the hooks, as well.

"Daisy, get a towel," Violet said.

Daisy had just resumed her seat and looked like she wanted to argue, but the tone of command in her sister's voice didn't allow any room for disagreement. She stood up with a sigh, left the room for a moment, and then came back with a large, fluffy towel that she spread on the floor to soak up the water dripping from Pollard's hat and slicker.

He was a tall, well-built man in his thirties with dark hair, deep-set eyes, a prominent nose, and a dark mustache and spade beard. He had a ruthless, predatory look about him. A black gun belt was strapped around his lean waist and a black-butted gun rode in the holster.

"All right," Violet said, "why are you here, Linc? We weren't expecting to see you tonight."

Pollard smiled and asked, "You're not gonna offer me something to warm me up?"

"There's still some coffee in the pot, but it's been sitting for a while."

"I was thinkin' more along the lines of a drink."

"You're out of luck," Violet told him. "There's not a drop of whiskey in the house."

"Well, then, I guess I'll have to settle for the coffee."

Violet turned to look at Daisy, who said, "Of course. I'll get it. Why not?"

She left the room again.

Violet said to their visitor, "If your clothes are wet, I don't want you sitting on the good furniture. Take that ladder-back chair over there. It won't hurt it to get damp."

Pollard picked up the plain wooden chair Violet had indicated, turned it around, and straddled it. Violet went back to the armchair where she had been sitting. She laid the revolver on the table next to the needlework she'd set aside.

Daisy came back with a cup and handed it to Pollard, who took a sip and nodded in approval.

"That'll warm a man's bones on a night like this," he said.

"We're still waiting to hear why you came into town tonight," Violet said. "We weren't scheduled to meet again for another three days."

Pollard took another drink from the cup and said, "This is actually the second time I've been to Big Rock today."

"Oh?" Violet said coolly.

"Yeah, I was here early this afternoon. Just taking a look around, you know, since nobody here has any idea who I am. I saw you two hussies carrying on with a couple of cowboys in broad daylight."

Pollard's tone was light, but the look in his deep-set eyes was brooding and angry.

Daisy had sat down again. She said, "You're spying on us now, Linc?"

"Just keepin' up with things, like I said. We're partners, after all. I have to look after you gals." His lips pulled back from his teeth in what might have been taken for a smile, but it was equally likely the expression was a snarl. "That's the way Whisper wanted it, right? He wanted to make sure his little girls got looked after good and proper."

Violet stared right back at him. Her expression was chilly as she said, "What he wanted was for the gang to carry on successfully, and that's why he put me in charge. Not you, Linc. Me."

For a moment, tension filled the air in the parlor. There was no sense that violence was about to erupt, but no real guarantee that anger wouldn't be let loose, either. Violet and Pollard sat there with their dueling gazes while Daisy remained to the side, watching both of them warily.

Abruptly, Pollard threw back his head and laughed. "Aw, shoot, Vi, don't get your back up," he said. "I know you're Whisper's favorite. You're his daughter, after all."

"Stepdaughter," Violet corrected him.

"Maybe, but he's the one who raised you. You don't even remember your real pa, do you?"

"I don't," Daisy said.

"I remember him," Violet said. She shrugged. "But not well, I'll admit. He died when I was only six years old."

"Well, Whisper's the one who asked you to get the bunch back together and put you in charge, so I won't go against that. I owe the old man a lot. You don't have to worry. Every time one of the boys starts sayin' he's not sure about takin' orders from a woman, I set him straight, and mighty quicklike, too."

Violet nodded. "I appreciate that, Linc."

His expression hardened as he went on, "I'm still not sure it's a good idea for you to be cozyin' up to some scruffy cowboy, though."

Violet looked at him for several heartbeats, and then she laughed, much like he had a few minutes earlier.

"Why, Linc, I do believe you're jealous," she said.

He scowled. "I've made no secret of the fact that I'm sweet on you, Violet. And as far as I knew, the feelin' was mutual."

Violet's tone was scathing as she said, "So the big bad outlaw who doesn't mind wrecking a train and killing a bunch of people gets his feelings hurt over his girl kissing another fellow."

"Violet," Daisy said warningly.

It was too late. Pollard was on his feet. Some of the coffee left in the cup sloshed out as he set it down on the seat of the ladder-back chair. He stepped around the chair and said, "I want to know why in blazes you two are carryin' on with those cowboys."

Violet stood up, too, and her chin jutted out just as defiantly as Pollard's.

"We're not carrying on with them, as you put it," she said. "Do you know who those cowboys are?"

Pollard shook his head. "How would I know? Just saddle tramps hopin' to spark a couple of pretty girls, looked like to me."

"They ride for Smoke Jensen," Violet said.

Pollard's eyes widened. "Jensen!" he said. "Do you know the reputation he has?"

"Yes, of course I do. Do you think I didn't prepare for possible trouble before we ever decided to come to this area? Jensen represents the biggest threat to our plans, so what better way to keep up with what he's thinking and doing than by becoming friendly with two of his closest associates?"

"Besides," Daisy put in, "they're very sweet and they're teaching us how to shoot."

"Teachin' you how to shoot," Pollard repeated. He grunted. "That's a good one."

"I managed to seem like an amateur," Violet said, "and we decided to let Daisy go ahead and display her natural skills. Trust me, Linc, Pearlie and Cal aren't the least bit suspicious of us."

"I reckon not, what with the two of you actin' like butter wouldn't melt in your mouths." Pollard stood there for a moment, obviously turning over in his mind everything he had learned tonight. Finally, he said, "Does Jensen have any idea where we've been hidin' out?"

Violet shook her head. "No, you gave them the slip completely after the train job and with those cattle you rustled. Did you *have* to wreck that train, Linc? I thought you were just going to hold it up and grab that shipment of money from the express car."

Pollard appeared to have calmed down a little since finding out who Pearlie and Cal were. He might still be jealous, but he seemed willing to accept that the Caldwell sisters had a good reason for playing up to the two Sugarloaf hands. He picked up the cup, wiped away the drops of coffee that had spilled on the chair, and resumed his seat.

"That job didn't play out like I intended," he said. "When we blew two of the legs on the water tank, it was supposed to fall on the tracks like it did, but I thought we had allowed plenty of time for the locomotive to stop before it got there." Pollard frowned and shook his head. "The blasted engineer must not have been payin' as much attention as he should have. Or maybe the brakes didn't work right. I don't have any way of knowin'. But we were ready to close in and take over the train as soon as it stopped. It just didn't. Stop, I mean."

"I knew what you meant," Violet said. "So, people were killed."

"Not that many, considerin'. Shoot, it could have been a whole lot worse. You know that."

Violet nodded. "I suppose that's true. Even so, it drew more attention than I like. It stirred people up and made them angry, more than a simple holdup would have. The railroad is liable to send Pinkertons to try to hunt you down. We don't need that complication."

"I'm not worried," Pollard responded with a dismissive wave of his hand. "Like you said, we're good at givin' folks the slip. Nobody's gonna track us down, Vi."

"They had better not. Whisper always thought the law would never catch up to him, but look where he is now: in the Kansas State Penitentiary, serving a twenty-year sentence. He'll never get out of there alive."

"You're wrong about that," Pollard said. "It's just a matter of time. No prison can hold Whisper McReady. He'll bust out, you just wait and see." The outlaw's face creased in a satisfied smile. "And when he does, he'll find that between the three of us, the McReady gang is as good as ever and hankerin' to clean up more loot!"

Chapter 14

Linc Pollard left the house a short time later after finishing his coffee. He'd hinted that since it was still thundering and lightning and pouring down rain outside, the sensible thing for him to do would be to spend the night, but Violet slammed the door on that idea right away.

"It's risky enough you came here tonight," she told him. "We're not going to take a chance on ruining our reputations by having somebody catch a glimpse of a strange man leaving our house in the morning."

"You think anybody saw me comin' in here?" Pollard asked.

"They'd better not have," Violet replied in a flat, slightly menacing tone.

"Don't worry, they didn't," Pollard said. "This was the only light showin' anywhere back here. Everybody else in this part of town turned in a long time ago."

They couldn't be sure of that, but Violet knew that in all likelihood, Pollard was right about not being seen. Even so, before he left she was going to blow out the lamp, just to make sure that no one spotted him as he departed.

His hat and slicker were still damp but no longer dripping. As he put them on, Violet moved closer to him and said, "You know the plan for the next job, right?"

"Of course I do," Pollard said. "I've been doin' this a long time, Vi. You don't have to worry about me. Whisper always trusted me, and you should, too."

"I do trust you. I just like to make certain everyone knows what they're doing."

He put his hands on her shoulders and said, "I always know exactly what I'm doin'."

As if to prove that, he bent down and kissed her.

Violet didn't pull away. She put enough enthusiasm into her response to satisfy him for the time being, although the feeling wasn't completely genuine. Pollard was somewhat handsome in a cruel way, but he didn't actually appeal to her much.

He was also fairly good at carrying out her plans, notwithstanding the disaster that the train robbery had turned into. Even though she would have preferred it if no one had been killed, at least Pollard and the rest of the men had gotten that money shipment from the express car like they were supposed to.

Pollard broke the kiss and stepped back with a smug smile on his face.

"Why don't you come to the hideout next time instead of sendin' little sis?" he suggested. "I'd like to spend more time out there with you."

"We'll see," Violet said, although in truth she didn't intend to do any such thing. The setup they had was working so far, and she didn't see any reason to mess with it.

Pollard started to turn toward the door but paused. "When are you gonna be seein' those cowboys again?" he asked.

"Why do you ask? So you'll know when to spy on us?"

"I'm just curious, that's all," Pollard replied in a surly voice. "Maybe you've got a good reason for playin' along with 'em, but I don't have to like it."

"No, you don't," Violet told him. "But you have no reason to worry about it, Linc. It's not like I'm going to run off with Pearlie Fontaine."

"Is that his name?" Pollard's brow furrowed. "Seems like I've heard of him. I think he's a hired gun."

"He's the foreman on Smoke Jensen's ranch. If he used to hire out his gun, he's put those days behind him."

"Maybe." Pollard didn't sound convinced. "You just be careful, Vi. You might be gettin' in over your head."

"Not likely," she said. She looked over her shoulder at her sister. "Daisy, blow out the lamp."

Daisy leaned over the table to do as Violet said. Darkness closed around the room like a fist, relieved only when lightning flickered outside.

"You can go now," Violet told Pollard.

She couldn't see his face in the gloom, but she assumed he didn't care much for being dismissed like that. That was just too bad. He needed not to forget who was actually in charge of the Whisper McReady gang.

Or maybe now it was the Caldwell Sisters gang . . .

The door opened, and she caught a glimpse of Pollard in a lightning flash as he ducked outside. A little bit of rain sprayed through the opening before Violet could close the door behind him. She felt it lightly against her face.

"Do you want me to light the lamp again?" Daisy asked.

"Unless you want it burning, just leave it out."

"I don't need it. I think I'm going to bed."

"I might sit up for a while longer, but I don't need the light, either. I'm not going to work on anything."

"Fine." Daisy hesitated, then went on, "You'd better be careful, Violet. There's only so far you can push a man like Linc Pollard. If he wasn't so loyal to Pa, you couldn't get away with talking to him the way you do."

"We've gotten away with plenty," Violet said. "We're going to get away with even more before it's all over."

"When is that going to be? How long are we going to stay here?"

"We just got here. There are a lot of things we can accomplish before it's time to pull out. Besides, I've started considering a few other ideas."

"Oh? Like what?"

"Don't worry about that right now," Violet said. "Let me think about it."

Daisy didn't respond for a moment. Then she said, "All right. You've done a good job of taking care of us so far."

"And I'll keep on doing a good job. Good night, Daisy."

"Good night."

Daisy left the parlor, heading down a short hall with a small bedroom on each side.

The intensity of the storm outside had lessened somewhat. Earlier, the thunder and lightning was almost constant, and the booming and crackling had seemed to be right on top of Big Rock. Now, nature's violence had moved away a little, but the lightning was still frequent enough that Violet had no trouble finding her chair. She sat down and stared at the window as the bright, silvery glare pulsed in the heavens.

And as that inconstant light filled her senses, it seemed to surround her and take her back, back, to a time years earlier. She was little more than a girl, and yet she was a woman, too, because she was alone in the world then except for her sister, and Daisy was her responsibility. Their mother was gone, and their stepfather was in prison.

Anyway, even if he hadn't been locked up, Whisper McReady was hardly the kind of man to care about his dead wife's daughters. He had never seen much of them because he'd always been gone from home, off robbing and killing and leading one of the most vicious bands of desperadoes who had rampaged across the frontier. He was an outlaw, plain and simple, and truly cared for little in this world except the next job, the big payoff, the pile of loot he could get his greedy fingers on. Pollard had said that McReady raised the girls instead of their real father, but that wasn't actually true. He hadn't raised them at all.

But even so, Violet had learned from him. She liked to think that she had learned well . . .

Cottonwood, Kansas

The settlement of Cottonwood didn't amount to much. It sat on the eastern fringes of the Arikaree Breaks, a rugged area of canyons and ravines, gullies and buttes, that formed a barrier of sorts between Kansas and Colorado. Those badlands that lay west of Cottonwood between the Arikaree River on the south and the North Fork of the Republican River weren't good for anything. The range to the east wasn't particularly promising, either, but with good fortune and a vast amount of backbreaking, soul-destroying labor, a man might make a go of ranching or farming. If he was lucky.

The breaks actually were good for one thing: They provided enough places for the gang led by the notorious Whisper McReady to hide and set up ambushes for any star packers foolish enough to venture in there.

When they weren't hiding from the law, Cottonwood was handy enough to provide liquor, gambling, and women for McReady's men. If they needed to, they could duck back quickly into the breaks.

That was what brought Violet Caldwell to Cottonwood.

She drove the rented buggy along the settlement's single street. The horse's hooves sent up puffs of dust with every step. Dust lay thick in the street, except in the places where piles of dung had disturbed it.

A block of buildings stood on each side. To Violet's right were the Cottonwood Hotel, Ingersoll's Dry Goods and Emporium, Hector's Butcher Shop, and Bailey's Domino Parlor and Barber Shop. At the far end of town stood a livery stable and an attached corral.

To the left was the office of Dr. N. L. Swanson, Lester's Apothecary, the Cottonwood Land and Cattle Company, and finally, occupying as much space as the other three establishments on that side of the street put together, the Royal Flush Saloon.

That was Violet's destination.

Dwellings were scattered haphazardly behind the businesses, some built of sod, others clapped together from tin, tar paper, and roughhewn lumber. Cottonwood certainly wasn't an impressive place.

It wasn't busy, either. The only hitch rails in town where any horses were tied up were those in front of the saloon. Half a dozen bored-looking mounts stood there, their tails swishing back and forth lazily.

Violet brought the buggy to a stop in front of the land office rather than trying to crowd in at the hitch rails. The office appeared to be permanently closed. The windows were grimy and fly-specked, and she could see cobwebs gathered thickly inside them, obscuring the view even more.

As Violet was tying the buggy horse's reins to one of the posts holding up the awning over the rough boardwalk, a man pushed aside the batwings in the saloon's entrance and sauntered out of the Royal Flush. Another man followed him. They stopped on the porch and looked around at the sunblasted town, lazy arrogance obvious in their posture.

One of them straightened abruptly and nudged his companion with an elbow as he looked along the walk at Violet. The other man turned to stare at her. Both wore range clothes and broad-brimmed hats and had gun belts strapped around their lean hips.

As Violet came closer, their hard-planed, beard-stubbled faces were familiar to her. She didn't actually recognize them; she wasn't sure she had ever laid eyes on either of these two before. But she knew the type of men they were, knew it very well, indeed.

Grins that were right on the edge of being lustful leers spread across their faces. One of them, the taller and scrawnier of the two, stepped forward and reached up to pinch the brim of his hat as he said, "Why, hello there, miss. Dang, you sure brighten up the scenery in this miserable little burg. What brings you to Cottonwood?"

"I'm looking for someone," Violet said, keeping her face impassive and her voice flat and level. These men were looking at her as if she were a soiled dove, and that made her angry. Her face wasn't painted, and she was wearing a conservative gray traveling outfit and hat. They had no right to regard her in such a sordid fashion.

But she was here for an important reason and she didn't intend to let anything turn her aside from it. Certainly not two ill-mannered louts like these.

"Well, you've found me, honey," the man said. "What say we go back inside and have a drink?"

He reached out and closed his hand around her left arm. His grip wasn't tight enough to be painful, but its firmness said that he meant business.

Violet was carrying a small, woven bag in her right hand. She lifted it and pressed the bag against his belly.

"Feel that?" she asked. "It's the barrel of a derringer, and this is a cheap bag, so I don't mind shooting through it. A .41 caliber slug at point-blank range won't do your guts any good at all."

Chapter 15

The man's eyes widened in surprise. He was angry, too, and that made his angular jaw clench.

"You dirty little—" he began.

"Shut your mouth and let go of me," Violet interrupted him before the obscenities could spew from him. "Is Lincoln Pollard in there?"

That surprised the man even more than the derringer poking into his belly.

"You know Linc?"

The other man turned and plunged back through the batwings. "Linc!" he said. "Linc, you better get out here. There's some crazy woman lookin' for you, and she's gonna shoot Dooley!"

"Lady, you be careful with that derringer," the first man said as he released her arm. He swallowed hard. "You don't want to get nervous."

"I'm not the least bit nervous," Violet told him.

That was a lie. Every nerve in her body was stretched so taut it was about to twang like a guitar string. But she wasn't going to let this outlaw, or anyone else, see that. With a supreme effort of will, she forced herself to appear as calm as if she stuck a gun in a man's stomach every day and twice on Sundays.

A tall man with a dark spade beard slapped the batwings aside and hurried out onto the boardwalk. His right hand gripped the butt of the holstered gun on his hip.

"Dooley, what in blue blazes have you got yourself—"

He stopped short and stared at Violet for several heartbeats. Then he said in a shocked voice, "Violet? Is that you, Vi? It can't be!"

"It is," she told him. She smiled. "Hello, Linc. It's good to see you again."

He grinned and took a step toward her with his arms spread, as if he were about to hug her. He stopped again and said, "Uh, maybe you might want to put down that gun. Dooley ain't very smart, and he's sure not much to look at, but I'd hate to see him get a bullet in the guts."

"All right." Violet took away the bag from Dooley's stomach and lowered her arm. The outlaw's eyes rolled in relief as he stepped back.

"I sure didn't mean to insult you, ma'am," he said hurriedly. "I hope you'll forgive me."

"Of course, Mr. Dooley. I'm not one to hold grudges."

"Well, I'm mighty thankful for that."

Pollard gave Violet a hug, patting her lightly on the back with one hand as they embraced.

Then he stepped away and jerked a thumb over his shoulder as he spoke to Dooley. "Go on back inside. I want to talk to Miss Caldwell in private."

"Sure, Linc. Be happy to." Dooley tugged on his hat brim again. "I surely am sorry, ma'am."

Violet just smiled and nodded. She was grateful when he went back into the saloon, even though she wouldn't be surprised if he and the other men were lurking close by the entrance, trying to overhear what was going on outside. Outlaws were just as nosy as anybody else.

Pollard put his hand lightly on her arm and steered her away from the batwings.

"Vi, what are you doin' here?" he asked. "I hoped I'd see you again one of these days, but I sure never expected it to be here in Cottonwood. This is no place for somebody like you."

"Why not?" Violet asked. "I'm Whisper McReady's stepdaughter, aren't I? You and the rest of those men in there rode with him, didn't you?"

"Well, yeah, but you're . . . you're a lady."

"Maybe not as much of one as you think."

Pollard shook his head. "I'll never believe that. You and your sister are just like your ma, and Miz McReady was one of the finest ladies I ever knew. Whisper was lucky to marry her."

"He certainly was. I won't deny that." She changed the subject by asking, "What have you and the rest of the men been doing since Whisper was arrested and sent to prison?"

She knew the answer to that question, at least part of it, but she wanted to know what Pollard would say.

"Not a whole bunch," he replied with a slightly dispirited note in his voice. "Mostly just tryin' to lie low and get by. We've pulled a few jobs, you know, for eatin' money." He shook his head. "It wouldn't have been as hard if we'd known where Whisper stashed most of the loot from our jobs, but you know how he never shared that hidin' place with nobody."

"No, he didn't," Violet said.

"It's sure not the same without Whisper," Pollard went on. "He was always the one who came up with the ideas for what we ought to do next. I've been tryin' to keep the bunch together, usin' everything I learned from ridin' with him, but it ain't been easy, Vi. It may be gettin' time for all of us to split up and each man fend for himself."

"Don't do that," Violet said sharply. "There's no need. Things won't be exactly like they were before, but they can be better. A lot better."

He shook his head, frowned, and looked confused. "I don't see how."

"I've been to the prison," Violet said.

"The prison?" He still looked confused. "I don't understand—"

"I've seen Whisper. He gave me a message for you."

Now Pollard looked surprised. "You went to the penitentiary? I thought your ma didn't want you to do that."

"My mother has passed away, Linc."

"Yeah, I heard. I'm mighty sorry, Violet. I wondered how you and Daisy were gettin' along."

"It hasn't been easy for us, either. That's why I went to see Whisper in prison. And he had the perfect idea."

Pollard waited to hear what she was going to say.

"He wants me to take over the gang and run it."

Pollard just stared at her as if she had spoken in some foreign language.

Violet went on, "He wants me to plan the jobs and handle all the loot. I visited him quite a few times, and we talked as long as we could every time I was there. He said he was teaching me everything he knew. He wrote long letters to me about the same thing." She smiled. "It was quite an education, I must admit."

"You've got letters from Whisper?"

She shook her head. "He gave me strict orders to burn them so that no one would ever be able to prove Daisy and I are involved. But I committed everything in them to memory, Linc." Her voice rang with sincerity. "I can do this. The gang can be successful again. As successful as it ever was."

Pollard cocked his head to the side and gave her a dubious frown. "I don't know," he said.

"You don't believe me?"

"Of course I believe you," he said quickly. "The idea sounds like something Whisper would come up with. He always was one to think of things that nobody else would. That's what made him so good at plannin' the gang's jobs. Whenever we pulled one, it took folks by surprise." Pollard shook his head. "I just wish it had worked out a little better than it did."

"If you believe me, then what's the problem?"

The outlaw hesitated, then said, "I hate to talk so plain, Vi, but some of the fellas won't like takin' orders from a woman."

"They like making money, don't they?"

"Well, sure."

"If they go along with my plans, they'll make money. I swear that, Linc. I want to at least put the idea up to them."

Pollard scratched at his jaw for a moment with indecision still obvious on his face, but then he nodded and said, "That's fair enough, I suppose. Do you want me to say something to 'em first?"

"I can speak for myself," Violet said.

"All right, then. If that's the way you want it, come on."

They walked into the saloon, Pollard going first and holding the batwings aside for her. Men scurried back to the bar and to some of the tables, confirming Violet's hunch that they had been trying to eavesdrop.

Not counting the bald, middle-aged man in a dirty apron behind the bar, only half a dozen men were in the saloon, Violet saw as she looked around the squalid place. Her stepfather's gang had been much larger than that, she recalled. At times, as many as thirty outlaws had ridden with Whisper McReady. The bunch really had fallen on hard times, as Pollard had said.

She recognized a couple of them, and after a moment she came up with their names: Bill Wickham and Seth Layne. Wickham was an older man with a weathered face and salt-and-pepper hair. He was the oldest member of the gang other than Whisper himself.

She supposed the others were all men who had fallen in with

the group later on, when she hadn't been around much, or possibly after Whisper was sent to prison and Lincoln Pollard had taken over the gang.

All of them stared at Violet. She was a very attractive young woman, of course, which was more than enough to explain their fascination with her, but she was sure the ones who knew her had told the others that she was Whisper McReady's stepdaughter.

"You boys listen here," Pollard said. "You all know who this young lady is. She's got something to say to all of you, and I expect you to behave yourselves and listen to her."

Dooley, the man who had gotten the derringer shoved in his belly, looked at the others and said, "If you fellas are smart, you'll do like Linc says."

Mutters of agreement came from several of the other outlaws.

Pollard looked over at Violet and nodded. She smiled, took a deep breath, and stepped forward.

"Thank you, Lincoln. The rest of you know who I am." She nodded to Layne and Wickham and added, "Hello, Seth. Hello, Bill. It's good to see you again."

Layne dragged off his hat and grinned. "Mighty nice to see you again, too, Miss Violet."

Wickham's response was a curt, "Hello, Vi." She recalled that he never had seemed to like being around her or her mother or sister. He didn't think respectable women ought to be associating with outlaws. He was probably right about that.

Violet didn't really consider herself respectable, though. Not anymore.

She forged ahead, saying, "I've come to see you today because I have a message from my stepfather. I've been visiting Whisper in prison, and he's made a decision about the future of this bunch."

"How can he make any decisions?" Wickham asked. "He's locked up and will be for a long time to come."

"Let Violet finish, Bill," Pollard said, his tone a little sharp.

Wickham shrugged.

"Whisper wants the gang to continue," Violet said. "He appreciates everything that Linc has done to keep you together, but he believes that a change is necessary, that someone else needs to be in charge from here on out."

"And who might that someone else be?" Wickham said.

"Me," Violet answered without hesitation. Her voice was strong and level, and so was the blue-eyed gaze she swept over the men as they looked at her.

For a long moment, silence hung over the room. Violet thought she could almost hear her heart pounding in her chest as well as feeling it.

Then Bill Wickham said, "That's loco. No woman can lead an outlaw gang."

"I can," Violet responded immediately. "And if Whisper didn't think I could, he wouldn't have sent me here."

Wickham looked at Pollard and said, "Linc, you agree this idea is crazy, don't you? Surely you don't want to turn things over to a . . . a girl!"

"That was my first thought," Pollard admitted, "but once I thought it over, it sure does sound like something Whisper would come up with. He always liked to keep folks off-balance, and I don't know what else would do that more than what Vi's talkin' about."

One of the other men Violet didn't know asked, "What are you gonna do, ma'am, put on pants and ride with us?"

"Blast it," Pollard said, "don't be so disrespectful—"

Violet stopped him by holding up a hand. "I won't be doing anything like that," she answered the question coolly. "I can do us all a lot more good in other ways. My sister and I will move into a settlement, get the lay of the land in that area, and identify the best jobs for you to pull, and then I'll pass along the information to Linc so that all of you can carry out your part of the deal."

"I remember Daisy," Seth Layne said. "She's just a kid."

Violet shook her head. "Not anymore. She's all grown up now."

Pollard asked, "Does she know about you comin' here and suggestin' the two of you work with us?"

"Of course. We don't keep any secrets from each other. She's as much in favor of this arrangement as I am and will do her part, make no mistake about that."

"What do you mean when you say you'll move in somewhere?" Pollard wanted to know.

"Exactly that. Daisy and I are both good seamstresses. How could we be otherwise when we learned from our mother? She was the best seamstress I've ever known. We'll show up in a town, open a dress shop, and make ourselves part of the community. That will give us the opportunity to learn everything that goes on in the area." She smiled. "You know how women like to gossip. The ladies who come to our shop won't hesitate to tell us everything we need to know about their husband's businesses."

"Women do like to talk," one of the men said.

"No one will ever suspect us," Violet continued. "We'll be able to direct the gang's activities while keeping our distance from the actual jobs."

"How do you figure on doin' that?" Pollard asked.

"Daisy is an excellent rider. She can carry messages from town to wherever the rest of you are holed up. Again, no one will suspect an innocent young woman of being involved with criminals."

"That's how you hope it'll work out," a man said, "but you don't know that for sure."

"Nothing in this life is certain," Violet said. "But my stepfather believes the plan will work, and so do I. We just have to give it a chance."

Bill Wickham said, "If he trusts you so much, I don't suppose he told you where he hid that big pile of loot nobody ever found?"

Violet shook her head, and her regret was genuine as she said,

"No, he didn't. I suppose he felt like he had to keep some things to himself. In reserve for when he gets out of prison, so to speak."

Wickham grunted. "If he ever does."

"He will," Pollard said. "You know Whisper. Ain't no lockup ever been built that can hold him."

"The Kansas State Pen has so far."

"Well, just you wait."

Pollard's doglike devotion to her stepfather was sweet, Violet thought. She had counted on him to bring the others around, and so far, he wasn't letting her down.

"All I'm asking for is a chance to show that it can work," Violet said again. She looked around at the men. "Don't you think it's worth a try?"

Layne said, "It sounds good to me."

Dooley said, "I'm in. And I'm right sorry for actin' like a jackass earlier, Miss Violet."

She smiled at him and said, "That's all right, Dooley. Just don't let it happen again."

"No, ma'am, it sure won't."

Violet nodded. Might as well get them used to toeing the line, she thought. The others saw how respectful Dooley was acting now, and that would make it easier for them to follow his example.

Several of the others chimed in to say that they were willing to give the arrangement a try, and the rest nodded.

Except Bill Wickham. The old outlaw shook his head and said, "It still seems loco to me. I never heard of a woman leading an outlaw gang, especially one as young as Vi here. It'll never work, and I won't have any part of it."

Pollard's hand drifted closer to the butt of his gun. "Are you sayin' you're runnin' out on us, Bill?"

Wickham tensed. "I wouldn't call it that, but if the rest of you are determined to go ahead, you can do it without me."

The men closest to Wickham began easing away from him, getting out of the line of fire.

"I ain't sure it'd be smart to just let you ride off," Pollard said.

Wickham's face flushed angrily. "Are you saying I'd turn on you? After all we've been through together?"

Violet could almost smell powdersmoke in the air, and she didn't want that. She moved forward a step, although she was careful not to get between the two men, and said quickly, "Linc, there's no need for this."

"We can't afford to take a chance—" Pollard began.

"We won't be," she said. She looked at Wickham and went on, "Bill would never betray us, whether he's one of us or not. Would you, Bill?"

"Of course not," he said, scowling. He looked at the others. "We'll always be pards."

"Sure, Bill," Layne said. "I never figured it any other way."

That declaration brought mutters of agreement from the others.

"All right," Pollard said, still a little surly but willing to go along with what Violet wanted. "I reckon I believe you, too, Bill. I wish you'd change your mind, though."

Wickham shook his head. "I won't." He started toward the batwings. "So long, fellas. I wish you luck." Pausing beside Violet, he added, "And you, too, Vi. I hope this works out for you."

She squeezed his arm. "Thank you, Bill. That means a lot, coming from one of Whisper's oldest friends."

Wickham gave her a nod and left the saloon. A moment later, they all heard his horse's hoofbeats as he rode away.

"You know, for a second there," Pollard mused, "I kind of thought you might shoot him in the back of the head with that derringer of yours when he walked off, Vi."

"I thought about it," Violet said, and every man in the room knew that she absolutely meant it. Then she smiled and went on,

"Now, let's talk about how all this is going to work. You're going to need to find some more men, Linc . . ."

It had worked, in fact, for quite a while now. The gang had grown. It wasn't as large as it had been at its peak under Whisper McReady's leadership, but it was getting to that point.

The loot they had accumulated had piled up nicely as well. She and Daisy wouldn't need to keep doing this forever, Violet thought as she sat in the darkness of the parlor in the little cottage behind the dress shop. Lightning flashes still lit up the window from time to time, but they weren't as frequent as they were earlier. Raindrops pattered on the window now instead of lashing at the glass.

The storm was moving on. And so were Violet's plans, especially the one beginning to form in her mind that promised a possible end to all the risks and hard work. A single, simple stroke, a big payoff that, combined with what the sisters had already put away, would allow them to disappear and put the outlaw life behind them, once and for all. That life was exciting, challenging, even enjoyable in a way, but everything had to come to an end sooner or later.

And as far as Violet could see, there was only one real, potential obstacle standing in the way of her scheme.

Smoke Jensen.

Chapter 16

The spread of the railroads across the frontier had had a significant impact on the business of the stagecoach lines, but many people still wanted to go where the steel rails didn't run. Because of that, quite a few stage lines were still active, including the one that ran through Big Rock and continued on north and south.

Several coaches stopped at the settlement each week, so one morning several days later, Smoke wasn't surprised when he heard pounding hoofbeats and rattling wheels down the street from where he stood on the front porch of the mercantile. Sally had just gone into the store.

Then Smoke realized the stagecoach sounded like it was moving faster than normal. A few startled shouts rose from bystanders to disturb the midday calm.

Smoke wheeled around and walked at a brisk pace toward the stage station in the next block.

The big Concord coach came to a sharp stop in front of the building where the stage line's office was located. The abruptness of the halt made the coach rock back and forth a couple of times on the broad leather thoroughbraces that ran underneath it. A cloud of dust swirled around the vehicle and the team of sturdy horses hitched to it.

Ed Ferguson, the station's manager, hurried out of the office and paused to wave a hand in front of his face, trying to disperse the dust. Smoke heard him call up to the man on the driver's box, "Pidge, what in blazes are you doing? You can't drive like that in town."

Then, as the dust cleared some and Ferguson squinted up at the box, he went on in a surprised tone, "You're not Nate Pidgeon! Who are you? Where's Pidge?"

Smoke was acquainted with Nate Pidgeon, the veteran jehu who handled the reins on this run most of the time, and the man who had brought the stagecoach into town definitely wasn't him. Judging by the tweed suit, white shirt, colorful cravat, and derby hat the man wore, most likely he was one of the passengers. A salesman, by the look of him.

The man wrapped the reins around the brake lever and climbed down from the box as more townspeople began to gather around the newly arrived coach. He took off his hat and slapped it against his coat, evidently trying to remove some of the dust from both, but he didn't have much luck with that.

"The driver's inside, wounded," he told Ferguson. "I don't know how bad it is, but he needs a doc, that's for sure."

Ferguson rushed to the coach door and jerked it open. Smoke was close enough by now to look inside. He saw Nate Pidgeon lying on the floor between the seats. His head was in the lap of a middle-aged, competent-looking woman. Two other passengers, both men in suits, were inside the coach.

Pidgeon had a dark bloodstain on his shirt under the long duster he wore. He had been shot through the body. But he was conscious and able to say, "Road agents . . . Ed. They stuck us up . . . at Wilson's Hill."

Talking made Pidgeon cough. Droplets of blood came from his mouth and spattered on his chin and chest.

Ferguson leaned into the coach and said, "Take it easy, Pidge. Don't try to say anything else. The doc's on his way."

As a matter of fact, Dr. Colton Spaulding had just arrived, having been summoned by a townsman who had seen the stagecoach racing into town and figured something must be wrong. Spaulding pushed through the crowd, calling on them to step aside. Smoke pitched in, using his broad shoulders to move people out of the way and clear a path for the medico.

"Let me take a look," Spaulding said to Ferguson, who moved back so the doctor could lean into the coach. With a swift, sure touch, Spaulding pulled up Pidgeon's bloody shirt and examined the bullet hole.

Then he turned and said in a loud voice, "I need four men to take this man to my office, quickly but carefully. I may be able to pull him through if we don't delay."

Alerted by the commotion that something was wrong, Monte Carson had left his office and hurried along the street, too. He strode up and said, "I need to talk to the driver and find out what happened."

"Later, Sheriff," Spaulding said. "If my patient survives."

Smoke could tell that Monte didn't like being put off like that, but he accepted the necessity of it. Together with Smoke, he helped disperse the crowd, except for the four burly townies who got a good grip on the wounded man, lifted him out of the stagecoach, and carried him down the street toward the doctor's office.

Once that had been done and the other passengers had climbed down from the stage, Monte held out a hand toward them and said, "You folks stay right there. I want to talk to all of you." He turned to Ferguson. "Ed, did Pidgeon tell you anything about what happened?"

"He just said that outlaws held up the stage at Wilson's Hill, Sheriff. That's all I know."

"That's exactly what happened, Sheriff," said the man who had driven the stagecoach into Big Rock. He pulled a large handkerchief from his pocket and used it to mop sweat and dust from his beefy face. "We were rolling along as nice as you please and had just gotten to the top of the hill when somebody started shooting at us. The coach stopped all of a sudden, and I think the driver might've gotten off a shot or two in return, but then it got quiet until some men rode up on horses and yelled at us to get out of the coach."

"What's your name, mister?" Monte asked.

"Phil Quisenberry. I deal in dry goods. I started out driving a freight wagon, so I figured I could handle this team and bring the coach on into town, once the outlaws rode off and we put the driver inside."

Monte looked at the other passengers. "Do the rest of you agree with Mr. Quisenberry's story so far?"

One of the men nodded and said, "That's the way it happened, all right, Sheriff. We got out of the stage. There was nothing else we could do."

The female passenger spoke up, saying, "Poor Mr. Pidgeon was lying on the ground, wounded. Those thieves shot him right off the driver's box."

"Don't I know you, ma'am?" Monte asked.

"I'm Thelma Armstrong. My husband, Jonas, and I have a ranch down along the New Mexico border. My sister lives north of here. I pass through Big Rock from time to time when I've been visiting her."

"Of course. I remember you now, Mrs. Armstrong."

Smoke wasn't surprised that the woman was a ranch wife. She had that tough, hardy look about her.

He knew Monte wouldn't mind if he asked some questions, too, so he said, "How many bandits were there?"

"Eight or ten, I'd say," Quisenberry replied. The others nodded in agreement. "I didn't get an exact count. And there were several others nearby, hiding behind rocks and trees while they covered us with rifles. I saw the barrels sticking out. They were probably the ones who shot the driver."

"More than likely," Monte said. "What can you tell me about the ones you saw?"

"They all wore long coats and had bandannas tied over their faces, so you couldn't see much. With their hats pulled down, you couldn't even get a good look at their eyes." Quisenberry shook his head. "I'm sorry, Sheriff, but I can't really describe any of them."

"Nothing unusual about their voices?"

"Only one of them talked, as far as I recall. And he just sounded rough and mean when he was ordering us to hand over all our valuables."

"Did they loot the express box?" Smoke asked.

"Yeah, but there wasn't much in it, just some mail, mostly."

Monte frowned and said, "Why'd they go to the trouble of holding up the stage, then? That doesn't sound like a big enough payoff to make it worth their trouble."

Quisenberry pointed to one of the other passengers, who had been sort of hanging in the background behind the rest, looking nervous. "Ask him."

Monte beckoned the man forward. "What's he talking about, mister?"

This man was pale and slender, dressed in a tweed suit and bowler hat. He was clearly uncomfortable as he said, "They were after my sample case."

Monte grunted. "What were you carrying? Diamonds?"

"That's right."

Monte looked surprised. He hadn't intended the question seriously. He said, "Really?"

"I deal in fine jewelry," the man said. "I represent a firm in Denver, and I had taken several thousand dollars' worth of samples to a ranch in Wyoming. The owner wrote to my firm requesting that someone bring a nice selection to him so he could purchase some jewelry for his wife."

"Why didn't you go on the train, at least as far as Cheyenne?" Smoke asked. "Seems like that would have been safer."

The man sighed. "My boss got the idea that no one would ever suspect someone like me of carrying jewelry worth that much. I mean, just look at me. No one would think I was carrying anything valuable."

He had a point, Smoke thought. Such a meek little man didn't look like an important courier of valuable gems.

"But the outlaws knew what you had?" Monte said.

"They must have known. They demanded my sample case right away."

"Somebody else who works for your boss sold him out," Smoke said. "That's the only thing that makes sense."

The little man sighed and nodded. "I'm afraid you're right, sir."

"They'd better not try to blame what happened on the stage line," Ed Ferguson said. "The company is insured against loss, but not when the passenger doesn't tell us they're carrying something valuable. If we'd known, we would have put a shotgun guard up there with Pidge!"

"Doesn't sound like it would've done much good against a gang of that size," Monte said. "More than likely, it would've just gotten another man gunned down." He rubbed his jaw. "I'd better ride up there and take a look around. Smoke, you want to come along?"

"Let me tell Sally what's happened and where I'm going. I'll get Pearlie and Cal to come with us, too."

"Those two rode into town with you today?"

"Just try to keep them away. Any excuse to come into Big Rock is a good one these days, ever since the Caldwell sisters came to town!"

"Let me do the talkin'," Pearlie had said to Cal a short time earlier as they paused on the walk just outside the dress shop.

"Why? Because you're such a silver-tongued devil and I'm not?" Cal wanted to know.

"I got more experience dealin' with ladies, that's all, on account of I'm older."

"Older doesn't necessarily mean wiser, or smoother with women."

"Just follow my lead," Pearlie said. "Gals can't be rushed. They're like balky ol' mules when it comes to that."

Cal nodded sagely. "Yeah, that'll win them over, sure enough. Compare them to mules. Old mules, at that."

Pearlie snatched his hat off his head. "Dadblast it, that ain't what I said! Just hush."

"If you think you're going to swat me over the head with that hat, you'd better think again—"

Before either of them could say or do anything else, the shop's front door opened and Violet Caldwell stood there smiling at them.

"Are you boys going to stand out here and argue all day, or are you going to come inside and say hello?"

Cal grabbed his hat and took it off, too, as both cowboys turned toward the attractive blonde.

"Uh, good mornin', Miss Violet," Pearlie said quickly. "It sure is nice to see you again."

"I thought we were going to dispense with that formality. You can just call me Violet." Her blue eyes twinkled as she added, "Or even Vi. I don't mind when my friends call me that."

"I reckon that means we're friends?"

"Of course we are!" Violet stepped back and held the door open. "Now, come on in. Daisy and I don't bite. Well . . . not unless we're asked to, nicely."

That comment made Cal's face start to get warm again. Being around the Caldwell sisters seemed to have that effect on him. He looked down, hoping Violet wouldn't notice, as he followed Pearlie into the shop.

Daisy was inside, adjusting a dress on one of the dressmaker's dummies in the window. She smiled and said, "We saw you walking toward the shop, but then it looked like you weren't going to come in. Is something wrong?"

"No, nothing's wrong," Cal assured her. "Nothing at all. We were just talking about, uh, ranch business."

Violet said, "It looked like you were disagreeing about something."

"Naw, I was just tryin' to set the kid straight on a few things," Pearlie said. "You know how it is when you work with youngsters."

"Indeed, I do."

"And what do you mean by that?" Daisy asked, sounding a little aggrieved, but the smile on her lips said plainly that she wasn't actually offended. She linked arms with Cal and went on, "I think we should go for a walk and leave these two old-timers to do whatever it is people do at their advanced age."

A stroll with Daisy sounded like a good idea to Cal. He put on his hat and said, "That's a mighty fine suggestion. Unless you ladies would like to get in some more target practice. That's why we rode in with Smoke and Sally, to see if you wanted to work on your shooting some more."

"Oh, it's too nice a day for that," Daisy said. "The air smells too fresh to clutter it up with powdersmoke. I'd much rather you show me around town, Cal. There's still a lot about Big Rock that I don't know."

"Go ahead, you two," Violet told them. "I want to get Pearlie's opinion on some fabrics."

Pearlie's eyes widened. "Oh, now, I ain't exac'ly what you'd call qualified to talk about somethin' like that—"

"Nonsense. You're a man, and it's well-known that women dress to please men. So, you can tell me whether or not you think a particular fabric would make a nice-looking gown."

Pearlie swallowed and then nodded. "I reckon I can give it a try," he said, "but don't put too much stock in anything I might come up with."

Cal and Daisy left the dress shop and walked up the street arm in arm. Daisy asked about some of the businesses they passed, and Cal filled her in on as much as he knew about them.

"It's hard to believe that ten years ago, this town wasn't even here," she commented. "It's certainly grown quickly, and prospered, too."

"That's what happens when you have good folks living in a place," Cal said. "Smoke sort of set a good example for the whole valley, and people tried to live up to it."

"I've heard that he used to be an outlaw, and a notorious gunfighter."

"There's nobody better with a gun," Cal said. "That part of the story is true. And it's true that for a while, there were posters circulating that claimed he was wanted by the law. But they were put out by crooked lawmen working for enemies of his, fellas who hoped that somebody would kill him and keep him from coming after them."

"That didn't work, though, did it?"

Cal laughed. "Not hardly. Smoke caught up to those varmints. Or maybe I should say, justice caught up to them. Only it was Smoke delivering it from the barrel of a gun."

"Such things just seem almost unbelievable, coming from a genteel background like Violet and I do."

"I'm sorry," Cal said hurriedly. "I didn't mean to frighten or upset you—"

"I'm not upset, and I'm certainly not frightened." It was Daisy's turn to laugh. "It would take a lot more than that to scare me, Cal."

"I imagine it would."

She changed the subject by asking, "How long have you worked for Mr. Jensen?"

"A few years. It seems longer because there's so much happening all the time. There's always one ruckus or another brewing." He shrugged. "That's just the way it is around Smoke."

"Wouldn't you like to have your own ranch someday instead of working for someone else, no matter how much you might admire them?"

"Well, sure," he answered without hesitation. "I suppose most cowboys think about being their own boss."

"I think it's a very good thing for a man to have some ambition."

"I agree with you. I've already learned a lot, riding for the Sugarloaf. One of these days . . ."

"You'll have your own place," she finished for him. "With a family of your own."

"That's the dream, all right," Cal said, nodding slowly.

"Of course I imagine having your own ranch would take a lot of money."

"I'm working on it," he told her. "A lot of cowboys come to town and blow through their wages every month when they get paid, but I've never been much of one for drinking and gambling."

"What about girls?" Daisy asked with another laugh. "They can be expensive, you know."

"I don't care for a lot of carrying on. I sort of take that stuff seriously. Since I don't have a bunch of things I care to spend money on, I save most of my wages, so that when the time comes I'll be able to pay for a spread of my own."

Daisy squeezed his arm and laid her head against his shoulder for a second. "I think you're a very fine, sensible young man, Calvin Woods," she said, her voice solemn now. "Some girl is going to be very lucky when you set your sights on her."

Cal had to swallow hard before he was able to say, "Thank you. That's a mighty nice thing for you to say. And I think you're a, uh, mighty nice girl, Daisy."

They had come to a stop on the boardwalk. Daisy still held his arm, but she raised her head to look up into his eyes. Their faces weren't very far apart. If he leaned down right now, he'd be able to—

Instead, a commotion made him look up. His gaze traveled back along the street toward the other end of the settlement, where the stage station was located. The coach had come in, Cal noted. Caught up in his walking and talking with Daisy, he hadn't been aware of its arrival in Big Rock or, to be honest, much of anything else other than the beautiful blonde beside him.

But he saw now that Smoke was talking to Sheriff Monte Carson and several other people, and Cal's instincts told him that something was wrong.

Then Smoke turned away from Monte and started up the street, striding determinedly, and Cal knew that this interlude, pleasant though it had been, was over.

Chapter 17

After a brief detour into the mercantile to let Sally know what was going on, Smoke spotted Cal standing at the other end of town with the younger Caldwell sister. Her fair hair was hard to miss, shining as it was in the sunlight.

He didn't see Pearlie, so he figured his foreman was still at the dress shop with Violet Caldwell. Since he would come to it first as he moved along the street, he decided to stop there and see if his guess was correct.

He didn't have to check in the shop. Its door opened before he got there, and Pearlie stepped out to meet him. Pearlie held his hat in one hand, but he put it on as he said, "You look like somethin's wrong, Smoke. Is there trouble?"

"That's right. The stagecoach was held up, and the driver, old Nate Pidgeon, was badly wounded."

Violet had followed Pearlie from the shop and stood now in the open doorway. When she heard what Smoke said, she gasped and pressed a hand to the crisp bosom of the dress she wore.

"That's terrible!" she said. "Will the poor man be all right?"

Smoke touched a finger to the brim of his hat, his natural chivalry prompting him to make the respectful gesture.

"I don't know, ma'am," he said in response to her question. "Dr. Spaulding said he might be able to pull Pidge through, but I expect it'll take time and a considerable amount of luck. Pidge isn't a young man anymore."

Violet shook her head and looked distressed.

"It seems like there's been a lot of trouble since Daisy and I came to Big Rock."

Quickly, Pearlie put a hand on her arm and said, "Now, don't you go to worryin', Vi."

"I'm just afraid we may have moved to a place where there's too much violence."

"Naw, it ain't like this all the time," Pearlie assured her. "Big Rock is plumb civilized. So's the whole valley. It's just that, well, this is still the frontier, sorta, and you gotta expect a few wild things to crop up from time to time. But it's a good place to live, I swear it is, and you and Daisy are gonna be safe."

"Well, if you say so." Violet didn't look or sound particularly convinced by his reassurances, though.

By now, seeing that something was going on, Cal and Daisy had come from the other end of the street to join them in front of the shop. Cal asked, "What's wrong, Smoke?"

In a few words, Smoke repeated what had happened, then said, "Monte is riding up to where the holdup took place to have a look around. I told him I'd come along."

"And so will we," Pearlie declared without having to be asked. "What about Miss Sally?"

"She's going to finish her shopping and head back out to the ranch in the buckboard."

Violet said, "By herself? Is that safe with so many thieves and gunmen roaming around the area?"

"Sally can take care of herself," Smoke said with a smile, "and she's well-armed."

"Yes, we're aware of that. She showed us her pistol. That's why Daisy and I bought weapons just like it."

"But just to be sure, Monte is going to have one of his part-time deputies ride with her when she goes back to the Sugarloaf. She'll be fine."

"I certainly hope so," Violet said. "She's been a good friend to us since we moved here."

Smoke just nodded. He knew how warmhearted and friendly Sally was. She never met a stranger.

Pearlie turned to Violet and said, "Cal and me will come by and see you ladies again some other day, Vi, and we'll get in more shootin' practice, too. Right now, though, we got to give Smoke a hand."

"Of course." She gave his arm a squeeze. "Thank you for your help with those fabrics."

"Oh, it, uh, it weren't nothin'," he said. "I'm mighty glad to give you a hand, anytime."

She smiled at him and rubbed her hand along his upper arm for a moment.

Daisy said to Cal, "And thank you for the walk, even though it was cut short. We'll finish it another time."

"We sure will," he said.

Daisy came up on her toes a little and gave him a quick kiss on the cheek, then followed her sister back into the dress shop.

Pearlie cleared his throat and said, "Reckon we'd best get the horses."

As they started toward the mercantile, where their mounts were tied at the hitch rail, Smoke said, "Those young ladies seem to be the affectionate sort, at least where you boys are concerned."

"Aw, they're just friendly that way," Pearlie said. "It don't mean nothin'."

"I wouldn't be so sure about that," Smoke mused. "It looked to me like they're quite taken with you two. And you called her Vi."

"That's what her friends call her, she said."

"So the two of you are friends."

"I ain't never denied it," Pearlie said. "Ain't nothin' wrong with us bein' friends, is there?"

Smoke laughed. "I'm just joshing you a little. There's nothing at all wrong with you two being friends with the Caldwell sisters. They seem like fine young ladies."

"You don't think they're maybe a little too forward?" Cal asked.

"There's a time and a place for that," Smoke said with a shrug. "But as well as you're getting along, I don't see anything wrong with it. That just means you're all comfortable with one another." He looked at Pearlie. "What was that about you helping Violet with some fabrics?"

Pearlie waved dismissively. "Oh, that didn't amount to nothin'. She just had some bolts of material and wanted to know if I thought they was pretty."

"Were they?" Cal asked.

"Never you mind about that! We got some stagecoach bandits to chase, don't we?"

"We do," Smoke agreed, growing more serious. "And I hope we're able to follow their trail this time."

Seth Layne rode hunched over in the saddle, clutching the reins in his right hand while his left forearm pressed across his midsection. His eyes were big and round with pain, and beads of sweat stood out on his pale, strained face.

"I'm sorry, Seth," Linc Pollard said as he rode alongside the young outlaw. "I can't tell you how sorry I am."

"Save your breath, Linc," Layne said through clenched teeth. "I knew this day was gonna come sooner or later." A grunt that might have been a grim laugh came from him. "At least this way I won't die sittin' in a rocking chair on some blasted porch like ol' Bill probably will."

Dooley rode on the wounded man's other side. Like Pollard, he was ready to reach out and steady the wounded man if he should start to fall.

"It was just puredee bad luck, the way that ricochet caught you, Seth," Dooley said. "We shoulda blasted that jehu off the box quick-er'n we did."

"He only got off a couple of shots," Layne said. "Just bad luck, you're right about that. My luck was bound to run out one of these days." He looked over at Dooley. "Yours will, too, if you don't get out of this game."

Pollard swallowed the irritation that welled up inside him. Sure, Layne was gutshot and dying, and that was a shame, but that didn't mean he had any right to be spreading despair and strife among the other members of the gang. They all knew the risks they were taking by riding outside the law. As long as they were smart, the payoffs outweighed those risks.

They had been smart today, using the tip Violet had gotten from one of her contacts in Denver to grab that sample case full of diamonds and other valuable jewels. The stagecoach had been traveling slowly at the top of the hill, there were plenty of hiding places along the trail, and the driver should have hauled back on the reins and put his hands in the air as soon as the first warning shots went over his head. It was a perfect setup for a robbery.

But no, the stubborn varmint had had to grab the gun on his hip and try to put up a fight. The plan had been clear on that point: If the driver did anything other than surrender immediately, shoot to kill.

Unfortunately, Seth Layne had raised up from cover more than he should have to aim his rifle, and the driver's second wild shot struck the top of the rock and ricocheted right up into Layne's belly.

With his guts torn up like this, there was no way he could survive.

Pollard had considered going ahead and firing a bullet through his brain to forestall what was likely to be considerable misery, but Layne had asked them to put him on his horse, and Pollard had gone along with it.

It might be getting time to reconsider that decision, he mused.

Up ahead on the right was a large clump of boulders. Once they were past it, they would cut east, hit the creek that flowed along the western edge of the big tableland, and use it to throw any pursuers off their trail. They had done it before, and Pollard knew they could do it again.

From there, they would cross the plateau, drop down the other side, and head for the hidden cave where they had been holing up since coming to this part of the country.

Getting there would take most of what was left of the day. Pollard didn't figure Layne would last that long.

"Wait a minute," Layne grated. Awkwardly, he pulled back on his reins and brought his mount to a halt. Pollard and the others didn't have much choice other than to do likewise.

"What is it, Seth? Is there somethin' we can do for you?" Pollard asked.

"Yeah." Layne's voice was getting weaker. "Help me . . . fort up in those rocks."

Pollard frowned. "What are you talkin' about?"

Layne nodded toward the boulders. "I'm gonna stay here," he said. "Leave me a rifle . . . and a couple of pistols . . . and I'll stop any posse that comes along . . . on your trail."

Pollard's frown deepened as he leaned back in the saddle and considered what Layne had said.

"That's a loco idea, Seth," he said. "You ain't in good enough shape to do that."

"I'm not in . . . good enough shape . . . to do anything else. I can't ride anymore. But if I stay here . . . I can slow them down, anyway. Give you fellas time to make it to the creek . . . and up onto the plateau." Layne's lips stretched back from his teeth in a grimace. "Lemme do just one more thing . . . for the boys, Linc."

Dooley said, "Blast it, Seth, we're gonna get you back to the hideout and patch you up—"

An obscene oath from Layne interrupted him. "That'll . . . never happen," the wounded man managed to say.

"He's right," Pollard agreed, his voice flat and hard now. "He won't make it." He paused. "But are you sure you want to do this, Seth?"

"I'm sure," Layne said. "Just help me get into the rocks."

Pollard looked at the other men and nodded. Several outlaws dismounted, lifted Layne from the saddle, and half carried him into the nest of boulders.

Layne looked around, pointed, and said, "Set me on that one . . . behind that flat rock. I can put my rifle and pistols there."

It was a good location, with a boulder behind him for his back to rest against and the stone slab in front of him where his weapons could lay within easy reach. A gap between two of the boulders gave him a space through which to shoot. The rocks around him would provide some cover. Not much, but he didn't need much. He was a dead man no matter what happened. He just wanted to send some of his enemies across the divide ahead of him.

They left Layne's own Winchester and Colt with him, as well as a spare revolver, all of them fully loaded. Dooley got the canteen off Layne's saddle and placed it next to the guns, too.

"Don't do that," one of the other men said. "When a man's shot in the belly like Seth is, drinkin' just makes it worse."

Layne grinned. "Nothing's gonna make this much worse, but I appreciate the thought. Leave the canteen, Dooley. You never know, I might get thirsty."

Dooley reached down and squeezed Layne's shoulder.

"You're a good man, Pard," he said. "One to ride the river with, that's for sure."

Several other outlaws stepped up, patted Layne's shoulder, shook his limp hand, and said their rough goodbyes. Pollard was the last one after the others had returned to their mounts.

"We're takin' your horse with us, Seth," Pollard said.

"Good. No reason not to. I'd rather he be taken care of."

"He will be," Pollard promised. "If the hurtin' gets to be too much and that posse ain't here yet, well, you got a Colt right there with a full wheel."

"I won't need it . . . for that. I can hold out until they get here, Linc."

Pollard looked at the huge bloodstain on the front of Layne's shirt. He said, "Sure you will, and we're obliged to you, Pard. You're goin' out the right way, that's for dang sure."

"I know. You tell . . . Vi and Daisy . . . I'm sorry for lettin' them down."

"You didn't let nobody down, Seth. Not ever." Pollard squeezed the dying man's arm. "So long."

"So long," Layne husked.

Pollard stood up and joined the others, who were already mounted. He swung up into the saddle and jerked his head to indicate that they should move out.

"That's a mighty brave thing Seth's doing," Dooley said after they had ridden out of earshot.

"A mighty foolish thing, you mean," Pollard said, his voice cold and callous now. "He won't last another half hour. He'll be dead long before any posse might come along here."

"Now, you don't know that, Linc. At least he's trying to do something to help us."

"Yeah, I guess. Ten to one, though, after a little while, he's gonna be hurtin' so bad he'll look at those Colts so close to hand and change his mind about usin' one of them on himself."

Dooley shook his head. "Not Seth. He's got too much sand for that."

Pollard didn't look over at the other outlaw. He kept his eyes fixed on the trail ahead of them as he said, "His sand ran out with all of his blood. I'd bet a hat on that."

Behind them, nestled in the rocks, Seth Layne licked his dry lips and gazed back the way they had come from, waiting.

Chapter 18

The posse from Big Rock numbered eight men: Smoke, Pearlie, Cal, Sheriff Monte Carson, Louis Longmont, one of Monte's regular deputies, Dave Olney, and Fred Ketchum, who worked for the stage line as a hostler and considered the wounded driver, Nate Pidgeon, to be a good friend.

Monte warned Ketchum not to let his desire for vengeance on the men who had shot Pidgeon cloud his judgment.

"You can come along," Monte had told the man before they left Big Rock, "but I'm in charge and you do what I say."

"Of course, Sheriff," Ketchum agreed. "That'd be true whether me and Pidge were friends or not, wouldn't it?"

"Just don't forget in the heat of the moment," Monte said. "Assuming we catch up to the outlaws who robbed the stage."

They didn't have any trouble locating the spot where the holdup had taken place. All of them were familiar with Wilson's Hill and knew how the road climbed a fairly steep slope to the crest. The stagecoach would have been rolling along slowly when it finally topped the hill. When the shooting started, the driver would have had no chance to whip his team into a gallop and try to escape from the ambush.

Smoke pointed to a dark stain on the dirt. "That's Pidge's blood where he fell," he said.

Pearlie rode over to some rocks not far from the trail and studied the ground behind them. "Looks like one of the bushwhackers waited here. I can see the marks from his knee where he knelt down. Got a couple of empty rifle shells he didn't pick up, too."

"What about the horses?" Monte asked. "The riflemen who were hiding had to leave their mounts somewhere."

The men spread out to look around. A few minutes later, Cal called to the others and waved them over to him.

The young cowboy pointed behind a screen of trees and said, "They had a man holding the horses back there. You can see plenty of prints."

"Anything unusual about any of them?" Smoke asked.

Cal shook his head. "Not as far as I could see, but you and Sheriff Carson ought to take a look at them. You have more experience at that sort of thing than I do."

"So do I," Pearlie pointed out.

"Well, there's nothing stopping you from looking at them," Cal said.

Pearlie snorted and joined Smoke and Monte in studying the hoofprints left by the bushwhackers' horses. There were prints in the road, too, around the spot where the stagecoach had stopped, but there were so many that they were just a muddle, with nothing distinctive about them.

The three trackers spotted several nicks and other marks in the prints that might allow them to identify similar tracks if they found them later on. That was the only thing they noticed that might prove to be helpful, though.

"The whole bunch gathered up and headed north after the robbery," Smoke said, pointing out the trail left by the outlaws. "They weren't trying to cover their tracks. They just wanted to put some distance between themselves and this spot. But more than likely, the trail will get harder to follow later on."

"Only one way to find out," Monte said. "Let's go."

They headed north. That was the way the stage road ran, but it wasn't long before the tracks left by the gang veered off to the east. Several miles away in that direction lay the large plateau, and beyond it rose the mountains.

"They're headed in roughly the same direction as those rustlers we tracked a while back," Smoke commented as the posse jogged along. "The men who wrecked and looted that train could have disappeared up in this part of the country, too."

"It's all the same bunch," Monte declared. "I know we can't prove it yet, but I'm convinced that's the case."

"I can't argue with you," Smoke said. "Seems that way to me, too. There's not much up in those parts except that bare tableland, no place to hide there, and then some rugged country between the plateau and the mountains."

Monte nodded. "That's where we'll find them, in those badlands."

"It would take a month to comb through all those gullies and ravines," Pearlie said. "I've done some huntin' up in there. It'd be mighty easy for a fellow who didn't want to be found to get lost up there. And there are plenty of places they could hide and see us comin', too."

"If they did, they'd move," Smoke said. "Or else set a trap for us."

Monte looked frustrated. "Are you saying we'd need the army to root them out?"

"Maybe not the army," Smoke replied with a faint smile, "but more than just the eight of us, I'm afraid."

"Should we turn around and head back to Big Rock?"

"Not just yet. We can ride on a ways. You never know what you might run into."

"Ain't that the truth?" Pearlie muttered. "Problem is, a lot of the time when you run into somethin', it ain't anything good."

With that comment casting a slight pall over the group, they rode on, following the tracks left by the fleeing outlaws. As Smoke had predicted, the trail became harder to follow the longer they rode. It appeared that the gang sought out rocky stretches where their horses wouldn't leave as many marks. Smoke's keen eyes kept picking out the trail, though.

After a while, Smoke noticed something else. Several large black birds were wheeling slowly, high in the sky ahead of them. Their wings flapped only occasionally. Most of the time, they just glided with effortless, graceful ease.

Monte saw them at the same time and said, "Look at those buzzards up there, Smoke."

"I see 'em. They've got their eye on something."

Smoke lowered his gaze to study the ground roughly underneath where the buzzards were circling.

"Got to be a carcass o' some kind," Pearlie said. "Could be a dead animal. Or it could be a dead man."

Monte said, "If whatever's ahead of us was already dead, those ugly scavengers would be down on the ground having themselves a feast. They're keeping an eye on something, but I reckon it's probably still alive."

"None of those stagecoach passengers said anything about an outlaw being wounded," Smoke said. "But it's possible they wouldn't have known about it." He leveled an arm and pointed at a clump of boulders several hundred yards away that seemed to be the most likely place for the buzzards to be watching. "There could be somebody holed up in there. We'd better spread out."

The men had just started to move their horses to put some distance between them when a rifle cracked. Smoke saw the muzzle flash from those boulders he had just pointed out, and at the same time the bullet sizzled between him and Pearlie.

"Yee-oww!" Pearlie yelped as he dug his bootheels into his mount's flanks. "That was too close for comfort!"

The members of the posse scattered. The rifle blasted twice more, but none of the men or horses fell. The range was still pretty far, and if the man holed up in the rocks was wounded, as the circling buzzards seemed to indicate, he might be weak and not able to aim as well as normal.

Monte called for Olney and Ketchum to follow him but stay spread out. They pounded off to the right.

Smoke, Pearlie, Cal, and Louis Longmont had battled side by side many times in the past, so they knew what to do without any of them having to think about it. They circled to the left, staying well apart, and hunted for cover.

There was none to be found as good as that nest of boulders, but enough rocks and trees were scattered over the landscape to offer some shelter. Smoke and Louis swung down from their saddles while their horses were still moving, taking their Winchesters with them. Each of them dropped to one knee behind tree trunks.

Twenty and fifty yards away, respectively, Pearlie and Cal had dropped from their saddles as well and stretched out on their bellies behind some rocks that were considerably smaller than the boulders where the ambusher was holed up. As long as the two cowboys stayed low, though, the rocks would give them some protection.

Off in the distance, Monte Carson and the other two members of the posse had sprawled on the ground, as well.

Smoke aimed his rifle at the boulders and cranked off three rounds as swiftly as he could work the Winchester's lever. He couldn't see whoever had taken those shots at him and his companions, but he knew the man had to be in there somewhere. The other men from Big Rock opened fire, as well. Smoke heard the sharp whines of bullets ricocheting from the boulders, blended with the rolling thunder of the rifle blasts.

It was an ugly symphony of violence, one that Smoke had heard played too many times in his life.

After a minute or so, the shooting slowed down, and then Monte shouted, "Hold your fire! Hold your fire!" The other men followed that order, and the thunderous echoes gradually died away.

The silence that followed had an echoing quality of its own. No more shots came from the boulders.

Smoke knew they had poured enough lead into the bushwhacker's nest that the man was dead, more than likely. It would have been nice to take him alive so they could question him, but under the circumstances, with the rifleman hunkered down in rocks like that, trying to force him out probably would have resulted in innocent men being hurt or killed.

The ambusher had called the tune. The results were his responsibility.

"What do you think, Smoke?" Louis called over to him. "I don't mind trying to draw his fire if he's still alive in there."

"Let's wait a few more minutes," Smoke said. "That could be just what he's trying to get us to do."

Eventually, though, they would have to risk it if nothing else happened. Time dragged by, and finally, Monte Carson called to the others, "I'm going in!"

"Monte, wait—" Smoke began.

"Blast it, I'm the sheriff. It's my responsibility."

Monte was in charge of the posse, and even though Smoke was never shy about offering his opinion to his old friend, he wasn't going to countermand the lawman's orders, either.

"Just be ready to duck," he called back to Monte.

With a nod, Monte stepped out from behind the tree where he had taken cover. Holding his rifle at a slant across his chest, ready to snap it to his shoulder and fire, he started forward.

It was about a hundred and fifty yards to the boulders, and it was a *long* hundred and fifty yards, Smoke thought, as he tensely watched Monte's advance.

"Louis, keep an eye on those rocks," Smoke said. "If you see anything move in there, even a little, open up on them again."

"Those were my thoughts exactly, Smoke," the gambler said. His cheek was nestled against the smooth wood of his Winchester's stock, and his eyes were fixed on the clump of boulders.

Smoke knew Pearlie and Cal were also prepared to give Monte plenty of covering fire if he needed it.

The haze of powdersmoke that had hung over the rocks was breaking up and blowing away on the breeze. Nothing happened during the few minutes it took for Monte's cautious approach. Those minutes seemed longer to Smoke, dragging out the way they did.

At last, Monte was close enough to poke the rifle barrel between two of the boulders and lean in to take a look. After a moment, he straightened up, took off his hat, and waved it over his head to let the others know there was no threat.

Smoke and the others caught their horses and led them to the boulders. Dave Olney brought Monte's mount as well as his own.

"He's dead, all right," Monte told them as they came up. "Funny thing, though. I don't see any fresh wounds on him, just a big bloodstain that looks like it came from him getting hit earlier. It happened during that holdup would be my guess, and he finally gave out."

"Then Pidge did for one of the varmints, after all," Ketchum said. "I'm kind of glad of that, anyway. He'll be happy to hear it when we get back to Big Rock, assumin' he's still alive."

Smoke looked through the gap and over a large slab of rock at the still form slumped behind it. The dead man had been fairly young, probably in his midtwenties. His face was pale, and the suffering he had endured today had etched trenches into his cheeks. His eyes were open, staring sightlessly.

Monte was right about the bloodstain. It covered almost the entire front of the shirt the outlaw was wearing. It had dried and darkened, however, supporting Monte's suggestion that the injury had happened earlier.

Pearlie said, "How in blazes did we throw so much lead in there without at least one o' the ricochets hittin' him?"

"Odd things can happen where bullets are concerned," Smoke said. "I've seen men blaze away at each other from ten feet apart and miss with every shot."

"Yeah, that's true, I reckon. I've heard tell of things like that, myself." Pearlie looked around at the others. "Anybody recognize this hombre?"

"Never saw him before," Olney said.

"Me either," Ketchum said.

Monte rubbed his jaw and frowned in thought. "There's something about him that's familiar," he said after a few seconds. "Like I've seen him somewhere before, but I don't know when or where."

"The most obvious place would be a wanted poster," Smoke said.

"That's what I'm thinking, too. When we get back to Big Rock, I'll look through the posters in my desk and see if I can find him."

Olney said, "That'll take a while. There's a lot of them in that desk."

"Maybe I ought to get you to go through them and file them all proper-like," Monte said.

"Now, let's not get carried away, Sheriff."

Cal said, "What are we going to do with this fellow?" He nodded toward the dead man.

"We need to keep trailing the rest of those outlaws," Monte said. He glanced up at the black-winged shapes still swooping high overhead, riding the air currents. "I don't cotton to the idea of leaving a man to the buzzards, though, even an outlaw, unless it's a matter of necessity."

Smoke said, "We can put him down in that hollow in the boulders and cover him up with smaller stones. That'll keep him until we either come back through here or can send the undertaker out from town to pick him up."

Monte nodded. "That'll work. Let's get busy."

It didn't take long to arrange the body and then pile stones on it to keep the buzzards and any other scavengers from disturbing it for a while.

As the posse mounted up and rode away, Pearlie said, "If that fella was gutshot durin' the holdup and stayed alive long enough to bushwhack us, he must've been a mighty stubborn hombre."

"I was thinking the same thing," Louis said. "The amount of determination he demonstrated is impressive."

Smoke said, "I suppose he figured he was helping his friends by staying behind to slow us down. Even an outlaw can have courage and a sense of honor."

Ketchum turned his head and spat. "You sound almost like you admire the varmint, Mr. Jensen. I can't forget that him and the rest of his bunch may have killed poor old Pidge."

"We'll keep our hopes up for Pidge," Monte said. "Smoke, are you still seeing these tracks?"

"For now," Smoke said.

However, it wasn't long before the trail led into a creek bed. The same creek that the men who had ambushed Pearlie and Cal had used to throw pursuers off their trail, just a different stretch of the stream, Smoke thought.

The fact that the outlaws who had held up the stagecoach had used the same tactic was interesting, he told himself. He wasn't sure what it might mean, but he had a hunch that it meant *something.*

Although the searchers rode up and down the creek for more than an hour, they didn't find what they were looking for.

"The blasted devils have given us the slip again," Monte said, his voice harsh with frustration.

"It's only a matter of time until we dab a loop on them," Smoke said.

"I hope you're right."

When they got back to the rocks where they had left the body of the dead bushwhacker, several buzzards were sitting on the boulders, apparently waiting patiently. Pearlie yelled at them, waved his hat in the air, and scared them off. They hopped awkwardly a few times and then rose into the air, transforming instantly from their ungainly forms on the ground to the sleek, graceful gliders of the air.

"Ugly, filthy critters," Pearlie said with a scowl as he clapped his hat back on his head. "I don't like 'em."

"I don't reckon anybody does," Monte said. "Dave, you ride double with Fred. We'll put the carcass on your horse and carry him back to town."

"Wrap him up in a blanket first," Olney said. "I don't want him getting blood on my saddle."

It was almost evening when the posse got back to Big Rock with their grim cargo. Dave Olney took the body to the undertaking parlor belonging to Tom Nunnley, which was adjacent to the hardware store also owned by Nunnley. Fred Ketchum headed for the doctor's house to check on Nate Pidgeon. Louis Longmont invited the others to his restaurant and saloon for a drink, but Monte said, "I want to take a look through those wanted posters while that fella's features are still fresh in my mind."

"I'll come with you," Smoke said. "Pearlie, Cal, you can go with Louis."

Pearlie said, "You reckon you could have your cook rustle up a steak, Louis? It's been a long day, and I'm a mite empty. I'm sure this boy is, too. He's got a hollow leg."

"Speak for yourself," Cal said.

"I thought I just did."

Longmont chuckled. "I'm sure we can arrange for a hearty meal. Come along, gentlemen. Join us later if you'd like, Smoke, and you, too, of course, Monte."

Smoke and Monte went to the sheriff's office. Monte hung up his hat and gestured toward the coffeepot sitting on the stove in the corner.

"Poke up the fire in there if you want, Smoke. Might be some coffee left in the pot. It'll be strong enough to get up and walk around on its own hind legs by now, though."

Smoke grinned. "Just the way I like it. Once I get the fire going, I'll help you look through those reward dodgers."

Monte sat at the desk while Smoke took a stack of the posters to the old sofa on the other side of the office. Smoke thumbed back his hat and started paging through the sheets of paper.

Ten minutes had gone by before Monte slapped down a poster on the desk and said, "I knew I'd seen him before." He poked a finger at the drawing on the paper. "Name's Seth Layne. Wanted for murder and robbery in half a dozen states and territories. Says here he's known to ride with the Whisper McReady gang."

Smoke stood up and came to the desk. Monte turned the wanted poster so he could see the crude picture. Even though it wasn't a perfect likeness, it was good enough for Smoke to recognize the man who was now lying on a table over at Tom Nunnley's.

"That's him, all right," he said. "What gang did you say he rode with?"

"Whisper McReady's bunch."

"That's an odd name."

Monte grunted. "McReady was an odd duck. Vicious as could be, but at the same time mighty smart. It took the law a long time to catch up to him."

"Why did they call him Whisper?"

Monte sat back in his chair and said, "Because when he was

young and just started out riding the owlhoot trail, he got in a fracas with another fella and got shot in the throat. It didn't kill him, but it left him unable to ever raise his voice above a whisper again."

"You talk like he's dead," Smoke commented.

"Not dead, but he might as well be. He couldn't have anything to do with the gang Layne was riding with now." Monte looked up at Smoke. "For the past couple of years, Whisper McReady's been locked up in the Kansas State Penitentiary."

Chapter 19

With its tall limestone walls and massive entryway with guard towers rising above it, the Kansas State Penitentiary was a very impressive structure, although it had an understandably grim air about it. It had been built by some of the very convicts it wound up housing, and for the past dozen years, hundreds of vicious criminals had been imprisoned behind its walls.

However, unless they were being punished for some infraction of the warden's rules, the men were allowed to have visitors from time to time.

With a couple of burly guards following close behind him, Whisper McReady shuffled into the big visiting room with its long tables and hard wooden chairs. A screen of close-set metal bars ran down the center of each table, and there were wooden partitions between the seats on the prisoners' side.

Guards armed with thick clubs stood here and there, but generally, the visiting room was a peaceful place. None of the convicts wanted to lose the privilege of seeing someone from the outside world.

McReady had to shuffle because leg irons were clamped around his ankles. His hands were cuffed in front of him. They weren't taking any chances with him, despite the fact that he was getting older, in his early fifties now. He was stocky and mostly bald, with a short, silvery beard and large ears that stuck out from his head at right angles like jug handles.

Jug, in fact, had been his nickname when he was a kid. One boy had taken particular delight in yelling, "Look, here comes Jug!" and braying with coarse laughter, until the day McReady had cornered him behind a barn, held him down, and sawed his ears off with a dull butcher knife he had stolen from his drunken mother.

McReady could still hear the boy's screams and feel the hot spatter of blood on his hand.

That was the day McReady had taken off on his own, shaking off the dust of that squalid little Iowa town even though he was only twelve years old.

It hadn't taken him long to steal a gun, and once he had a gun in his hand, there was no stopping him.

Until he was brought here in chains.

He hadn't had a visitor in a long time and had no idea who might be here to see him today. All he knew was that the guards had come to get him and brought him here.

Early on during his incarceration, newspaper reporters had shown up now and then, wanting to interview him about his career robbing banks and trains. He supposed they had done stories already about the Reno brothers, the James brothers, the Youngers, and the other famous gangs and now wanted something about the McReady gang.

Also, they had tried to worm information out of him about that big pile of loot he was rumored to have stashed somewhere. They tried to be so subtle about it, but McReady knew what they were doing. They never got a thing out of him. And over the months, those visits had stopped.

Today, the guards ushered him along the table to the chair waiting for him. As McReady stopped behind it, he looked through the bars and was surprised to see a familiar face on the other side of the table.

"Bill, what in blazes are you doing here?" he asked in the husky undertone that had given him his name. Even though being shot in the throat had hurt like the devil, being called Whisper was better than being called Jug.

Bill Wickham, the gray-haired, leathery old outlaw who was McReady's best friend, if a man such as him could be said to have friends, smiled and said, "Howdy, Whisper."

One of the guards pulled out the chair. The other put a hand on McReady's shoulder and ordered, "Sit."

McReady sat.

He scraped the chair closer to the table as the guards stepped back far enough that they couldn't overhear what was said as long as McReady and his visitor were careful about it. Leaning forward, McReady asked again, "Bill, what are you doing here? This is a prison. You shouldn't be here."

Wickham glanced around and said, "I won't lie to you. It's more than a mite uncomfortable being behind these walls. But something's been eating at me for a long time, and I figure it'll keep on gnawing until I do something about it."

McReady frowned, which made him look even more intimidating than he usually did.

"You're not here to confess, are you?" he asked. "You're not the one who told that posse of U.S. Marshals where to find me?" The question was even more threatening voiced in McReady's harsh rasp.

"What?" Wickham leaned back, and his eyes widened in alarm. "Good grief, no! Don't even think that. I'd never double-cross you, Whisper, you know that."

"I didn't think so, but I don't know what else you could be talking about that would be bothering you."

Wickham swallowed and said, "It's about your daughters. Step-daughters, I mean."

"I know what you mean. Those girls are the only kin I've got left, even if it is just because I married their ma." McReady cocked his head a little to the side. "You'd better not be here to tell me that something's happened to them."

"No, no, they're fine, or they were the last time I saw them, a couple of years back. I've tried to keep up with them since then, and nothing's happened to them as far as I know."

"Well, then, what is it?" McReady asked, impatience edging into his distinctive voice.

Wickham cleared his throat and went on, "Violet came to see us."

"Came to see who?"

"The gang. We were in Cottonwood, taking it easy between jobs. Me and Linc Pollard and some of the other boys. Several of 'em you wouldn't know, because they started riding with us after you, well . . ."

"After I got put in here," McReady finished for him.

"Yeah, that's right."

McReady shook his head. "Violet shouldn't have gone to Cottonwood. She doesn't need to be in a place like that. It's not proper."

"I agree with you."

"What in the world was she doing there?"

"She said you sent her."

Surprise made McReady frown and lean back sharply in his chair. The movement prompted one of the guards to move a step closer, but then he relaxed when he saw that McReady wasn't trying to get to his feet.

After taking a moment for the news to sink in, McReady said, "She claimed I told her to go there?"

"That's right. She told us she'd been visiting you here in prison regular-like, and that you'd taught her everything you knew."

"Everything I know about *what*?"

"About leading an outlaw gang," Wickham replied.

McReady was even more thunderstruck now. It was a full thirty seconds before he could find the words to continue the conversation. "Violet never came to see me, and neither did Daisy. I told Emmaline I didn't want them here. She didn't want that, either. She told me she was going to forbid the girls from coming."

For a moment, unaccustomed emotion welled up inside McReady. He had to look down at the table as he forced those feelings away.

"Of course, after she passed, she couldn't stop them from doing whatever they wanted, I suppose," he went on, "but they didn't come here, not either of them. I haven't seen them in years." McReady grunted. "Daisy was just a kid the last time I saw her. I reckon she's grown up some since then."

"But you never told Violet you wanted her to take over the gang?"

"Never! Do you think I've gone loco? A girl can't run an outlaw gang!"

"That's what I tried to tell Linc and the other fellas," Wickham said, "but they wouldn't listen to me. Violet convinced them she was telling the truth, and they agreed to go along with her, at least for a while, so they could see how it worked out."

McReady's hands clenched into fists. His jaw was clenched just as tightly as he said, "That's crazy!"

"They thought that's what you wanted, Whisper. Violet got them to believe that. I was the only one who didn't go along with it. I walked out."

"You're lucky Pollard or one of the others didn't shoot you in the back."

"Believe me, I worried about that," Wickham said. "But something about the whole deal just seemed off to me. I didn't want to call Violet a liar, but I had a hunch I shouldn't be part of it. And now I know why."

"She was lying," McReady said. "The blasted little minx. I never really trusted her. She always acted so sweet, such a little goody-good, but you could see something in her eyes if you looked for it. A little devil, that's what she really was." He sighed. "But you said she and Daisy are all right?"

"They are," Wickham said. "The gang's pulled a dozen jobs since Violet took over. Not all of them have gone perfect, but they've gotten away with loot every time. Some pretty big payoffs, too."

McReady stared across the table at his old friend, once again unable to speak for a moment. Then he said, "She's actually running the gang?"

Wickham nodded. "And doing a good job of it, from what I hear. I haven't been riding with them, you understand, but I keep track of what they're doing as best I can. You know how it works, Whisper. Word always travels fast along the hoot owl trails."

"Why did you come here today?"

"Like I told you, the whole thing's been eating at me. I wanted to know the truth. I thought that maybe if it really was your idea, I'd go back to the gang." Wickham's shoulders rose and fell. "Life hasn't been treating me so good. At my age, it's hard to do much of anything that pays well."

"But now you know I didn't have anything to do with it."

"Yeah. I guess it was all Violet's idea."

And a daring idea it had been, McReady thought. Anger was beginning to bubble up inside of him. What kind of girl was so sure of herself that she would walk right into a den of thieves and announce that she was taking over? And what sort of men would let her get away with such a bold move?

McReady could almost admire Violet's guts, but at the same

time, he was furious with her. He had worked hard for years to build up that gang. She'd had no right to just waltz in and take charge like that.

Not only that, but the loot they had gotten from the jobs they'd pulled without him, well, by rights, some of that ought to be his. Just because he was locked up didn't mean it wasn't his gang anymore.

Those resentful thoughts were going through his head when one of the guards approached again and said, "Time's up, McReady."

"Not yet," McReady rasped.

"You don't get to decide that," the guard said. He clamped a hand on McReady's shoulder. "Come on."

Angrily, McReady wrenched free and leaned close to the bars again. He reached out with his shackled hands and gripped those bars tightly.

"Where are the girls?" he demanded of Wickham. "You said you'd been keeping up with them? Where are they?"

"Blast it, McReady," the guard growled. He reached for the club hanging from a loop at his waist, and the second guard began to move in, as well.

"I don't know for sure," Wickham said quickly as he half rose to his feet on the other side of the table, "but I heard about some jobs I'm pretty sure they pulled."

The guards took hold of McReady's arms and jerked him up, out of the chair. His eyes locked desperately with Wickham's as he tensed himself and waited, knowing that he might feel the clubs smashing into him at any moment if he didn't cooperate.

"Colorado," Wickham said as the guards started to drag McReady away. "I think they're in a place called Big Rock!"

Chapter 20

After a day or two, Dr. Spaulding declared that Nate Pidgeon had passed the crisis and would pull through. That was good news, but it was the only positive thing to come out of the stagecoach holdup. The posse's failure to catch up to the thieves was a disappointment, especially to the jewelry salesman, who had lost the sample case full of gems.

A week or so later, as soon as they could find the time from their duties on the Sugarloaf, Pearlie and Cal headed back into town to see the Caldwell sisters. As they dismounted and tied their horses in front of the shop, the door opened and Violet ushered a couple of well-dressed, middle-aged women out of the business. There were smiles and laughter all around as the women took their leave.

"Customers?" Pearlie asked as he and Cal stepped up on the boardwalk.

"That's right," Violet said, "and Daisy is helping two more inside. Thanks to Mrs. Jensen and several other ladies who are friends of hers, word is finally getting around about our work and we're lining up quite a few jobs, as well as selling dresses that are already made."

"That's mighty fine news," Cal said. "It's good to see that you're busy."

"Yeah, but we were hopin' maybe you gals would want to take a ride and do a little more target shootin' today," Pearlie said. "From the looks of it, though, you're gonna be stuck here at the shop all day."

Violet laughed. "I wouldn't call it being stuck. But, on the other hand, we might be able to get away for a while. If you could give us a half hour or so . . . ?"

"Sure, we can do that," Cal answered without hesitation. "We'll go get a cup of coffee at Longmont's and then come back. How's that sound?"

"It should be fine unless something else comes up."

"Well, if it does, Pearlie and I will understand. Won't we, Pearlie?"

"Sure, I reckon. But I was hopin' to spend some time with you today, Vi."

She rested a hand on his arm for a second. "Perhaps you will. Come back in a little while and we'll see."

With a smile, she went back into the shop and closed the door. Pearlie and Cal turned to walk along the street toward Louis Longmont's restaurant and saloon.

Pearlie heaved a disappointed sigh, but Cal said, "I guess if we're going to be paying court to a couple of successful businesswomen, we can't expect them to drop everything just to spend time with us."

"Maybe not, and I'm mighty happy their shop is doin' well. But I hope we get to take that ride with 'em before we have to get back out to the Sugarloaf."

"Yeah, me too. But Louis has the best coffee in Big Rock, so we might as well take advantage of the chance to get a cup."

"I ain't gonna argue with that."

To get to Longmont's, they had to pass the Brown Dirt Cowboy Saloon, a considerably lower-class establishment than the one owned by the gambler, but it was popular among punchers who rode for the ranches in the area. The batwings swung outward just before Pearlie and Cal reached them, and two men sauntered out onto the boardwalk.

All four men stopped short at the sight of one another. Chuck Dade and Jasper Hendryx glared at the two Sugarloaf hands. Pearlie and Cal returned the hostile stares.

Dade's nose was no longer bruised from the earlier fracas, and the swelling in it had long since gone down. He sneered and said, "Can't we go anywhere without runnin' into you two polecats?"

"I thought I smelled somethin'," Pearlie said, "like maybe a couple of ol' boar hogs. But I reckon it was just you two hombres."

"Don't you ever work at your jobs?" Hendryx snapped back at him. "Or does Smoke Jensen pay you just so he can keep you around like a couple of pets?"

"That must be it," Dade jeered. "These two ain't fit to do a real man's work."

Cal's jaw jutted forward and his hands clenched into fists as he moved a step forward. "Get out of our way," he said.

Dade jerked his chin toward the edge of the boardwalk. "There's the street," he said. "Plenty of room for you boys out there. Just be sure you don't step in anything."

Hendryx laughed and said, "I ain't sure they'd know the difference if they did."

None of them looked ready to give an inch. The four men continued glowering at one another for a long moment before Pearlie said, "I don't know what brings you boys to town, but Cal and me are gonna be spendin' the afternoon with a certain pair of mighty good-lookin' sisters."

"You lie!" Dade exclaimed. "Startin' out, you may have fooled those fine young ladies into thinkin' you were decent fellas, but

I'm sure they've seen through you by now. They're bound to have figured out you're just a couple of no-good, dumb-as-dirt saddle tramps!"

Pearlie's breath hissed between his teeth. He sounded a little like a tea kettle building up steam to boil over. The fingers of his right hand hooked as they hovered near the butt of the gun on his hip.

"I don't cotton to bein' called a liar," he said.

Dade and Hendryx both crouched a little and leaned forward. Their hands weren't far from their guns, either. The air was thick with impending violence, as if a thunderstorm was about to break loose.

In the hope of heading off a gunfight, Cal said quickly, "We can stand here jawing at each other all day, and it's not going to help anything—"

"Is there some trouble here?" a firm voice asked from behind him.

Pearlie, Dade, and Hendryx all straightened from their angry stances and moved their hands away from their guns. Cal looked over his shoulder and saw Monte Carson standing there in a watchful attitude, with his thumbs hooked in his gun belt.

"No trouble, Sheriff," Dade said. "Jasper and me were just havin' a talk with these two fellows."

"Seems to me like there have been several conversations among you boys lately," Monte said. "They don't seem to end well." His voice hardened a little as he went on, "Were you going into the saloon or coming out of it?"

"We're, uh, comin' out of it," Hendryx said.

"That's right," Dade added. "We need to get back to the Three Sevens."

Monte looked at Pearlie and Cal and asked, "How about you?"

"We're on our way to Longmont's for a cup of coffee," Cal said.

"Well, don't let me stop you. Any of you. You can all just go on about your business."

"Thanks, Sheriff." Dade jerked his head at his companion. "Come on, Jasper."

They stepped off the boardwalk and went to their horses, tied at the hitch rail in front of the saloon. As they untied the reins and swung up into their saddles, they kept shooting angry glances toward Pearlie and Cal.

Then they pulled the horses around and heeled them into brisk trots that carried them out of Big Rock.

"Those two boys don't like you," Monte said to Pearlie and Cal.

"I don't reckon they do," Pearlie said.

"It looked to me like they were fixing to slap leather, in fact."

Pearlie shook his head. "Naw, it wouldn't have gone that far, Monte. They would've backed down. They have to know that neither one of 'em is as fast on the draw as me and Cal."

"They might know it," Monte said, "but sometimes when a man's pride gets ruffled enough, he's too stiff-necked to care about that. He's willing to take his chances."

Pearlie shrugged. "Maybe."

"This is still about those Caldwell sisters, isn't it?"

"Maybe," Pearlie said again.

Monte sighed and said, "I don't like any unnecessary killing in my town. I'd be obliged if you'd steer clear of Dade and Hendryx in the future."

"We weren't planning on running into them today," Cal said. "We were just walking down the street and there they were, all of a sudden."

Monte nodded. "Those things happen. But in the future, if you see them in time . . ."

"We'll try to avoid them."

Pearlie didn't make any such promise.

As he and Cal walked on to the restaurant, he muttered, "I still ain't convinced they didn't try to bushwhack us that day."

"Seems pretty unlikely to me, the way it all played out," Cal said.

"Then who tried to part our hair with some rifle slugs?"

Cal shook his head. "I don't know. Smoke thinks it might have been some of those outlaws, afraid that we were about to stumble on them."

"Could be, but I ain't convinced."

Louis was glad to see them, as always, and they enjoyed the next half hour as they sat at the gambler's personal table at the back of the restaurant's main room and sipped some fine Cajun-style coffee with him as they chatted.

Then Pearlie and Cal headed back to the dress shop, hoping that Violet and Daisy had been able to clear their schedule enough to take that ride out to the creek and practice some more with their pistols.

And if any smooching happened to be involved in the afternoon's activities, well, that would be all to the good, too.

As soon as the two cowboys walked into the shop, they knew at least one of their hopes was soon to be realized. Violet and Daisy were both dressed in riding outfits and looked ready to go.

"Did you get horses for us?" Violet asked.

"Not yet," Pearlie told her, "since we didn't know for sure you'd be able to leave."

"We can all go down to the livery stable together," Daisy suggested as she put the sign in the window stating that the shop was closed for a while, and that they would be back later that afternoon.

The same saddle mounts the sisters had ridden the other time were available. It didn't take long to get saddles on them. Then Pearlie, Violet, Daisy, and Cal rode out of Big Rock, the four of them lined up side by side, with the two cowboys flanking the young women.

Cal kept an eye out for Chuck Dade and Jasper Hendryx, just in case they had doubled back to Big Rock after Monte told them to leave earlier. He didn't catch sight of them anywhere. Chances were, they actually had ridden back out to the Three Sevens, as they said they were going to.

Violet and Daisy were both in happy, talkative moods, so the conversation was a lively, enjoyable one as they rode to the creek where they had practiced before. Once they were there, they dismounted and tied the horses. Pearlie picked out a different tree on the other side of the creek to serve as a target this time.

"See that big knothole about six feet up the trunk?" he asked as he pointed to the distinctive marking. "You can shoot at that."

"It's not really that big," Violet said. "In fact, it's going to make a pretty small target."

"No smaller than that limb you were shootin' at last time, and you were able to hit it. Give 'er a try."

"I'll go first," Daisy declared as she drew her pistol from the pocket of her riding skirt. She took out a handful of cartridges, as well, broke open the little revolver, and loaded it with swift, easy movements. Pearlie and Cal traded a glance as Daisy snapped the gun closed, stepped to the bank, and raised the Smith & Wesson to aim at the knothole on the tree.

Clearly, she had practiced loading, even if they hadn't been out here to do any shooting for a while.

Cal didn't have to give her any tips. He just watched, impressed, as Daisy smoothly fired three rounds, not rushing them but not taking a lot of time between shots, either. The first two bullets struck the tree just below and to the left of the knothole. The third one hit the target.

She lowered the gun and turned to beam at Cal. "That's pretty good, isn't it?" she asked.

"It sure is," he told her. "You have a good eye and natural instincts, I'd say. But we already knew that from last time."

Pearlie said to Violet, "You give it a try now. You don't need me to load for you, do you?"

"Of course not," she replied. She opened the revolver and thumbed shells to it just as deftly as her sister had a few minutes earlier.

Violet aimed and fired three times. All three rounds struck the knothole at an outer edge. None of them were bull's-eyes, but it was still fine shooting.

Pearlie let out a low whistle of admiration.

"Are you sure you gals ain't been sneakin' out here to do some practicin' on your own?" he asked as Violet lowered the gun.

"No, we just have a knack for picking up on things quickly, especially things that require a deft touch," she said. "It's really not that different from being a seamstress, you know. In order to be good at sewing, you have to have a clear eye and the ability to make your fingers do what you want them to."

Cal said, "I think this is the first time I've ever heard sewing compared to shooting a gun, but I guess I can see what you're talking about."

"I suspect a seamstress'd make a better gunfighter than a gunfighter would make a seamstress, though," Pearlie said.

"We're hardly gunfighters," Violet said, "but I'd like to think that Daisy and I are developing the skills to take care of ourselves."

Cal nodded. "I'd say you are. Why don't you try it again, Daisy?"

She smiled and lifted the gun. "I'd be happy to. It's loud, but I like this!"

For the next half hour, the sisters took turns shooting at the knothole. They missed occasionally, but most of the shots were hits. Pearlie and Cal continued to be impressed.

After Violet had placed a bullet very near the center of the knothole, she said, "I think that's enough for today."

"Of course you think that," Daisy said. "You just made the best shot so far, so you want to quit while you're ahead."

"I wasn't aware that it was a competition," Violet responded, coolly arching an eyebrow.

Daisy laughed. "With sisters, isn't it always?"

Pearlie stroked his chin and said, "We didn't do no wagerin', but if we had, I would've bet on you, Vi."

"And I would have bet on you," Cal told Daisy.

"Oh, you just feel like you have to say that," she said.

"No, I mean it—"

While Cal was still talking, Daisy turned quickly to the creek bank, raised the Smith & Wesson, and fired four shots as fast as she could cock the hammer between them. And that was fast, because the echoes of one shot had barely started before Daisy squeezed off the next one. Those echoes merged into one rolling peal of gun-thunder.

Cal's eyes widened as he watched splinters flying from the target tree. All four rounds from Daisy's gun slammed into the knothole, fairly close to the bullet hole in the center that Violet's last shot had left. As the reports died away, Daisy lowered the gun and turned to Cal with a smile.

With an annoyed edge in her voice, Violet said, "Now you're just showing off, Daisy."

"I know, and I should be sorry, I suppose. But I'm not. I just needed the proper motivation."

Daisy touched the gun's barrel to see how hot it was, then, satisfied that it wouldn't cause a problem, slid the little revolver back into her pocket.

"Now, that's enough for today," she went on. She linked her arm with Cal's. "But I'm not ready to go back to Big Rock just yet. It's an awfully nice day. Why don't we take a walk along the creek?"

Cal started to glance at Pearlie to see what the older cowboy thought of that suggestion, but he stopped himself. He was a grown man, he thought. He could make up his own mind what he was going to do.

And right now, he wanted to take that walk with Daisy Caldwell.

"We'll be back in a little while," he told Pearlie. He and Daisy strolled along the creek bank through the sun-dappled shadows cast by the trees.

Behind them, Violet said, “It really is a nice day, Pearlie. Why don’t we sit here under this tree for a while and enjoy it?”

“I ain’t gonna argue with that idea, ma’am.”

“Oh, please,” Violet said. “When you’re sitting under a tree beside a creek with a pretty girl, you don’t need to call her ma’am, no matter how chivalrous you are.”

That was the last Cal heard as he and Daisy walked around a bend in the stream. The trees would have cut off his view of Pearlie and Violet if he had looked back, which he didn’t.

As they walked, Daisy asked about some of the bushes and trees they passed, wanting to know what kind they were. She pointed out some colorful birds flitting around in the branches over their heads and asked what they were called. She laughed when she spotted a squirrel sitting on a limb, chattering at them. She seemed to be having a good time, and Cal really enjoyed seeing the smile on her face.

After several minutes, she stopped and turned to look at him. “I’m about to do something that’s going to make you think I’m terribly forward, Calvin Woods.”

His voice was a little strained as he said, “I, uh, was thinking about maybe doing something that’s a little forward, myself.”

“I wish you would,” she murmured as her arms came up and went around his neck. He slid his arms around her waist and urged her closer.

Except for birdsongs and that squirrel chattering, the next few minutes were pretty quiet along the creek bank as Cal and Daisy embraced and kissed. Cal firmly ordered himself not to get too carried away, but it was difficult not to when his arms were full of a beautiful young woman and her warm, sweet lips were pressed to his.

However, he managed not to do anything improper. This was just some sparking, he thought. Nothing to be ashamed of.

After a while, Daisy sighed, rested her blond curls against his chest for a moment, and said softly, "I've been thinking, Cal."

"Thinking about what?"

"When we were talking before about you having your own ranch . . ." She lifted her head to gaze solemnly up into his face. "It would be a lot better if you had somebody to share that place, wouldn't it?"

"You mean like a partner? To tell the truth, Pearlie and I have talked about pooling our money and going in together to buy a spread—"

"I mean like a wife," Daisy said, breaking into the words tumbling out of his mouth.

Cal stiffened. She couldn't help but feel his response and went on, "Did I say something wrong?"

Quickly, he smiled down into her blue eyes and shook his head. "No," he told her. "Just stirred up a few memories, that's all. But it's nothing to worry about."

"Are you sure?"

"I'm sure." He bent his head and kissed her again. "Reckon I was just a mite surprised by the idea."

"I told you I could be forward," she said. "But maybe that's moving a little too fast. We should think about this."

"We definitely should," Cal said.

"And I'm sure you would have rather brought up the subject of marriage yourself. I mean, there are traditions to uphold. That's something the man usually does."

He nodded and said, "Next time we come out here to practice with those guns, we can take another walk like this and talk about it some more."

"Oh, I'm looking forward to that," Daisy said, her smile widening to a happy grin. "I suppose now, though, we ought to go back and join Violet and Pearlie."

"More than likely we should," Cal agreed. He linked arms with her again, and they headed along the creek toward the spot where they had left the other couple.

Cal took pains to insure that they made plenty of noise as they approached, talking and laughing, just in case Pearlie and Violet might be doing a little sparking of their own.

Sure enough, Violet looked a little flushed when they came in sight. She was sitting with her back propped against a tree trunk. Pearlie was sitting close beside her, but not improperly so. And he had a grin on his face, too, just like Cal did.

"Everybody ready to head back to Big Rock?" Cal asked.

"Yes, we really should be getting back," Violet said. "We shouldn't have been away from the shop this long." She glanced over at Pearlie. "But I think it was worth it."

"Yeah, I reckon it was," he said. He got to his feet, extended a hand to her, and helped her up.

They untied the horses and let them drink from the creek, then mounted up and rode toward the settlement. The atmosphere was a little different now, Cal sensed. Things had changed this afternoon. He felt as if events were suddenly rushing along at a faster pace than he had expected.

But sometimes, that's how life was, out here on the frontier. It was an uncertain world, and when something good came along, something worthwhile, maybe the smart thing for a fellow to do was to grab hold of it and hang on for all he was worth.

Chapter 21

As soon as they were in the back room of the dress shop, with the front door firmly closed behind Pearlie and Cal and the curtain pulled over the opening between the rooms, Daisy turned to Violet and said in a quiet but intense voice, "I won't do it."

Violet drew the pistol from her pocket and placed it on one of the tables. She laughed and said, "You already did. I could tell from the look on Cal's face when the two of you walked up that he's totally besotted with you. He'll do anything you ask him to, dear, and be absolutely thrilled to do it."

"And I suppose you've got Pearlie bewitched the same way?"

"Of course, I do. He's totally under my spell, if that's the way you want to put it. Was there ever any doubt?"

Daisy shook her head. "I suppose not. But it's not fair to them, Vi. It's just not."

Violet had started to turn away, but she swung sharply back around toward her sister. The self-satisfied smile dropped off her face. Anger blazed in her eyes.

"Fair?" she repeated. "Was it fair for our mother to marry a vicious outlaw who treated her and us terribly? When he wasn't ignoring us and practically abandoning us? We're just following the example our stepfather set for us. We're taking what we want, and if anyone gets in our way, it's just too bad!"

For a moment, the two young women glared at each other. Then Daisy's stubborn defiance faded, and she dropped her eyes, no longer able to meet Violet's baleful stare.

She mustered up the courage to mutter, "I still don't see why we have to betray them so badly."

"Because that's the only way we'll ever get them to part with all their hard-earned money." Violet began to pace, caught up in the tension created by the argument. "Sure, we could play things along and get them to spend some on us here and there. They're just simple cowboys, Daisy, eager to do anything to gain the favor of the girls they're smitten with. But that would take forever, and it would never amount to enough to make all the effort worthwhile."

"I wouldn't exactly call what I've been doing with Cal an effort," Daisy said.

"Granted, he's young and handsome. More so than Pearlie is, although I'll admit Pearlie does have a certain roughhewn charm. He's actually quite likeable, in his own way. But it doesn't matter. They have what we need, and we're going to get it."

"We're making money from the jobs Linc and the other men are pulling."

Violet rolled her eyes dismissively. "They're doing all right for now, but we've carried them about as far and as long as we can. Sooner or later, no matter how well thought out the plans are that we give them, Linc's going to make a mistake that's going to ruin everything, and you know it. Wrecking that train like he did was almost enough to ruin everything. He drew too much attention to the gang. For all we know, the railroad has already sent detectives out here to look for the men responsible for the crash. And if the law ever catches up to Linc and the others, do you really think they won't betray us to make things easier for them?"

Daisy sighed and said, "I suppose they would."

"Of course they would. There's no honor among thieves, no matter what the old saying claims. That's why we have to start making plans now to leave this life behind. It's time, Daisy. And we can get enough money from Pearlie and Cal to disappear from Big Rock and go somewhere that nobody will ever find us. Not the law, and not the rest of the gang."

Daisy knew that Violet was right. From the moment her sister had laid out the plan for her, she had had no doubt that it would work. The first steps of playing up to Pearlie and Cal, encouraging the romantic dreams that lonely men everywhere had lurking inside them, planting the seeds of the idea of buying a ranch of their own . . . those had been simplicity itself.

And when the time was right, Daisy was sure the two men would continue to be just as easily manipulated. They would turn their life's savings over to Violet to purchase the ranch she claimed to have found for them. The ranch that didn't really exist and never would . . .

Then the two of them would be gone, never to be seen again. Violet had suggested that they travel to San Francisco and use the money to establish themselves there. With what they would get from Pearlie and Cal, combined with their share of the loot from the robberies pulled by the gang, they would be able to live in comfort for the rest of their lives.

That was the plan, anyway.

"If we knew where Whisper hid all that loot of his, we wouldn't have to steal from Pearlie and Cal," Daisy said.

"It's not stealing when you take money from someone who's too foolish and blinded by emotion to keep it," Violet said. "That's just the way of the world. You might even call it justice."

"It's not justice to break their hearts."

"If their hearts are weak enough to be broken, it is."

She was wasting her time, arguing with Violet, Daisy knew. Violet had always been convinced she knew more than anyone else, and even though she could be warm and charming when she wanted to, inside she was as cold and hard as ice. Daisy didn't want to admit that, even to herself, but she knew it was true.

Whisper McReady probably didn't know it, but he had taught his older stepdaughter very well, and Violet had been a willing student.

Daisy wondered if he would be proud.

More than a week had passed since Linc Pollard had heard from the Caldwell sisters. The members of the gang were getting restless. They were eager to know what their next job would be and when they would be pulling it.

They needed a chance to ride into a town, drink whiskey, play cards, and spend time with some soiled doves, too. Sitting out here in these badlands, hunkered under a big stone overhang that might as well be a cave, could be wearing on a man's nerves.

Pollard's nerves were certainly feeling that strain as he sat next to the campfire, sipping from a cup of coffee and smoking the quirley he had rolled a few minutes earlier after supper. It was already dark outside, although the stars weren't visible through the tons of rock looming over their heads.

A breeze drew the smoke off through some cracks in the overhang farther back. This area was big enough for all the men. The horses were kept in a rope corral a short distance away, watched over by a couple of guards.

Two more lookouts were posted up the canyon. Only one trail led in here, and it ended at the beetle-browed bluff that formed the overhang. That meant the place would be easy to defend, but if they were ever penned in here, there was no back door for an escape.

You always had to trade one thing for another in this life, Pollard had told the men when they found this spot and established their hideout here. Nothing came without a price, or at least the potential of one.

The campfire crackled and danced. A ridge on the far side of the canyon cut off any view of it, so it was safe to let the flames leap high. Even though the days could be mighty warm at this time of year, the thin air cooled off quickly at night, so the warmth from the blaze felt pretty good.

Other than the four men on guard, the two dozen remaining members of the gang were sitting around talking, playing cards, cleaning guns, and mending clothes.

It was too bad they couldn't get Vi and Daisy to do that for them, Pollard mused. But it wasn't wise for there to be too much contact between the gang and the sisters. Pollard had taken a big enough chance visiting them in Big Rock on the night of that big storm.

If the weather hadn't been bad enough to keep folks off the streets, and if he hadn't been so annoyed by the way they were cozying up to those two cowboys, he wouldn't have risked the visit. And they were still pretending to be smitten with Jensen's men. Pollard had spied on them from a distance and seen them out there at the creek.

When Vi let that blasted saddle tramp put his arms around her and then kissed him, it was all Pollard could do not to rush in and shoot the son of a buck. Vi had to have figured out by now that he was in love with her.

Maybe she just didn't care.

Sitting around brooding wasn't going to accomplish anything, Pollard told himself sternly. He snapped the butt of his cigarette into the flames. He had finished the coffee. He tossed the dregs in the fire and dropped the cup in the wreck pan to be washed.

Then he strode over to the opening to get some fresh air.

He hadn't been standing there more than a minute when he heard rapid footsteps approaching through the darkness.

There hadn't been any alarm from the guards, but that might be what this was. Pollard stepped out from under the overhanging rock and rested his hand on the butt of his gun as he walked forward to meet whoever was hurrying toward the camp.

"Who's there?" he called. "Sing out or get a hole blowed through you."

"Hold your fire, Linc. It's just me."

Pollard recognized Snub Dooley's voice, but he didn't relax. Dooley was one of the men who had been posted to sentry duty a hundred yards out on the trail.

"What's wrong?"

Dooley was panting a little from the rapid pace at which he'd been moving. He came up to Pollard, stopped, and announced, "Riders comin'."

Pollard stiffened even more. "How many?"

"Don't know for sure. We didn't see 'em, just heard their horses. Half a dozen, anyway, maybe more."

Pollard bit back a curse and a groan. "A posse?"

"Don't know," Dooley said again. "We gonna bushwhack 'em just in case?"

Pollard didn't like the idea of murdering folks when he didn't know who they were or what purpose their deaths would serve. Sometimes, though, it was necessary, and tonight might be one of those times.

He turned his head, called the names of five of the outlaws.

"Grab your rifles and come on!" he told them.

The urgency in his voice communicated itself to the men. They scrambled to their feet and rushed out of the cavelike camp, bringing their Winchesters with them.

Together with Pollard and Dooley, they ran out to join the other man who was on guard duty.

When they reached the spot where that man should have been, Pollard hissed a command to stop. He looked around. Quite a few rocks and clumps of brush littered the canyon floor here, which was what made it a good place for the guards to hide.

"Jarboe!" he called quietly. "Jarboe, where are you?"

No response came back to him. Pollard listened intently for a moment, then turned to Dooley and said, "I don't hear any horses headed this way."

"They were there, Linc, I swear it," Dooley said. "Jarboe and me heard 'em plain as day. We even waited a little spell to make sure they were comin' this direction instead of just passin' by in the night, before I ran back to camp to fetch you."

"Well, where are they now?" Pollard demanded. "And where's Jarboe?"

A new voice spoke in answer, a voice that Pollard hadn't figured he would ever hear again, not truly.

"If Jarboe's your sentry, he's right here," the instantly recognizable voice declared. "Don't get trigger-happy, or he'll be the first one to die." A heartbeat's pause, and then the voice added, "And you'll be next, Linc."

At the first words out of the darkness, Pollard had started to draw his gun. But as he realized who was speaking, he let the iron slip back into leather.

"Whisper!" he exclaimed. "Whisper, is that really you?"

Several dark shapes appeared, stepping out of the concealment of some brush into the silvery starlight that filled the canyon. As one of those shapes came closer, Pollard recognized not only the voice but also the large, prominent ears sticking out from the man's head under a low-crowned hat.

"If we'd been a posse or a cavalry patrol, you'd all be dead now," Whisper McReady said. "Two guards wouldn't have been enough to stop us."

"The canyon's narrow," Pollard said, instantly feeling defensive even though McReady had been back for only a moment. "I figured it would be easy to defend."

McReady snorted. "A dozen men could overrun two sentries without any trouble, and that's if the man in charge didn't mind losing a few riders. If he wanted to cut his losses down to nothing, he'd just send a good scout out ahead to take care of the guards." McReady jerked a thumb over his shoulder. "A scout like Banjo there."

One of the men with McReady stepped forward, pushing another figure in front of him. Pollard recognized Jarboe. The man called Banjo had an arm looped around Jarboe's neck, holding him tightly, while with his other hand he rested the point of an Arkansas toothpick against the side of the erstwhile guard's head.

Even in the starlight, Pollard could see Banjo's gap-toothed, dim-witted grin over Jarboe's shoulder. It told him Banjo wouldn't hesitate to shove that big knife into Jarboe's brain. He'd probably even enjoy it.

Pollard swallowed hard and said, "How about tellin' your man to let him go, Whisper? Jarboe's a good hombre. He ain't done nothin' wrong."

"Except for letting himself get caught." McReady half turned and flicked a hand toward the prisoner as he ordered, "Let him go, Banjo."

When Banjo took the knife away from his head and released the grip on him, Jarboe sagged from the strain of being that close to death and almost fell. Dooley stepped forward and took hold of his friend's arm to steady him.

"We've had a long, hard ride to get here," McReady went on. "We could do with coffee and something to eat."

"Sure, sure," Pollard said quickly. "Come on back to the hideout with us. You can bring your horses and put them with ours."

He told Dooley and Jarboe to remain on guard and ordered three of the men who had come out with him to stay there on watch, too. Then Pollard turned and led the way toward the big, overhanging bluff.

With a confident, almost arrogant stride, McReady moved alongside him. Somebody else would bring the boss outlaw's horse, Pollard supposed. When he looked over his shoulder, he saw five men following them, leading the mounts.

"How in the world did you get here?" Pollard asked the man beside him. "The last I heard, you were locked up in the Kansas State Pen."

McReady let out a raspy laugh. "You think the prison's been built that can hold me if I want out bad enough?"

"You know, I've said the same thing, Whisper. The very same thing! I told the boys you'd bust out and just show up one of these days, and now here you are."

"You're still surprised to see me, though."

"Well, yeah, I reckon I am. A fella can be convinced that something's gonna happen, but he's not really expectin' it until it actually does."

"So you figured you'd just keep bossing the gang from now on."

Again, Pollard felt a surge of mixed defensiveness and anger at McReady's tone.

"I just wanted to keep the gang together until you got back," he said. "The only way to do that was to go on pullin' jobs. We needed the money. I never thought of myself as the boss, but somebody had to take charge. I figured I could do as well as anybody."

"You've kept the gang together," McReady said. He sounded as if he made that admission reluctantly. However, he didn't make any comment on whether he thought Pollard had done a good job.

That was just his way, Pollard told himself. McReady never was the warm, friendly type of hombre who was quick to praise the men who rode with him. Just the opposite, in fact.

When they reached the camp, several of the men called out startled greetings to McReady. They had ridden with him before but clearly hadn't expected him to return.

As the light from the fire washed over the newcomers, Pollard got another surprise. Bill Wickham was among them. Pollard hadn't recognized him until now. Wickham grinned at him and said, "Hello, Linc."

"Bill, it's, uh, it's good to see you again."

"How about that coffee and grub?" McReady asked.

Several members of the gang took turns handling the cooking chores. Tonight, the one responsible for that was an outlaw named Willard Jackson. He had been with the gang when McReady was leading it, so he recognized the impatient tone of voice in which McReady asked that question and hurried to get food and coffee ready for him. Luckily, quite a bit of stew still remained in the pot from tonight's supper.

Once the new arrivals had bowls of stew and cups of coffee and were sitting around the fire, Pollard said, "I really want to hear how you managed to get out of prison, Whisper. You busted out, right? They didn't let you go for some reason?"

"No, they didn't let me go," McReady said, and his contemptuous tone made it clear what he thought of the question. "But money can buy almost anything, and I knew where Bill could lay his hands on enough to get the job done. He'd been coming to see me, so we worked out a plan. He paid off a guard to smuggle in guns to me and a few other fellas, and then that same guard looked the other way when the time came for us to bust out." McReady let out a harsh laugh. "That's when the greedy fool got his real payoff. Since his head was turned, I put a bullet in the back of it."

Pollard had no trouble believing that McReady was capable of such ruthless treachery. "And then you and those other fellas shot your way out?"

"Yeah. Bill had horses waiting for us. Since then, we've been on the run, but before we got here, we shook off the last of the pursuit. Nobody knows where we are now."

"Well, that's just great, Whisper. Now that you're back, and we've got some new men to throw in with us, the gang will be better than ever."

"Ready for me to take over from you, is that right?"

Something about the mocking tone in McReady's voice worried Pollard. He said, "Yeah, I reckon so. You were always the boss—"

"And you never were," McReady cut in. "You were never smart enough for that. Tell the truth, Linc. My daughters have been running everything, haven't they?"

Pollard glanced at Wickham and knew that the old outlaw had told McReady everything about Violet's visit to Cottonwood. McReady was acting like he didn't know about it, though, which confused Pollard.

"Sure, Vi and Daisy have been helpin' us out with information and plans," Pollard said, "but when we pull a job, I'm the one who gives the orders. That's how you wanted it, right? That's why you sent Vi to find us in the first place?"

McReady glared at him and said, "I never sent Vi to find you, and she never came to visit me in prison. She lied to you about everything, and you just swallowed it whole, you fool!"

Chapter 22

It was time for another of the monthly town socials, and when Saturday of that week rolled around, Pearlie and Cal cleaned up, slicked up, and looked forward to seeing Violet and Daisy Caldwell again.

They had been out to the creek with the sisters twice more to practice shooting, although other interests actually were uppermost in the minds of all four. Each time, the young women fired some shots at various targets across the creek and demonstrated that they had become fairly skilled in the art of gun handling.

Once that was done, the couples split up for walks along the creek and some passionate kissing, followed by serious conversation.

When it was time to leave for town, Smoke escorted Sally out of the ranch house and helped her onto the buckboard, then climbed aboard and sat down beside her. He was going to be handling the reins this time, instead of riding into Big Rock on horseback.

Pearlie, Cal, and the other hands who were going into town

emerged from the barn leading their horses and came over to the buckboard. The cowboys were laughing and joking, clearly eager to reach Big Rock and get started on the evening's recreation.

Smoke grinned at them and said, "You boys go ahead. There's no need to wait for us. In fact, I'd rather you get a good lead on us so we won't have to eat your dust."

"Are you sure, Smoke?" one of the men asked. "We can follow the buckboard, if you'd rather."

"And make you rein yourselves in when you're rarin' to go?" Smoke laughed. "No, that's all right. We'll come on at a leisurely pace and see you fellas later."

A couple of them jerked off their hats, waved them over their heads, and shouted in pure exuberance. The men wheeled their horses and galloped off, heading for Big Rock.

Sally laughed as she watched them go. "Oh, my, to be young again," she said.

"What are you talking about?" Smoke asked her. "You're still young, and so am I."

"Yes, but we have responsibilities, and that makes you feel older than you really are. We have to be sane and sober and sensible."

Smoke let a mock shudder run through his body. "Sounds like pure torture to me."

Sally laughed again and then looked over to where Pearlie and Cal were still sitting nearby on their horses.

"Why didn't you two charge on into town with the others?" she asked them.

The two cowboys looked at each other. Smoke could tell they were a little uncomfortable about something. They wanted to talk but were unsure which of them should start, he figured.

Knowing those two, they had planned out ahead of time how to approach him, but now that the time had come, they didn't know what to do.

He said, "You fellas are smart enough to know that sometimes you have to bite the bullet and go ahead. So, whatever you have to say, just go ahead and say it."

They glanced at each other again, and then Pearlie said, "We need to tell you somethin', Smoke, but I ain't sure of the best way to do it."

"Straight out usually works."

Pearlie nodded. "Yeah." He took a deep breath. "There's a mighty good chance Cal and me are gonna be leavin' the Sugarloaf."

"Oh, no!" Sally exclaimed. "Does that mean you're not happy here?"

Pearlie and Cal both looked horrified at that suggestion. Cal said quickly, "That's not it at all, Miss Sally. Why, I've been happier here than any other place I've ever been in my life."

"The same's true for me, ma'am," Pearlie said. "It's just that our, uh, circumstances may be about to change."

"We hope to know more about that before the evening is over," Cal added.

A big grin suddenly split Smoke's face. "You two boys are about to ask the Caldwell sisters to marry you, aren't you?"

Sally looked over at him in amazement. "Marriage?" she said. She turned back to Pearlie and Cal. "I knew you'd been, well, keeping company with them, but I didn't have any idea things had gotten serious enough to talk about marriage!"

"It sure didn't start out that way," Pearlie said. "But we've been teachin' those gals to shoot, you know—"

"We haven't had to teach them much," Cal broke in. "They're just naturally good shots. It comes from being seamstresses, Violet says. Their eyes and hands work well together."

Sally nodded and said, "I can see how that would be true."

"Anyway," Pearlie went on, "we've been takin' them out to the creek to practice, and when they've had enough shootin', we take walks with 'em along the stream . . ."

His voice trailed away as his face flushed. Both cowboys looked so uncomfortable and embarrassed that it was all Smoke could do not to bust out laughing.

He suppressed that urge and instead said solemnly, "There's nothing more natural than for a man and a woman to get mighty fond of each other. If that's what's happened, fellas, you should count yourselves lucky."

"Oh, we do," Cal said. "Sometimes I feel like we're the luckiest hombres on the face of the earth."

Sally said, "Just because you're married, that doesn't mean you'd have to leave the Sugarloaf. A lot of ranch hands are married, aren't they? We could build quarters for you so you wouldn't have to stay in the bunkhouse."

Smoke looked shrewdly at the two punchers and said, "I have a hunch it's more than that. There came a time in my life when I had a hankering to own a spread of my own."

Sally's face lit up. She asked them, "Is that it? You want to have your own ranch?"

"It'd be a mighty fine thing, I reckon," Pearlie said. "I never gave much thought to the idea when I was younger. I mean, before I came here to work."

That was because Pearlie was a hired gun before coming to the Sugarloaf, Smoke reflected, and men in that line of work seldom devoted much thought to the future. They knew the odds of them living long enough to have to worry about something like that were pretty slim.

"I've considered it," Cal said. "If things had worked out differently with Susannah Bolton, there's no telling what I might have done. But that's in the past, and it seems to me that it's time to look to the future instead."

Smoke nodded and said, "That's always a smart thing to do. Yesterday's gone, as they say."

"Violet and Daisy are both very sweet," Sally said. "And they're hard workers, too. You can tell that from the fine job they're doing with their dress shop."

Pearlie bobbed his head. "Yes'm, a couple o' scraggly ol' critters like me and Cal would be mighty lucky to get hitched up with such a fine pair of ladies."

"Speak for yourself," Cal said with a laugh. "I don't think I'm all that scraggly."

Smoke was glad that the uncomfortableness felt by the two cowboys seemed to have eased quite a bit. He said, "You're going to ask them tonight?"

"That's the plan," Cal said. "Assuming that the situation feels right. I mean, we've already discussed the possibility with them, but there haven't been any official proposals yet."

"Well, for goodness' sake, try to put a little romance in it," Sally told them. "It's not like you're discussing buying a herd of cattle."

"No, but you'll have to do that if you start your own spread," Smoke pointed out. "I reckon I could give you a pretty good price on some Sugarloaf stock. Which brings up another question, and if it's none of my business, just say so. Do you have the money to buy a ranch?"

Cal said, "If we put together what we've saved and go in as partners, we can come up with enough. We were thinking about the old Diamond Y spread."

Smoke nodded again. "It's been just sitting there the past six months since Orville Yeager died. I know his widow would like to sell it. She ought to make you a good deal on it. Have you talked to Joel Montgomery at the bank? He was going to handle selling it for her, since he and Orville were friends."

"Things ain't got that far along yet," Pearlie said.

"We have to talk to Violet and Daisy first," Cal added.

"Of course you do," Sally said firmly. "You can't make a big decision like that without consulting the women who'll be sharing it with you."

Cal asked, "Does this mean we have your blessing? Both of you?"

"Good grief, you don't need our blessing," Smoke said. "We're not your folks."

"You're as close to it as I'm ever likely to have again," Cal said with heartfelt simplicity.

Sally looked both flustered and touched. "That's an awfully nice thing to say, Cal," she told him.

"And you're mighty like a brother to me, Smoke," Pearlie said. "There ain't nobody in this world whose opinion I respect more."

"As far as I'm concerned, it's a good idea," Smoke said. "Now, I'll be honest with you. I'd hate to lose both of you as members of my crew. But I figure you'll more than make up for that loss by being mighty fine neighbors."

Pearlie grinned. "I sure hope it works out that way."

"So do I," Cal said. "But I don't reckon we'll ever know if we don't get to that social and dance with Vi and Daisy a little before we pop the question."

"Well, then, let's get to town," Pearlie said as he turned his horse. He started out at a brisk trot, with Cal riding alongside them. Grinning, Smoke flapped the reins hitched to the buckboard team and headed down the road after them.

"I think tonight may be the night," Violet said as she studied her reflection in the mirror. She tucked a stray tendril of blond hair back into place. She and her sister were in Violet's bedroom in the little cottage behind the dress shop.

Daisy said, "Get these buttons, will you?" She turned her back toward Violet and revealed that the light blue dress she wore wasn't fastened yet.

Deftly, Violet began slipping the buttons through their holes. She said, "What do you think? Is Cal all primed and ready for the big moment?"

Daisy didn't answer for a few seconds. Then she said, "I think he is. I'm just not sure I want him to be."

Violet finished buttoning the gown and stepped around Daisy so that she could give her sister a stern look.

"I don't want to hear any more talk like that," she said. "We can't let any doubts ruin this for us now. We've worked too hard for it, Daisy. You know we have."

"We've pretended to let them teach us how to shoot, we've gone on walks with them next to a pretty little creek, and we've let them kiss us." Daisy shook her head. "I don't really see how any of that is hard work, Vi."

"Do you love Calvin Woods?" Violet asked bluntly. "Be honest, now."

Daisy hesitated again. "Well . . . not really. But I'm very fond of him. He's a sweet boy."

"I'm not in love with Pearlie, either, although as I said before, he does have a certain rough charm. We don't owe either of them anything, Daisy. Not a thing."

"That doesn't mean it's all right to steal from them."

"It's not stealing if they're getting something in return."

Daisy frowned in confusion and asked, "What are they getting in return?"

"A lesson. They're learning not to be so trusting." Violet turned toward the door. "Come on. As eager as they are, they'll probably be waiting for us when we get there. And if Cal does propose, what are you going to say?"

Daisy drew in a breath. "I'll say yes. And then we'll talk more about them buying that ranch for us."

"That's my girl," Violet said with a smile. Daisy followed her out of the room.

It was early evening when Smoke, Sally, Pearlie, and Cal arrived in Big Rock. A strikingly lovely red and gold arch from the sun that had set not long before lingered in the western sky.

Buckboards, buggies, farm and ranch wagons, and men on horseback filled the street, nearly all of them heading toward the town hall. Pedestrians thronged the boardwalks. The often monotonous day-to-day life of frontier communities was enlivened considerably by frequent socials and dances. Big Rock was no exception.

"I'm not sure how close we'll be able to get with the buckboard," Smoke said to Sally. "We may have to walk a little way."

"I don't mind. That'll give me a chance to stretch my legs before the dancing starts."

Smoke grinned. "You'd better call 'em limbs. Some of the proper ladies of Big Rock might be scandalized to hear you talking about your legs."

"As if I've ever been worried about scandalizing people," Sally said with a laugh. "Remember, everybody thought I was just a sweet, innocent schoolteacher when I married a notorious outlaw and gunfighter."

Smoke chuckled and said, "That's true."

Despite his lighthearted response, Sally's comment made his mind go back to the days when they had met in Idaho. That part of his life was filled with violence, bloodshed, tragedy, and grief, as well as righteous anger and justice. But Sally was the anchor that had gotten him through it. Sally, and his own strength and determination.

He stopped the buckboard in front of a store that was closed for the night and tied the team to the hitch rail. Pearlie and Cal had ridden out of sight by the time he and Sally reached the settlement, so he assumed they were already at the town hall and their horses were either in the large corral at the livery stable or tied somewhere along the street. He had spotted a few mounts belonging to other Sugarloaf hands.

Monte Carson came along the boardwalk just as Smoke was helping Sally down from the buckboard. The sheriff was dressed more nicely than usual. He stopped, tipped his hat to Sally, and grinned at the couple.

"Howdy, you two," he said. "Good to see you again."

"Any trouble so far, Monte?" Smoke asked.

"Everything's as peaceful as it can be. Of course, it's early yet. The social's just getting started."

Smoke linked his left arm with Sally's right as they strolled along the boardwalk toward the town hall. That left Smoke's right hand free to hang near the butt of the Colt .45 holstered on his right hip.

Maybe someday he would feel comfortable enough to come to town without packing iron, but he hadn't reached that point yet. And to be honest, he wasn't sure he ever would, or if, in fact, he wanted to.

Guns were a major part of his life. Without them, he never would have survived to meet Sally, let alone marry her and carve out their ranching empire together. He wouldn't have been able to avenge the brutal murders of his father Emmett, his first wife Nicole, and the infant son they'd had together, little Arthur.

Some folks liked to talk about what a wonderful day it would be when guns were no longer necessary in the West. But as long as there were bad men in this world—and there would *always* be bad men—there would be a need for good men with guns, too. That was how Smoke saw it.

This wasn't the time or place to be pondering such things, however, so he pushed those thoughts away. Monte was walking on Sally's other side. Smoke looked past her at the lawman and said, "Might be some changes coming up at the Sugarloaf."

"Oh, really?" Monte said. "What do you mean by that?"

In a warning tone, Sally said, "It might be a little premature to talk about that, Smoke." With her usual shrewdness, she had figured out that Smoke was talking about the impending proposals by Pearlie and Cal.

Monte took the comment to mean something else, though, and

broke into a huge grin. “Wait a minute,” he said. “You mean that you two are finally going to have—”

He didn’t get to finish the question, because they had almost reached the town hall, which sat there, large and impressive, with music and light spilling out its open front doors.

And at that moment, a knot of men also spilled out into the street, cussing and fighting for all they were worth.

Chapter 23

When Pearlie and Cal arrived in Big Rock, they took their horses through the livery stable and out the gate into the large and crowded corral behind the cavernous building. Pearlie dropped a couple of nickels in the bucket hung on a nail beside the gate. The bucket was unattended because the stable's proprietor knew he could count on the honesty of the punchers who brought their horses there.

"Ol' Patterson must make good money off all the hombres who put up their horses while the dance is goin' on," Pearlie commented.

"The hitch rails were already full," Cal said. "We didn't have much choice."

"Oh, I don't mind payin' him. Most of the stores close early on nights like this, so it's good that somebody in town is still makin' money."

As they approached the town hall on foot, they heard the buzz of talk from inside, along with the sounds of musicians tuning their instruments.

"I hope Bob lets that boy Len sing again tonight," Pearlie said. "He's got a mighty fine voice."

"I just hope I don't step on Daisy's feet when the music gets fast," Cal said.

Pearlie asked, "Have you ever stepped on a gal's feet?"

"Well, no, not that I recall."

"Then quit worryin'. You'll do fine." Pearlie paused. "Save your worryin' for what comes later."

Cal nodded solemnly. He knew exactly what Pearlie meant.

They had talked about how to proceed tonight and were in agreement that they would just enjoy the dancing for a while, and then, if Violet and Daisy seemed in a receptive mood, they would suggest stepping out of the town hall to get a breath of the fresh evening air.

A large grove of trees stood behind the hall, and it was a favorite place where couples went to be alone. Of course, they weren't actually alone, because the shadows under the trees were quite popular, but everybody knew to keep to themselves and not bother anyone else. It was the closest thing to privacy anybody was likely to get on a night such as this.

Once they were shrouded in that comforting darkness, Pearlie and Cal could ask their fateful questions of Violet and Daisy. Based on conversations they'd had during those walks along the creek, both of them were confident the ladies would say yes . . . but a fellow could never be sure of such a thing until the time actually arrived.

Quite a few people were going into the hall. Pearlie and Cal had to wait their turn as the crowd bottlenecked at the entrance.

While they were doing that, someone bumped into Cal's shoulder. The unexpected impact made him stumble sideways against Pearlie. Both of them almost lost their balance and fell, but their natural athleticism allowed them to recover as they clutched at each other for support.

The man who had jostled Cal laughed.

"Save your dancin' until you get inside. Have you been into the spiked punch already, Woods?" he asked. "Or are you just fumble-footed?"

Cal looked over and saw Jasper Hendryx giving him an ugly grin. Hendryx nudged Chuck Dade with an elbow. Dade smirked, too, clearly amused by his friend's feeble witticism and the near mishap.

Pearlie glared at the men from the Three Sevens and said, "I didn't know there was a travelin' carnival in town."

"Carnival?" Dade repeated with a puzzled frown. "What are you talkin' about, Fontaine?"

"Why, I figured you two must've escaped from the freak show," Pearlie told him.

Dade and Hendryx lost their grins. They glared defiantly at Pearlie and Cal.

"If you're in such a big hurry to get inside that you have to run over people, don't let us stop you," Cal said. "Come on, Pearlie. Let's step aside so they can go first."

Pearlie squinted in disapproval of that idea.

"I ain't much of one for steppin' aside," he said. "Not for these varmints, or anybody else."

"It's not worth the trouble it would take to educate them in good manners. Besides, we have more important things to think about."

Grudgingly, Pearlie nodded and said, "Yeah, you're right about that." He moved aside, slightly, and jerked his head toward the door. "Go ahead," he told Dade and Hendryx.

Scowling, the other two punchers moved through the doorway. They looked back over their shoulders, not in triumph but seemingly suspicious that the Sugarloaf riders had gotten the better of them in some fashion, even if they couldn't figure out how.

Cal said, "I didn't figure it would be a good idea to get our clean clothes all dirty and messed up before we even set eyes on Vi and Daisy."

"Well, you're right about that, I reckon," Pearlie admitted, "even though I would've liked to give that pair o' coyotes their needin's."

Dade and Hendryx headed for the table where the punch bowl rested. A large group of single men had gathered already along that wall of the building.

Technically, Pearlie and Cal were still single men, too, but neither of them felt that way, anymore. In their minds, it was only a matter of time before their matrimonial status changed for the better.

They turned in the other direction, toward the side of the hall where the ladies were congregating.

Cal didn't spot Violet and Daisy right away, but their bright, fair hair was hard to miss for long. He picked them out of the crowd, tapped Pearlie on the arm, and pointed to the sisters.

They made their way across the room toward Violet and Daisy, weaving in and out of the constantly moving stream of cowboys, townspeople, cattlemen, bankers and shopkeepers with their wives in finery, ranch wives in patched but crisply clean dresses brought out of trunks and wardrobes for the occasion.

A portly hombre who punched cattle for a living and played music for fun called, "Comin' through, comin' through," as he toted a big bass fiddle toward the front of the room, followed by more men in brightly colored shirts and bandannas, each carrying a guitar.

Pearlie knew all the musicians and nodded to them as they went by, saying, "Howdy, Bob, howdy, Tim, howdy, Len, howdy, Karl, howdy, Lloyd, howdy, Hugh. You gonna sing tonight, Len?"

The curly-haired cowboy looked back over his shoulder and grinned. "I sure am. Might even do some yodelin'!"

After the musicians had gone by, Pearlie and Cal continued toward the Caldwell sisters. They were close enough for Pearlie to call, "Howdy, Vi!" when a hand gripped his shoulder from behind and stopped him short. Pearlie's head jerked around so he could glare at whoever had grabbed him.

"Step aside, Fontaine," Chuck Dade said. "Jasper and I got first call on the ladies tonight."

Hendryx's barrel-chested bulk loomed up behind Dade.

Pearlie wrenched his shoulder free of Dade's grip and turned to face him squarely.

"What the devil makes you think you got first call on anything?" Pearlie demanded.

"You and this wet-behind-the-ears kid have gotten your way too much around here," Dade said.

"Hey—" Cal began in protest to the way Dade characterized him, but Pearlie overrode his resentful words.

"This kid, as you call him, has already accomplished more in his life than some two-bit saddle tramp like you ever will." Pearlie threw the retort in Dade's face. "And he's a heap better to ride the river with than you ever will be, you redheaded, monkey-faced jackanapes!"

"Why, you—" Hendryx blurted out as he pushed past Dade, following the exclamation with a few choice, colorful obscenities that made several ladies within earshot gasp and turn pale. He leaned forward, put both hands against Pearlie's chest, and shoved hard.

Pearlie had just enough warning to try to set his feet, so he only staggered back a couple of steps rather than falling. Cal caught hold of his arm and steadied him even more.

"You all right?" Cal asked.

"Sure," Pearlie said.

"Good."

Cal's previous hesitation about fighting had vanished. He stepped forward and whipped a hard, straight right into the middle of Hendryx's face. Blood spurted from Hendryx's nose as his head rocked back.

"Hey!" Dade yelled. He threw a right cross that smashed into Cal's jaw and knocked him to one knee.

Pearlie tackled Dade. They would have fallen to the floor, except for the fact that too many people were pressed around them. The crowd was trying to thin out already as men struggled to get out of the way. One bespectacled townsman held up both hands and shouted, "No fighting! No fighting!"

The next second, Pearlie and Dade, whirling around as they grappled with each other, crashed into the would-be peacemaker and knocked him sprawling. He yelped as a few people stepped on him in the burgeoning stampede. His spectacles had flown off when he fell, and the lenses were quickly stomped to powder.

Women screamed and men bellowed curses. With that many people so close together, keeping the hostilities contained to only the four cowboys was impossible. Punches were thrown at the battlers from the Sugarloaf and the Three Sevens but found other, unintended targets. The men who wound up on the receiving end of those punches struck back. Seemingly within seconds, a seething, chaotic melee filled Big Rock's town hall.

The only saving grace was that the floor had been cleared for dancing, so there were no chairs for anybody to pick up and wallop somebody else with.

Up toward the front of the room, the men with guitars had retreated to the wall in an attempt to stay clear of the brawl. The fellow with the bass fiddle had gotten caught in the middle of tides of battle that surged back and forth around him. Hugging the big instrument to himself to protect it, he darted one way and then another and seemed to be on the verge of breaking free of the fracas when his feet got tangled up and he pitched forward, landing on the fiddle in a tremendous crash of splintering wood and twanging strings.

Pearlie and Cal were still locked in combat with Dade and Hendryx. All four of them had found solid footing and stood there, slugging away at one another. Their faces were already bruised and bloody, but they weren't ready to stop fighting.

Pearlie threw a punch at Dade's head that the smaller man was able to duck. Dade lowered his head even more and bored in, hooking half a dozen short, powerful punches into Pearlie's midsection. Pearlie doubled over and looked sick.

That put him in perfect position for the uppercut Dade brought from his ankles. Dade's fist caught Pearlie under the chin and lifted him up and back, completely off his feet. Pearlie came down on his back and slid across the polished floor.

Blinking dazedly, Pearlie looked up and saw a face hovering over him. It seemed familiar, but from Pearlie's perspective, the hombre was upside down. It took several seconds for his vision to clear enough to recognize the man gazing down at him in a mixture of surprise and anger.

"Howdy, Smoke," Pearlie said, his voice weak but loud enough to be heard over the tumult filling the hall.

Smoke reached down and grabbed the front of Pearlie's shirt, which was clean only a short time earlier but was now spattered with bloodstains. He hauled the Sugarloaf foreman to his feet with seemingly effortless ease.

"What in blazes are you doing?" Smoke demanded. "Did you and Cal start this free-for-all?"

"No, sir!" Pearlie managed to say, even though he was still a little sick from those punches to the belly. "It was them two sons o'—"

He had lifted a hand to try to point out Dade and Hendryx as he spoke, but before he could finish the accusation, the townie whose spectacles had gotten busted to smithereens charged out of the crowd, howling like a panther and throwing wild, looping punches at whatever dimly seen shape happened to be in front of him.

Smoke and Pearlie jumped out of the way of the attack, and

Smoke grabbed the man from behind, swinging him around and off his feet.

"Whoa! Whoa, there! Take it easy, mister!"

The crazed townie continued flailing and kicking and yelling incoherently.

With Smoke occupied for the moment, Pearlie turned to look for Cal. He spotted his best friend hammering short, swift blows to Hendryx's face, driving the bigger cowboy backward in jittery steps. Once Hendryx was sufficiently off balance, Cal wound up and hit him with a more powerful blow. Hendryx went down like a falling tree and didn't move from where he landed on his back.

That was the beginning of the end of this social-turned-madhouse. Monte Carson and a couple of his deputies waded into the fight, tearing men apart, shouting for order, threatening to lock up the whole lot of them.

Monte had to pause for a moment when he came upon the bass fiddle player, sitting in the wreckage of his instrument and sobbing miserably. Then the sheriff shook his head and resumed his efforts to break up the fight.

It took about ten minutes, but finally the fists stopped flying and a strained silence fell over the hall, broken by harsh breathing, a few whimpers, and the muttering of the loco little fellow Smoke still hung on to as he threatened to murder all and sundry.

Frustrated beyond control, Monte roared into the silence, "Have all you idiots lost your minds?"

Chuck Dade dared to speak up, pointing a shaking hand at Pearlie and Cal as he yapped, "It was their fault, Sheriff, all their fault—"

"Shut up! I have a pretty good idea how it started. You, you, you, and you!" Monte jabbed a finger at Pearlie, Cal, Dade, and Hendryx in turn. "You're all under arrest! And this time it's gonna be more than a little fine! You'd better get used to being behind bars!"

The man Smoke was holding was finally running out of steam. When Smoke let go of him, the man slumped to the floor, where he sat cross-legged and put his face in his hands as he moaned.

"Monte, maybe—" Smoke began.

Monte turned sharply toward him. "This is the second social in a row these four have ruined. They've got to learn their lesson, Smoke."

Smoke sighed and nodded. "I can't argue with that. But there'll have to be a hearing—"

"There will be. First thing Monday morning. They can cool their heels in my hoosegow until then!"

Pearlie and Cal turned pleading gazes on Smoke. He knew they were thinking about the potentially life-altering plans they had made for tonight.

"Smoke, we were gonna—" Pearlie began.

"I know you were, but I'm sorry. Monte has the right to arrest you."

Monte snorted. "Durned right I do. This is the most clear-cut case of disturbing the peace I've ever seen. Not to mention assault and mayhem and malicious destruction!" He leveled a pointing finger at the door and ordered his deputies, "Take those four to jail and lock them up!"

Pearlie and Cal looked at Smoke again. He nodded and told them, "Go on with the deputies. Don't make things any worse than they already are."

With stricken expressions on their faces, Pearlie and Cal allowed themselves to be marched out of the town hall. Dade and Hendryx trudged along sullenly behind them. Hendryx was shaking his head a little, as if it were still ringing from the punch Cal had landed on it.

Smoke glanced over to where the women were huddled against the wall. Sally was there, talking to Violet and Daisy Caldwell and obviously trying to comfort and console them.

Violet and Daisy might not know for certain what they had missed out on tonight, but they probably had a pretty good idea. They looked disappointed, no doubt about that, but Smoke saw something else on Violet's face.

She was angry, too, and he wasn't sure what had brought on that reaction. Maybe just irritation at how foolish and bullheaded men could be, he thought.

There would be another time, but for right now, and for who knew how long in the future, all the big plans Pearlie and Cal had made would just have to wait.

Chapter 24

Somehow, the fight hadn't overturned the table on which the punch bowl sat. The bass fiddle was busted to pieces, but the guitars were all safe. After a while, things in the town hall settled down enough that the social was able to get started, although many of the men who had tangled earlier still cast hostile glances toward the ones with whom they had been fighting.

Gradually, between the music and the dancing, things got back to normal.

As Smoke swirled Sally around the floor, she said, "Poor Pearlie and Cal! They had such high hopes for tonight."

"Well, then, they shouldn't have let Dade and Hendryx prod them into a fight," Smoke said.

"I don't know exactly what caused the fight, but I really don't think they would have abandoned their plans unless they were forced to."

Smoke nodded and said, "Sometimes a fella gets backed into a corner and can't do anything except start swinging. That's true enough. I'm sure they tried to keep things from getting out of hand. It's just too bad they weren't able to do it."

Smoke caught a glimpse of Violet Caldwell as she went past in the arms of one of the local merchants. Violet had a smile on her face, but even in that brief moment, Smoke could tell the expression wasn't genuine. Violet was being polite to her partner, that's all.

She was probably upset about the disruption to the evening, too.

"You talked to the Caldwell sisters after that ruckus," he said to Sally. "Did they have any idea what Pearlie and Cal were going to do tonight?"

"The proposals, you mean?" Sally shook her head. "They didn't come right out and say that they knew the boys were going to ask them to get married, but I got the feeling they were expecting it. I could tell Violet wasn't happy things had gotten messed up."

"Yeah, I got that same feeling a minute ago when I saw her dancing with Tim Murchison."

"It's funny, though," Sally mused. "I could be wrong, of course, but it seemed to me like Daisy was almost relieved that something happened."

"That is a mite odd," Smoke agreed. "She and Cal seem to be a pretty good couple."

Before they could add any more to the discussion, the song came to an end. All the dancers stopped and clapped politely. The leader of the musicians stepped forward and announced that young Len was going to sing a few songs, adding that folks should feel free to continue dancing while he sang.

It turned out to be a pleasant evening, which wouldn't have seemed possible a couple of hours earlier during the big brawl. After the musicians had played "Goodnight, Ladies," the crowd began to drift out of the town hall, with a lot of laughter and talk still going on among them.

As Smoke and Sally left the hall, arm in arm again, Smoke

noticed that Violet and Daisy Caldwell were walking right in front of them. Sally called to the sisters, and they stopped to let Smoke and Sally join them.

"I'm sure sorry about the way things worked out this evening, ladies," Smoke said. "I hope you won't be too upset with Pearlie and Cal about what happened."

"I'm sure it wasn't their fault," Daisy said. "Those other two cowboys can be so obnoxious."

"Although it wouldn't hurt Pearlie and Cal to try to keep their tempers under control," Violet added, and Smoke could tell from the crisp, cool tone of her voice that she was upset. But she shrugged and went on, "It probably won't be too bad for them, though. I know the sheriff intends to keep them locked up until Monday morning, but I'm sure the judge will just fine them and let them go."

"More than likely," Smoke agreed. "Monte talked about keeping them in jail for a while, but I'm sure he'll change his mind about that once he cools off."

"Since tomorrow is Sunday," Sally said to Violet and Daisy, "why don't the two of you come out to the Sugarloaf and have dinner with us? We could all ride out there together in our buggy after church, and then Smoke could bring you back to town later in the afternoon."

"That's very sweet of you—" Violet began.

"We'd love to," Daisy broke in. "Thank you so much."

From the look that Violet gave her sister, Smoke had a feeling that she had been on the verge of graciously declining the invitation.

But now that Daisy had accepted, Violet smiled and said, "Yes, thank you. That sounds lovely."

Sally put out a gloved hand and squeezed Violet's arm for a second.

"I'm looking forward to it. We don't have company on the ranch nearly often enough."

The Caldwell sisters said their goodbyes and went on their way. Smoke said, "See you at church in the morning," and tipped his hat to them as they left. Then he and Sally headed for the buckboard they had left down the street.

"That was nice of you, inviting them for dinner like that," Smoke commented.

"I'd like for them to feel at home out here. And if they wind up marrying Pearlie and Cal, I'm sure we'll see a lot of them in the future. I hope we can all stay friends."

"I don't see why not. Whether those boys are working for me or not, they'll always be part of the Sugarloaf. The place wouldn't be what it is today without everything they've done to help us."

Sally nodded. "That's very true. They really are like family, aren't they?"

Smoke put his arm around her shoulders.

"They sure are," he said. "And they always will be."

"That was a very foolish thing to do," Violet said quietly as she and Daisy approached the cottage behind the dress shop. She could no longer hold in the feelings that seethed inside her.

"You mean it was foolish for Pearlie and Cal to get mixed up in a fight?" Daisy asked. "If that's it, I agree with you. They should have kept a tighter rein on their tempers." She shrugged. "But I don't see that it really changes anything."

"Maybe, maybe not," Violet said. "You know good and well they were going to propose tonight. Now they have time to sit in a jail cell and think about it! They might change their minds. We can't know what will happen." She shook her head. "But that's not what I was talking about. I meant accepting that invitation to have dinner with the Jensens was foolish."

Daisy frowned in puzzlement and said, "I don't understand. What's wrong with going out there to eat dinner with them?"

"I don't like the way Smoke looks at us," Violet snapped. "I've felt from the first time we met him that he's just too suspicious. Too smart. You know how he feels about Pearlie and Cal. He'll go to any length to protect them."

"He has no reason to be suspicious of us," Daisy said with a shake of her head. "But maybe he should be."

"Don't start that again."

"I just don't feel right about—"

Violet stopped and took hold of her sister's arm, pulling Daisy to a halt as well.

"When have I ever done anything other than try to take care of you to the best of my ability?" she demanded as she leaned closer. "Even before Mother died, who actually made sure that we always had a roof over our heads and food to eat?"

"You did, Vi. I won't argue with that—"

"And since she died, have I ever steered us wrong or let you down?" Violet went on. "I had to make moves to take care of us, Daisy, and they had to be bold moves. We're just two young women, alone against the world. Nobody's going to give us anything without demanding something in return, and you know it. We have to take what we need! If we want a place in the world for ourselves, we have to carve it out!"

"But maybe it doesn't have to be like that. Sally Jensen has been nothing but friendly to us and welcome us. The other ladies who've come to the shop have been nice, too." Daisy gestured across the little alley toward the building that held their dress shop. "We're doing good business, Violet, and people are treating us well. If we steal that money from Pearlie and Cal and just disappear, we'll have to throw away everything we've done here!"

Violet stared at her sister. Even in the dim light, she looked as if she couldn't believe what she was hearing.

"You want to stay here and eke out a pitiful living sewing dresses for women who think they're so much better than us?" Violet demanded after a moment, when she found her voice again. "That's truly what you want, Daisy? Scrimping and saving and scratching out an existence that depends on the generosity of other people? Or would you rather have enough money to live where we want, however we want, to never be worried about the future again?"

"You think we can get that by taking their life savings away from those boys?"

"They're not boys," Violet said, her lip curling into a sneer. "They're grown men, and I refuse to feel sorry for them. They went into this with their eyes wide open." With an effort, she moderated her tone a bit as she went on. "And they'll be fine, you know that. They'll be mad for a while, but they'll get over it."

"Their hearts will be broken."

Violet shrugged. "Nobody ever died of a broken heart. And even though we won't be here to see it, I promise you they'll recover quickly. As soon as the next pair of pretty girls comes along and smiles at them, they'll start chasing them and forget all about us."

"Maybe," Daisy said, although she didn't sound as if she were fully convinced.

"I'm absolutely certain that's the way it'll be. You know how easily distracted men are!"

Daisy didn't raise any more objections. She and Violet stepped up onto the small porch on the front of the cottage, ready to go inside and get ready for bed.

Violet stopped short. Some instinct jerked her head to the right. She peered along the alley behind the buildings in that direction, certain that she had heard something, or someone, moving around there.

Her hand dipped into the bag she carried. She closed her fingers around the butt of the little Smith & Wesson revolver she carried in it. She hadn't expected to need a gun at the town social, but it never hurt to be prepared for trouble.

Pearlie would be amazed if he knew how far she was willing to go if she ever found herself backed into a corner.

She stiffened even more as she caught a glimpse of movement against the faint glow that filtered back here from lights along the main street.

"What is it?" Daisy asked, sudden concern in her voice as she realized how tensely her sister was standing there gazing into the shadows.

"I thought I heard something," Violet said.

"It was probably just a cat," Daisy said. "They roam around back here all the time, looking for scraps of food."

"This was no cat. It was bigger than that."

Daisy laughed. "Some of them can make quite a racket, you know. Anyway, I didn't hear anything."

Violet didn't respond. She didn't explain she was basing her assessment that the lurker was larger than a cat not on the faint sound she had heard but rather on the fleeting glimpse she had gotten.

What she had seen had been as big as a man, and it had moved like a man trying to be stealthy, too.

"Well, is there anything?" Daisy asked after a moment.

Violet relaxed and let go of the gun. She took her hand out of the bag. Whoever it was, they were gone now.

"No, I must have been imagining things," she said. "There's nothing there."

But something had been, she knew, even though she didn't say so to Daisy. There was no point in worrying her sister now. The lurking figure had vanished and the night was quiet again, so quiet that Violet heard the stamping of a horse's hoof from one of the hitch racks on the street.

The glimpse of the lurker she had gotten was imprinted vividly on Violet's mind, though. She was convinced that for that split second, she had seen a man slipping from the alley into one of the passages alongside a building leading back to the street. He was broad-shouldered and wore a hat.

And underneath that hat, sticking straight out from the man's head, were large ears, each shaped remarkably like the handle of a jug . . .

But no, Violet told herself as she went into the cottage after Daisy and closed the door firmly behind her. That was *impossible.*

She kept telling herself that, hoping it would make the cold feeling in the pit of her stomach go away.

Linc Pollard jumped a little as two figures suddenly appeared beside him as if they had formed out of thin air.

"Dang it, Whisper, don't sneak up on a fella like that," Pollard said, a little embarrassed by his spooked reaction.

"Pay more attention so nobody can sneak up on you," Whisper McReady rasped.

The boss outlaw, accompanied by the dimwitted but canny and vicious young man called Banjo, had been gone for an hour, leaving Pollard and the other three members of the gang who had come with them tonight hidden here in this grove of trees about a mile outside Big Rock. This was a scouting expedition. McReady had wanted to get a good look at the town, or so he claimed.

Pollard had a hunch that McReady wanted to check on his stepdaughters, too. He said, "Did you see Vi and Daisy?"

"I saw them," McReady said heavily. "I watched them leave that dance and go back to the place they're renting, the one you told me about, Linc."

"Behind their dress shop?"

"Yeah." McReady scratched his jaw and frowned in thought. "Before that, when they were leaving the town hall, they had a pretty earnest conversation with a man and a woman." McReady described them. "Sound like anybody you know?"

"That could be Smoke Jensen, from what I've heard about him," Pollard said. "He's married to a mighty good-looking woman with dark hair, too."

"This lady fit that description," McReady agreed. "I wonder what they were talking about."

"There's no tellin'. Those cowboys the girls have been playin' up to ride for Jensen. I know Vi was a little worried about him. He's a big man in this valley, and whenever there's trouble, Jensen's usually around to put a stop to it. If Vi's acting friendly with him and his wife, it's because she wants to keep tabs on Jensen."

McReady nodded slowly and said, "She's pretty smart that way." He grunted contemptuously. "Too smart for her own good, obviously, if she thought she could just waltz in and take over what I spent so much time building up."

"I know you're mad, Whisper," Pollard said, "but you can't take it out on the gals. They're your kinfolks."

"Not by blood," McReady snapped. He waved a hand. "But getting mad is just a waste of time. I have my eye on something else, something that'll give us a mighty big payoff. That's really why I wanted to have a look around the town tonight."

That caught Pollard's interest. If McReady was concentrating on something else, he wouldn't be as likely to do anything to hurt Violet and Daisy. Even though he was a little angry with them himself because of the way they had lied to him, Pollard didn't want to see any harm come to them.

"What did you have in mind, Whisper?" he asked.

"That town has a bank and a lot of prosperous-looking businesses," McReady said. "There's a lot of money just sitting there, ripe for the taking."

"You mean—"

"I mean that tomorrow morning, while everybody's either sleeping late or singing hymns in church, we're going to hit Big Rock with the whole gang. That town's going to be ours, and we're going to clean every blasted cent out of it . . . and kill anybody who gets in our way."

Chapter 25

Smoke and Sally had dressed nicely for the town social the night before, but the next morning they donned their Sunday-go-to-meetin' finest to attend services at the Ranney Street Baptist Church in Big Rock.

Smoke had never been deeply involved with organized religion. A gunfighter he had met briefly during his early days on the lonely trails had mentioned feeling closer to the Creator whenever he was out far from civilization in the beautiful mountains and forests of the high country. That was where he did his best worshipping, the hombre had told Smoke as they ate supper together next to a campfire.

That message resonated immediately with Smoke, and he had never forgotten it. To feel truly close to the Creator, some fellows needed to be out in creation.

But that didn't mean he disliked going to church. He was friendly with a lot of the folks who attended, and E. D. Owen, the pastor, was a good man. Sally had numerous friends among the ladies and always enjoyed visiting with them after the services. The church did good work, too, caring for the less fortunate.

So, Smoke never complained about attending. He was ready to go this morning, wearing a brown tweed suit, a snowy white shirt with a gray silk string bow tie, and a tan Stetson Columbia hat. He went into the ranch house's foyer and took down the gun belt and holster that hung from a hook on the wall there. His familiar walnut-butted Colt Peacemaker rested easily in the holster.

He was buckling on the gun rig when Sally said from behind him, "You don't honestly believe there's going to be a shoot-out at church this morning, do you, Smoke?"

He smiled as he turned to face her and finished buckling the gun belt around his hips.

"More than likely not," he said, "but you can never be sure about such things. I know the day's coming when folks won't have to bring their guns to church, but I'm not sure it's here quite yet."

"You're probably right about that," she admitted. She returned his smile and went on, "Anyway, I know how uncomfortable you feel when you're not wearing a gun. What was it Preacher once said about you?" Sally lowered her voice in a gruff imitation of the old mountain man's tone. *"Smoke's been packin' iron for so long, he walks slanchwise when he ain't carryin' a gun."*

Smoke laughed. "I don't remember that, but it does sound like something Preacher would say." He let out a low whistle of admiration as his gaze took her in from head to toe. "Anyway, we shouldn't be talking about guns when you're standing there looking so lovely. That ought to be the only subject of discussion."

Sally laughed, too, and said, "My, aren't you the gallant one this morning."

"Just stating the facts, ma'am," Smoke assured her.

She did look lovely, in a conservative but elegant blue gown with a stylish hat of the same shade on her piled-up dark hair. She linked arms with Smoke and walked out of the house with him.

Earlier, one of the ranch hands had hitched a two-horse team up to the buggy and brought it from the barn to leave it in front of the ranch house. Smoke and Sally usually used the buckboard when they went to Big Rock, but the buggy was nicer, and since they were going to be having company today, it was the better choice. The Caldwell sisters could ride in the back seat when they came out here after church.

Smoke helped Sally into the vehicle, climbed up beside her, and took hold of the reins. He flapped them and called to the team, and they rolled away from the Sugarloaf toward town.

"How do you think Pearlie and Cal are doing this morning?" Sally asked.

"I'm sure by now they're wishing they had figured out a way to avoid getting in that ruckus," Smoke said with a chuckle. "But they're all right. Monte's jail isn't fancy, but it's clean and comfortable enough for what it is. And Lambert's provides the meals, so they'll be getting a good breakfast."

"I suppose that's one way of looking at it," Sally said.

None of the businesses in Big Rock were open on Sunday morning, although the restaurants and saloons would be operating later in the day. So, the streets weren't as busy as usual, though even so, quite a few pedestrians were on the boardwalks, and riders and wagons moved along at a brisk pace as folks headed for the several churches in the community.

"There are Violet and Daisy," Sally said as Smoke guided the buggy down the street. "Let's stop here and walk with them."

"That's fine with me," Smoke said as he drove on past the Caldwell sisters and then angled the buggy toward one of the hitch rails along the street. By the time he tied up the team and helped Sally down from the vehicle, Violet and Daisy had caught up to them.

"Good morning," Sally greeted them. "Smoke and I thought we'd walk on to church with you. Isn't it a lovely morning?"

"It is," Violet agreed. "It's so peaceful, you wouldn't think anything bad could ever happen."

"Well, I'm not expecting it to," Smoke said. "The pastor might get a little carried away dishing out the fire and brimstone, but that's about the worst that's likely to happen."

The three ladies all laughed at that.

Monte Carson was ahead of them on the boardwalk. He must have heard them talking, because he stopped and waited for them. Tipping his hat, he said, "Good morning, ladies. Smoke, you've got what they call an embarrassment of riches there, walking along with three such beautiful women."

Smiling, Sally said, "I'm used to flattery like that from Louis Longmont, but you're not usually so quick with a compliment, Monte."

"I reckon I'm just feeling chivalrous this morning," Monte said as he settled his hat back on his head and joined the group. When they reached the next corner, they turned left into Ranney Street and headed for the church, which stood at the edge of town with its whitewashed walls gleaming in the morning sun and dulcet tones pealing out from the bell in its steeple.

The front doors were open to welcome the members of the congregation, who were entering steadily. Pastor E. D. Owens stood to one side, smiling, shaking hands, and greeting the parishioners as they went in.

As Violet had commented, it was such a tranquil scene that it was almost impossible to believe anything bad might be about to happen.

Fifty riders waited a mile outside Big Rock. During the past several days, McReady had sent riders out in different directions to visit Cottonwood and other outlaw havens in the region and recruit new members for the gang. Until the previous night, Pollard hadn't had any idea what was going on or why McReady wanted to increase their numbers. Once McReady announced his plan to raid Big Rock, though, the effort made sense.

If you were going to loot an entire town, the more guns you had, the better.

Now they were waiting for the final report from Banjo, who had slipped into Big Rock to get the lay of the land. As they sat on their horses next to each other, Pollard asked McReady, "Are you sure you can trust that half-wit kid?"

"I'd trust that half-wit kid, as you call him, with my life," McReady snapped. "In fact, he saved my life when we were in prison. We were out in the yard one day when another convict with a grudge against me tried to stick a knife in my ribs. Banjo got in his way and stopped him. Got cut up pretty bad for his trouble, too. A while after that, some of the other men went after him, and I helped him fight his way out of that. He's been as devoted to me as a dog ever since then."

"I don't mean any offense, Whisper, but he's sort of an odd duck. What'd he do to get locked up?"

"He set fire to the orphanage where he grew up. His folks didn't want him, and the people at the orphanage didn't, either, but they didn't have any choice but to keep him. Plenty of terrible things happened to him there." McReady shook his head. "Stupid fools thought he was too dumb to ever try to even the score. They found out differently when they were surrounded by flames."

A shudder went through Pollard. He didn't say anything else. He reaffirmed a decision he'd already made, though: to never let Banjo come up behind him.

McReady leaned forward in the saddle and said, "That's him coming, now."

Pollard spotted the approaching rider. Banjo was easy to recognize. He wore a fringed buckskin jacket, and the brim of his battered old hat was pinned up in front. Long, greasy curls spilled out from under the hat. He grinned as he reined up in front of Pollard and McReady.

"Pert' near ever'body's gone to church, just like you said they would, Whisper," Banjo reported. "The doors are closed, and they're all inside singin' hymns."

"Not everybody in town, though," Pollard said.

McReady shook his head. "No, some of them will be sleeping off Saturday night's drunken spree. The soiled doves will be resting up for their evening's work. Some folks who aren't religious might be having a late breakfast. Probably the only ones in town actually accomplishing anything are the saloon swampers, who are cleaning up and getting ready to open later. Nobody's expecting *us*, that's for sure."

The previous night, around the big fire at the hideout, McReady had gathered the whole gang and gone over the plan for today's raid, handing out assignments as he did so.

There were five churches in Big Rock. Four men would station themselves outside each one and be ready to open fire and keep the congregations pinned down if they tried to get out.

Several two-man teams would go to each business, break in, and search for any cash or other valuables on hand. Groups of three men would take the saloons and loot them. Pollard was in charge of those efforts and would roam through the town, making sure everything went smoothly.

McReady and four other men would concentrate on the bank. One of the convicts who had broken out of prison with him, Mitch Steadman, was an experienced safecracker. If he wasn't able to open the bank's safe by listening to the tumblers as he turned the lock on the door, he would blow it open with a stick of the dynamite he carried.

"There's bound to be some shooting," McReady had said.

"Probably a lot of it. But let's keep things as quiet as we can for as long as we can. I'd like to get as much loot as possible in our hands before somebody starts the ball. But if you have to shoot, go ahead and shoot to kill. Those miserable townies don't deserve any mercy from us."

Grim nods had come from quite a few of the assembled outlaws.

"What about the dress shop?" Pollard had asked. "We're gonna leave it alone, aren't we?"

McReady had considered and then said, "Kick the door open, but don't bother going inside. It'll look like you did, and nobody's likely to know the difference. That way, if the girls want to stay in Big Rock without any suspicion falling on them, they can." He went on, "I don't owe them anything, either, not after the way they double-crossed me and tried to take over, but I don't suppose it'll hurt anything to take it easy on them. There won't be any money to amount to anything in that shop, anyway."

It seemed like a solid plan to Pollard. As McReady said, there was bound to be some shooting. They would never be able to get in and out of town without people knowing that Big Rock was being raided, and if there was one thing you could count on from frontier citizens, it was that most of them would fight back when threatened.

But the folks in Big Rock wouldn't be prepared to take on such a large, well-armed group of hardened gun-wolves and owlhoots. Some of the gang probably wouldn't make it . . . but the ones who did would get a big payoff from this job.

Now, with Banjo having brought confirmation that everything in the settlement was just as they expected it to be, there was no longer any reason to wait. McReady turned his horse, looked at the men gathered there, and asked in a loud voice, "Everybody know what he's supposed to do? You all know what your job is?"

Some of the outlaws nodded, others called out that they were ready to go. McReady gave them a curt nod in return and wheeled his horse back toward Big Rock. He raised his right arm and swept it forward like a cavalry officer calling for a charge as he jabbed his boot heels into his horse's flanks and sent the animal leaping ahead into a gallop.

The attack had begun.

Chapter 26

"They're still over there glarin' at us, ain't they?" Pearlie asked as he and Cal sat on their bunks in the jail cells. A wall of iron bars separated them, but they were close enough to talk quietly with each other.

"Yep," Cal replied. "You know the old saying about how if looks could kill, we'd be dead? That's sure true this morning."

"Well, they're the ones who started it. They ain't got no cause to be blamin' us."

The cellblock in the Big Rock jail had eight cells in it, four on each side of a center aisle. On one side, Pearlie and Cal were in the two cells closest to the door leading into Monte Carson's office. On the other side, Chuck Dade and Jasper Hendryx were in the two cells farthest from the door. The arrangement kept the prisoners from being directly across the aisle from each other, but of course, they were all in plain sight.

Dade and Hendryx stood at the doors of their cells, their hands wrapped tightly around the bars. They stared at Pearlie and Cal with pure hatred in their eyes. They had been doing that ever since they'd woken up this morning. The two Sugarloaf hands tried to ignore them, but it wasn't easy.

The faces of all four men displayed bruises and scrapes from the battle at the town hall the night before. Cal was sore, and he knew Pearlie must be, too. He didn't care about any aches and pains the Three Sevens men might have. However much they hurt, they had it coming.

"Nobody's gettin' in any hurry to bring us breakfast, are they?" Pearlie went on. "I don't know about you, but my belly's startin' to wonder if my throat's been cut."

"It's Sunday morning," Cal said. "Nobody's getting in any hurry to do anything. But I'm sure the grub will be along soon. Monte wouldn't let prisoners go hungry for too long."

"No, I don't reckon he would. Can't be soon enough to suit me, though."

A couple of minutes went by, and then Chuck Dade called, "Hey, Fontaine?"

Pearlie looked at him and asked, "What do you want?"

"You got the makin's?"

"What happened to yours?"

"I reckon my papers must've fallen out of my pocket durin' that tussle. I got tobacco, but nothin' to roll it in."

"What about your pard there?" Pearlie wanted to know. "Borrow some from him."

Hendryx said, "I don't use the stuff. I chew instead o' smokin'."

As if to demonstrate that, he leaned forward and propelled a gob of chewing tobacco through the bars and into a spittoon at the end of the aisle between the cells.

Then he grinned at them, exposing his stained teeth, and said, "Nice shot, weren't it?"

Pearlie rolled his eyes, shook his head, and took a small cloth pouch of Bull Durham from his shirt pocket. He opened the pouch and extracted the packet of rolling papers that nestled inside along with the tobacco. Cal was in the cell closest to the other prisoners, so Pearlie passed the papers through the bars to the younger cowboy.

"Toss them prayer books to that varmint so he'll quit botherin' us," Pearlie requested.

Cal stood up and went to the cell door. Diagonally across the aisle, Dade extended his arm through the bars as far as it would go. Cal reached through the bars in his cell and said, "All right, Chuck, here you go. Ready?"

"I'm ready. Toss it here, Woods. I'm about dyin' for a brain tablet."

As carefully and accurately as possible, Cal tossed the little packet, which had the same picture of a bull printed on it as the tobacco pouch. It was a good throw, but when Dade reached to catch the papers, he fumbled the packet, and it fell to the floor in front of his cell.

Dade let out a dismayed groan. "I told you to throw 'em good, blast it."

"You touched 'em," Pearlie said. "You flat-out dropped 'em. It ain't Cal's fault."

"And if you take off your belt and get down on your knees," Cal said, "you might be able to throw the buckle out there and drag the packet close enough to reach."

"I reckon I can give it a try," Dade said with a frustrated sigh. He started to unbuckle the belt around his waist.

Before he could do so, they all heard the front door of the sheriff's office open.

"Maybe that's our breakfast," Hendryx said excitedly. "It's durned well about time!"

The cellblock door was closed, but they could hear voices coming through it, including the one belonging to Ollie Nash, the deputy who was on duty this morning.

"When Ollie brings in our breakfast trays, he can pick up those cigarette papers for me," Dade said.

A minute later, the office door opened and closed again, and then the cellblock door opened. Deputy Nash, a lean, dark-haired man with an easy grin, came in carrying a tray.

"Here you go, Pearlie," he said. He passed the tray through the opening in the cell door designed for that.

"I'd complain about breakfast bein' so late, but I'm too weak from hunger," Pearlie gibed as he took the tray, which contained a plate with half a dozen thick strips of bacon, two large, flaky biscuits, a mug of coffee, and an apple.

"I'll be right back with yours, Cal," Nash said, turning back toward the door.

"That ain't fair," Dade complained. "You're givin' them their breakfast first because Smoke Jensen's friends with the sheriff."

"They're gettin' theirs first because they're closest to the door," Nash said over his shoulder.

"Well, that ain't fair, neither!"

Nash returned with a tray containing a meal identical to Pearlie's and passed it in to Cal. He was on his way back out of the cellblock again when all five men heard gunshots crashing somewhere outside. Nash stiffened in surprise at the sound, and then his hand moved toward the butt of the revolver holstered on his hip.

"What in blue blazes?" he muttered. After that brief moment of shock, he rushed out of the cellblock, pounded across the office, and threw the front door open.

"Hey!" Dade called after him as Nash ran out of sight. "What about our food?"

The shooting continued outside, with the reports slamming through the Sunday morning air.

"Whatever's goin' on out there, it's more important than your breakfast," Pearlie said. He set his tray on the bunk and stood at the cell door, trying to see through the cellblock door into the office and out the front door, which Ollie Nash had left open when he ran out. Cal did likewise.

"I don't like the sound of all that shooting," the young cowboy said.

"Nope, I don't, either," Pearlie agreed. "Sounds like a little war. I wonder if Smoke and Miss Sally came into town for church this mornin'. If they did, Smoke's likely to be right in the big middle o' whatever that ruckus is."

In addition to the guns going off, the jarring rataplan of rapid hoofbeats drifted into the jail. A lot of horses seemed to be charging down Big Rock's main street.

"It must be an Indian attack!" Hendryx cried.

"Don't be loco," Dade told him. "The Indians around here ain't hostile no more."

"It ain't been all that long since they were," Hendryx argued. "What else could it be?"

Before any of the prisoners could speculate on that, Ollie Nash reappeared. The deputy reeled through the doorway into the office. He still gripped his gun in his right hand, but his left arm was pressed across his belly. As Nash staggered across the room toward the cellblock, Pearlie and Cal saw the large, spreading bloodstain on his shirt.

"Ollie!" Pearlie yelled.

Gritting his teeth against the pain of the wounds where bullets had ripped through him, Nash stumbled through the door into the cellblock. He lurched against the bars of the cell closest to him, which was the one where Pearlie was locked up.

"Get . . . the . . . keys!" Nash rasped. "All you boys . . . gotta get out of here!"

Pearlie saw the ring of keys hanging from Nash's belt. He reached through the bars, got hold of the iron ring, and worked it free as the wounded deputy leaned on the cell door.

"What's goin' on out there, Ollie?" he asked as he reached

around and tried to fit the right key into the door lock. It was obvious that Nash was badly wounded, and even if the deputy didn't die, he was bound to pass out soon. The prisoners needed to know as much as they could about what was happening.

"Looks like outlaws . . . raidin' the town . . . lots of outlaws," Nash managed to say.

"See, I told you it wasn't Indians," Dade said to Hendryx, which seemed to Pearlie like an incredibly stupid and pointless thing to say under the circumstances.

He twisted the key, and the lock clicked open.

As it did, Nash slid down the bars to the floor and rolled onto his back. Pearlie jerked open the door and leaped out into the aisle. He dropped to one knee beside the deputy and said, "Ollie? Ollie!"

Nash's eyes were wide open but staring sightlessly at the ceiling. His gun had slipped from nerveless fingers and lay beside him. His other arm had dropped away from his body, revealing that he had been shot at least three times in the midsection. It was a wonder he had lived long enough to get back inside the jail.

A sudden sound from the open front door of the sheriff's office made Pearlie's head jerk up. He saw a roughly dressed, bearded man standing there holding a Colt. The gun began swinging up toward Pearlie.

Instinct made Pearlie's hand shoot out and scoop up the revolver Nash had dropped. Long years of surviving as a hired gun allowed Pearlie's muscles and nerves to work with blinding speed without him having to think about what he was doing. His thumb eared back the hammer and his finger squeezed the trigger, and the gun in his hand roared and bucked a split second before the intruder's.

The slug slammed into the stranger's chest and drove him backward. His arm had already started to rise as he toppled over, so his shot went harmlessly into the ceiling. He fell through the door and landed on the boardwalk outside.

Pearlie surged to his feet and dashed through the office. He slammed the door closed. He had left the key to the cell door in the lock, along with the others on the ring, so he couldn't lock the office door, but it had brackets on both sides, and a bar to keep it from opening. More than once, Monte had been forced to defend the place against outlaws and lynch mobs. Pearlie grabbed the bar from where it leaned against the wall and dropped it in the brackets.

Cal, Dade, and Hendryx were all yelling at him. He ran back into the cellblock, snatched the key from the first door, and began unlocking the others.

"Rifles and shotguns in the rack in the office," he barked. "Grab some of 'em. Monte keeps boxes of shells in the desk. I ain't sure exactly what's goin' on, but we'd better be armed."

Dade grabbed his arm and said, "I don't know what's goin' on, either, Fontaine, but for now, no hard feelin's amongst us, right?"

A grim smile tugged at Pearlie's mouth.

"No hard feelin's, Chuck," he said. "Normally, I don't mind whalin' the tar outta you two pelicans, but trouble's come to Big Rock, and for now we're all on the same side!"

Chapter 27

Smoke, Sally, and Monte sat in the same pew as Violet and Daisy. The church was mostly full, with only a few empty spaces here and there on the benches.

Many of the men were unarmed, but Smoke and Monte were hardly the only ones packing iron this morning. Only a few years earlier, most of the men who came to church brought rifles or shotguns with them, and when Pastor Owen had stepped up to the pulpit to preach his sermons, he had placed a loaded six-gun on each side of his opened Bible, just so they would be handy in case of trouble. Between the hostile Indians and the outlaw gangs that had roamed the region in those days, an attack of some kind was always possible.

Thankfully, those dangers had eased in recent years, and some members of the congregation no longer felt it was necessary to bring their guns along. But Smoke wasn't comfortable with that, and as a lawman, Monte was always armed when he was out in public, too.

The servicc opened with a prayer and a hymn, and then Owen

made several announcements about upcoming church activities. Then the piano player launched into another hymn, and everyone stood up to sing.

Smoke wasn't sure how good his voice was, but he enjoyed the hymns and participated enthusiastically. Having Sally, who was an excellent singer, right beside him made it even better.

After several more hymns, Pastor Owen moved behind the pulpit again and opened the thick, leather-bound Bible that sat upon it. He smiled at the congregation and raised his voice to say, "I never get tired of looking out from this pulpit on Sunday morning and seeing all of you here, my friends, for as the Lord said in the Book of Matthew, 'For where two or three are gathered together in my name, there am I in the midst of them.' And as the scriptures tell us in Ecclesiastes, 'Two are better than one; because they have a good reward for their labor. For if they fall, the one will lift up his fellow: but woe to him that is alone when he falleth; for he hath not another to help him up.' We are many more than two or three, and that gives us the strength—"

The church's doors were closed, but some of the windows were cracked open to let in fresh air, and just as the pastor was getting wound up to fully launch into his sermon for that morning, more than gentle breezes entered the sanctuary.

The roaring blasts of guns going off hammered the peaceful morning, shattering it.

Smoke was on his feet instantly, as was Monte. Their guns had appeared in their hands as if by magic.

"Stay here, ladies," Smoke told Sally and the Caldwell sisters. He and Monte dashed toward the rear of the sanctuary where the double doors were. Several of the other armed men were headed in the same direction. Others stood up, drew their guns, and protectively watched over the rest of the congregation.

"Everyone, stay calm," Pastor Owen said from the pulpit in his preaching voice, which carried to every corner of the building.

One of the men who had been closer to the doors reached it first and flung one of them open before Smoke and Monte could get there. The sheriff called, "Be careful!" but it was too late. A shot roared outside, and the man who had leaped into the doorway was thrown backward as a bullet struck his shoulder.

"Jonas!" a woman screamed as the wounded man spun around and collapsed.

"Everybody, down!" Smoke shouted. More shots rang out. Slugs whipped through the open door, and stained glass shattered as some of the gunfire found the windows.

Men, women, and children all dived for the floor. The solidly built pews offered quite a bit of protection, but it was still very dangerous in the church with so much lead flying around the room.

Smoke left the other door closed and pressed himself against it as he risked a look past its edge. He spotted spurts of powdersmoke and flashes of muzzle flame from an alcove at the end of the boardwalk on Ranney Street. He thrust his Colt's barrel around the door and triggered a couple of swift shots, not figuring he would hit anything but in the hope that he could distract the attackers for a moment.

As Smoke opened fire, Monte reached down, grabbed the wounded man's collar, and dragged him to relative safety between two pews.

"Got him, Smoke!" he called.

"Jimmy, kick that door closed!" Smoke said to a man on the other side of the open door.

Jimmy did as Smoke told him without exposing himself to the gunfire still lashing at the church. Smoke heard bullets thudding into the doors, but they didn't penetrate.

Those shot-out windows were still more than enough of a threat, though. The shooting had tapered off since the initial assault, but enough slugs still sizzled through the air to make everyone keep their heads down.

Monte scrambled over to one of the windows to risk a look out. He said to Smoke, "I think we've got a rifleman on three sides of the church, at least, maybe all four. My hunch is they're trying to keep us pinned down in here."

"Did you get a look at any of them?" Smoke asked.

"Not a good one, but enough to tell that they're white, not Indians."

"Outlaws, then," Smoke said. "A gang's out to tree the town. Probably the same one responsible for all the other trouble around here lately."

Monte nodded. "That'd be my guess. They got confident enough they're going for a real jackpot."

Shooting continued in other parts of Big Rock. That told Smoke the attackers were spread out all over town. He had no idea how many of them there were, but something had occurred to him. The settlement's defenders would stand a better chance of defeating the outlaws if Smoke could get out there among them, especially if he could free Pearlie and Cal from jail. Those two were fighting furies when it came to a battle.

Smoke glanced over at a small, enclosed area tucked away in a rear corner of the church. A narrow door opened into it. He knew that behind that door was a ladder that led up into the attic, and that provided a way into the steeple, where the church's bell hung.

It was highly unlikely the outlaws knew about that. He caught Monte's eye, pointed at the ceiling, and said, "I'm going up."

Monte looked confused for a second, then nodded in understanding. "Need help?"

"This is likely a one-man job," Smoke said.

Smoke holstered his gun and slid along the wall to the little door that accessed the ladder. Sunlight filtered down and dimly illuminated the cramped space, the walls of which almost brushed Smoke's broad shoulders as he climbed to the attic.

Boards had been laid across the ceiling joists to form a walkway leading to the steeple. He had to crouch as he climbed out onto that path because the roof was low at this point. It got higher and easier as he approached the middle of the building. He was able to stand up straight when he reached the steeple.

The structure rising above the roof was square, with a small window covered with a shutter on each side. Smoke pulled his bandanna from his pocket, reached up, and wrapped the cloth securely around the bell's copper clapper so that it wouldn't ring when the bell moved back and forth. That pealing sound might draw the attention of the outlaws and warn them that somebody was up here.

Instead, the clapper just thudded softly as Smoke shouldered the bell aside, grasped one of the bracing boards inside the steeple, and pulled himself higher. He was able to get hold of the top of the window frame on the back of the steeple and hung there as he drew a leg up. A couple of careful kicks knocked the shutter loose without making too much racket. He pushed it out and worked his way through the narrow opening.

When he slid down from the steeple onto the roof's peak, he spread his arms and legs on each side of the crest to keep himself stable. The wooden shingles were hot from the sun shining on them, but Smoke ignored that. Staying low so he wouldn't be as visible from the ground, he crawled toward the other end of the building.

He went to his belly again when he reached a point where he could see the pair of outhouses behind the church. A haze of powdersmoke hung over one of them. As Smoke drew his Colt and watched, a man leaned out from behind the outhouse, aimed a rifle at the church, and squeezed off a round.

The man moved the Winchester's lever down, but before he could pull it back up to throw another cartridge into the chamber, Smoke drilled him through the head with a single shot from the Colt. The man jerked, dropped the rifle, and fell beside the outhouse. He was dead when he hit the ground and didn't even twitch.

With gunfire still going on all over town, Smoke hoped none of the other outlaws around the church had noticed his shot. He holstered his iron again, swung around, and backed off the roof until he was hanging by his hands. It was a longer drop from where he was, but he figured he was less likely to be seen. He let go and fell.

Smoke landed with his usual lithe grace, went down, rolled, and came up on his feet with the Colt in his hand again. He pressed his back against the wall of the church and moved along it until he reached the corner.

From there, he could see several wagons parked on that side of the church. Another of the outlaws was using a wagon for cover as he peppered the building with slugs. Smoke couldn't get a good angle on the man's body from where he was, but when he knelt at the corner, he could see the owlhoot's legs under the wagon bed.

Smoke squeezed off a shot that tore through the rifleman's right knee and dumped him howling on the ground, in plain sight now behind the wagon. Smoke silenced him with a bullet to the chest that plowed through the man's heart, killing him instantly.

That accounted for two of the varmints, but there were still plenty more to go.

Bullets continued slamming into the front of the jail, so as soon as Pearlie, Cal, Dade, and Hendryx had armed themselves, they headed for the building's back door.

Pearlie had shoved Deputy Nash's Colt into the waistband of his trousers and grabbed one of the Winchesters from the rack. Cal and Dade also took rifles and filled them with cartridges from the boxes in Monte's desk, as well as stuffing their pockets with extra rounds. Hendryx chose one of the shotguns and thumbed shells into both barrels before sticking extras in his pocket.

"I never was a great shot with a rifle, but I can handle a scattergun pretty good," he said as they hurried along the aisle through the cellblock, stepping past the body of the unfortunate deputy.

Pearlie still had the keys. It didn't take him long to find the right one and unlock the back door.

"Get them guns ready," he told the others. "No tellin' what we'll run into outside."

"I'll go first," Cal said. "Pearlie, you open the door."

Pearlie looked like he wanted to argue, but he must have known it wouldn't do him any good. He jerked the door open, and Cal rushed out, swiveling from side to side as he swung the rifle back and forth.

"I don't see anybody," he called to the others after taking a good look around. "Come on."

They hurried after him, alert, heads jerking from side to side as they searched for potential threats.

"Where are we goin'?" Dade asked.

"If Smoke's in town this mornin', he's likely at the Baptist church," Pearlie said. "Let's head in that direction. Best stay off the street as much as we can."

The four men ran along the alley, heading for the edge of town, where the Ranney Street Baptist Church was located. Of course it was possible that Smoke and Sally hadn't come into Big Rock this morning to attend services, but if they had, that was where they would be. And there would be other men at the church who could pitch in to fight the raiders, as well.

They had gone behind several buildings when two men stepped around a corner ahead of them. The men wore long dusters and carried rifles, and Pearlie knew instantly he had never seen them before. That didn't necessarily mean they were outlaws, but the way they yelled startled curses and jerked their weapons toward the four former prisoners meant they weren't friendly.

"Spread out!" Pearlie yelled as he brought up the Winchester he carried. All six men opened fire at the same time, the sharp cracks of the rifles counterpointed by the dull, heavy boom of the shotgun in Hendryx's hands.

The double load of buckshot slammed into one of the men and flung him backward like a casual slap from a giant hand. The other outlaw staggered as Pearlie and Cal both caught him with rifle shots. The Winchester he held suddenly seemed too heavy for him to hold up. The barrel tilted toward the ground as he triggered his last shot. The bullet plowed a furrow in the dirt. The duster-clad hombre dropped the rifle and pitched forward.

The man Hendryx had blasted kicked a couple of times and then lay still. Pearlie and Cal both rushed forward, rifles poised to fire again as they checked on the downed men.

"Hey!" Hendryx yelled behind them. "Chuck's hit!"

"See how bad it is," Pearlie told Cal. "I'll make sure these varmints are done for."

Cal didn't hesitate to do as Pearlie told him. Pearlie was a veteran of numerous range wars, coolheaded and smart whenever gun trouble erupted.

When Cal turned to hurry back toward the men from the Three Sevens, he saw that Dade was down on the ground but struggling to get up. Hendryx was trying to help him.

"They just nicked me, blast it!" Dade said. "I'm all right."

He had a small bloodstain on the left sleeve of his shirt, Cal saw. Other than that, there was no sign of a wound. The bullet had hit him hard enough to knock him off his feet momentarily and the gash it left behind probably hurt like blazes, but Cal could tell that Dade wasn't seriously injured.

Once Dade was standing again, Hendryx broke open the shotgun and reloaded both barrels.

"You need me to help you get along, Chuck?" he asked as he closed the weapon.

"No, I don't need you to help me," Dade snapped in a surly voice. "I've cut myself worse'n this shavin'."

Pearlie called, "These boys are both dead. Come on."

Leaving the outlaws where they had fallen, the group resumed its rapid journey through the back alley. They reached Ranney Street and were about to turn left, toward the church, when a bullet whipped past Pearlie's head, followed instantly by another that kicked up dust from the ground at Cal's feet.

"Hunt cover!" Pearlie said.

Several men had just emerged from the building on the opposite corner, one of the lesser saloons in Big Rock. Catching sight of Pearlie and the others and knowing they weren't part of the gang, they had opened fire.

Pearlie had been a short distance ahead of the others when the shooting started. He knew he couldn't retreat into the alley without getting hit, so he threw himself to the ground behind a nearby water trough. The trough's sturdy sides offered plenty of protection from bullets, but it was small enough that Pearlie could barely move without exposing part of himself to owlhoot fire.

Cal ducked back and crouched behind a rain barrel at the end of the alley. Dade flattened himself on the ground on the other side, right up against the wall of a building. Hendryx turned and dashed the other way, moving back to some crates stacked beside the rear door of the building.

None of the four men had good cover, but it was the best they could do at the moment. Cal and Dade opened fire with their rifles. Hendryx wasn't in a good position to use the shotgun, and Pearlie couldn't risk raising up enough to bring his Winchester into play, not with the way lead was humming around that water trough.

They were pinned down, and with the outlaws across the street taking cover behind some wagons, Pearlie, Cal, Dade, and Hendryx were at a distinct disadvantage, even though the fight was at a standoff for now.

That didn't last long, because at that moment, an explosion roared out somewhere not far away, a powerful enough blast to shake the ground underneath the embattled defenders.

Chapter 28

Linc Pollard stood on the boardwalk in front of Lambert's Restaurant, rifle in hand, looking back and forth along the street. He was waiting for the men who had kicked open the restaurant's doors and gone inside to see what they could find.

Several footsteps sounded behind him. He looked around to see the other outlaws emerging from the building.

"Well?" Pollard snapped.

"Not much money, Linc," one of them said. He held up a cloth bag. "Got some good-lookin' rolls for later, though."

Pollard reined in the irritation he felt and nodded.

"Get on to the next place," he ordered. "There are still quite a few to clean out—"

The explosion from down the street interrupted him. A couple of the men with him yelled in surprise and alarm as the boardwalk trembled under their feet.

"What in blazes was that?" one of them shouted.

Pollard knew what it had to be. He snapped, "Keep doin' what you're supposed to," and broke into a run toward Big Rock's bank.

Whisper McReady was part of the crew charged with cleaning out the bank. Pollard could only hope the gang's leader hadn't been caught in the explosion.

On the other hand, if McReady was dead, Pollard figured he would be in charge again . . .

He saw black smoke coming out through the bank's shattered front window. A familiar figure stood on the porch, though, in a black hat and duster, holding a rifle. Pollard hurried up to him and asked, "What happened?"

"Steadman blew himself to smithereens, that's what happened," McReady replied. "Maybe he wasn't as much of an expert at using dynamite as he claimed to be."

"Was anybody else killed?"

McReady shook his head. "No, he told us all to get out before he lit the fuse." A raspy laugh came from the boss outlaw. "At least it blew the door off the safe, just like he said it would, and the blast didn't destroy too much of the money inside. The other boys are in there now, gathering it up."

"What about Steadman?"

"Not enough of him left to gather up," McReady said. "How are the other boys doing?"

"All right as far as I know. I've been circulatin' from place to place like you told me. Lots of shootin' around the church on the edge of town, so I guess the fellas there are doin' their job and keepin' everybody penned up in there."

The outlaw called Dooley came running up to them, panting a little from breathlessness.

"There's a place called Longmont's we can't get into," he reported. "Some varmint holed up in there is a heck of a shot. Every time he catches even a glimpse of one of the boys, he wings 'em."

"Keep trying," McReady ordered. "If you haven't gotten in there and cleaned it out by the time we're ready to ride, torch the place."

Pollard's eyes widened in surprise.

"If we set one of the buildings on fire, Whisper, it's liable to spread."

McReady's lip curled in a sneer. "If we've gotten all the money we can out of this town, what does it matter if it burns to the ground?"

Pollard's jaw tightened. He had killed numerous times during his career as an outlaw, and he never minded shooting it out with the law. He sort of figured that was part of the job on both sides.

But in these frontier settlements, a fire could get out of hand quickly and wind up destroying the whole town. That wasn't something he particularly wanted on what was left of his conscience.

McReady was the boss, though, and he gave the orders. Whatever happened, it wouldn't be Pollard's fault. That was cold comfort but better than nothing.

"I'll finish up here," McReady went on, as if Pollard hadn't raised any objection. "You go and hurry up the rest of the boys. I'd like to get out of here as soon as we can."

"We're headin' back through the Flat Rock country to the hideout?"

"That's right." McReady looked like something had just occurred to him. He said, "And I want you to find Violet and Daisy."

"Why?" Pollard asked.

"Because we're taking them with us." McReady rasped out a laugh. "They wanted to be part of the gang, so they blasted well can be!"

Smoke ran to the wagons that the rifleman on that side of the church had been using for cover. He was confident the outlaw was dead, but he quickly checked the man's body to confirm that.

From where he was now, he could see the buildings on the left side of Ranney Street. An alcove on the front of one of them offered protection to the rifleman taking potshots at the front of the church. Smoke saw the barrel of a Winchester sticking out but couldn't see the man who held it.

He drew a bead on the rifle barrel and carefully squeezed off the shot. The bullet struck the barrel and knocked the weapon flying out of the hands of the outlaw who held it. Without thinking, the man leaned forward out of the alcove and peered around for whoever had just fired at his position.

Smoke was ready for that and put a slug squarely between the owlhoot's eyes. The man pitched sideways to the ground in front of the building and lay there in a motionless heap.

That opened up a path for Smoke to reach the main street of Big Rock, where a lot of shooting was still going on. Before he broke cover behind the wagon, he took cartridges from the loops on his shell belt and replaced the rounds he had fired, plus thumbing a cartridge into the chamber that was empty, with the hammer resting on it earlier. With Big Rock under attack from what sounded like a small army, he wanted a full wheel.

Gun in hand, he hurried along the street. He had gone a couple of blocks when several men stepped out of the building ahead of him at the corner. They all wore dusters and had revolvers in their hands. They stopped short, jerked up the guns they held, and opened fire.

But they weren't shooting at Smoke. Instead, they blazed away at something across the street from where they were. Smoke ducked closer to the wall at his left and dropped to a knee, ready to fight, but none of the outlaws seemed to have noticed him. They were too busy trading shots with whoever was over there on the other side of the street. They darted behind some wagons and continued throwing lead in that direction.

From the corner of his eye, Smoke had seen a flicker of movement over there. He took a closer look and spotted someone lying on the ground behind a water trough. A little shock went through him as he caught a glimpse of the man's face and realized it was Pearlie who had taken cover there.

That was a stroke of luck. Smoke had hoped to reach the jail and free Pearlie and Cal, and here was his foreman, already on the loose and armed. Smoke could see that Pearlie had a Winchester with him, but the way bullets were flying around that water trough, he couldn't risk raising up so he could use it.

Rifle fire came from the nearby mouth of the back alley behind the buildings fronting on Main Street. That was Cal, Smoke guessed. Wherever one of those boys was, the other could usually be found close by.

The outlaws had Pearlie pinned down, but Smoke had the drop on them and they didn't even know it. He raised his Colt, but before he could trigger the gun, an explosion rocked Big Rock.

Smoke grimaced in surprise as he felt the blast shake the ground. His first thought was that the explosion came from the bank. The outlaws raiding the settlement might have used dynamite to blow open the safe. But that explosion had sounded and felt too big for that.

Whatever had blown up was bad enough, but Smoke had a more pressing problem right in front of him. Pearlie and Cal still needed his help. The outlaws had paused momentarily in their assault because they had been shocked by the blast, too, but now they resumed firing at the water trough where Pearlie had taken cover and down the alley where Smoke figured Cal must be holed up.

There were three owlhoots, and Smoke wanted to take out all of them as quickly as he could. Normally, he disdained the practice of fanning a revolver. It was inaccurate except for the most expert gunhandlers, and it could damage the weapon, too. But it was *fast*, and right now, that was what Smoke wanted.

He surged back up on his feet, took several fast steps toward the outlaws, and clenched his finger on the trigger as he slapped the hammer with his other hand.

The six shots rolled out in one continuous roar of gun-thunder. Trick-shot artists who practiced for hours on end could hit something that way, but they were just trying to put on a show. Smoke's accuracy came from long years of using a gun to protect those he cared for and to save his own life. It was deadly serious business with him.

The lead storm slammed into the three outlaws. With their bodies already ripped by bullets, they tried to turn and fight back, but as they did, more slugs crashed into them and bowled them over. They went down in bloody sprawls.

As the echoes of those shots bounced around the street, Smoke shouted, "Pearlie! Over here!"

Pearlie leaped up and turned toward the alley to shout, "It's Smoke! Come on, kid!"

Cal ran out of the alley, followed by two other men. Smoke recognized Chuck Dade and Jasper Hendryx. From the looks of the blood on Dade's sleeve, he had been wounded, but he didn't appear to be hurt badly. The sight of the cowboys from the Three Sevens told Smoke that they must have busted out of jail together with Pearlie and Cal.

As they came up to him, Smoke asked, "Are you boys all right?"

"Dade got nicked," Pearlie said as he jerked his head toward the stocky, redhaired puncher. "The rest of us are all right."

"How'd you get out of jail?"

Pearlie's rugged features turned grim as he replied, "Ollie Nash was the deputy on duty, and when the shootin' started, he went to see what was goin' on. The varmints filled him full o' lead, and he barely made it back to the jail to turn us loose before he cashed in his chips."

"I hate to hear that," Smoke said, shaking his head. "Ollie was a good man. But I'm glad you fellas aren't locked up anymore. We've got a big fight on our hands."

Cal asked, "Is the whole town under attack?"

Smoke nodded. "Seems like it. They had the Baptist church surrounded, but I managed to get out and whittle down the odds a mite. There's no telling how many more of them are running around Big Rock."

"What about Miss Sally?" Pearlie wanted to know. "Is she all right?"

"She's safe in the church, along with Monte and a bunch of other men. And the Caldwell sisters are there, too," Smoke added, knowing his men might be worried about Violet and Daisy.

"That's mighty good to know. What are we gonna do now?"

"I figured we'd do some more whittling on those odds," Smoke said, "and maybe find out what blew up a couple of minutes ago."

Violet and Daisy sat on the floor between pews with Sally Jensen. Their heads were below the level of the seat backs, so they were relatively safe from the bullets that still flew through the air inside the church from time to time. The firing had tapered off dramatically in the past few minutes.

"I wish I knew what was going on out there," Daisy said.

"Your husband must have been able to take care of some of those men shooting at the church," Violet said to Sally. "It sounds like there's only one gun going off out there now. Do you have any idea who the attackers could be?"

"The only thing I can think of is that it must be the same gang that wrecked that train and stole those cattle," Sally said. "Of course it might not be, but I think the chances of two different bunches of outlaws operating around these parts at the same time are pretty small."

Daisy wanted to glance at her sister, but she suppressed the urge. That was the first thought that had sprung into her mind, too, but why in the world would Linc Pollard do such a thing? He had been following Violet's plans for quite a while now, and Daisy just couldn't imagine him pulling a double-cross like this on his own. He wouldn't have wanted to put their lives at risk, either. Daisy knew he was sweet on Violet, even though he had never done anything about his feelings for her.

For her part, Violet couldn't forget who she had seen, or thought she had seen, in that darkened alley the night before.

How could Whisper McReady be back? He was safely locked up in the Kansas State Penitentiary. And if he had managed to get out of there somehow, would he launch an attack like this on Big Rock, knowing that it was bound to endanger his stepdaughters?

Violet's mouth tightened as that thought went through her mind. Whisper had never been close to her and Daisy, she recalled. He had loved their mother, or at least claimed to, but the girls didn't really mean anything to him. If he thought he could collect a big payoff by raiding the settlement, he would do it, and if anything happened to the Caldwell sisters in the process, that would just be too bad.

Sally saw Monte Carson gathering some of the men from the congregation around him. Monte had a serious look on his face as he spoke to the men, and they were equally solemn and determined-looking.

Sally knew something was about to happen. She wanted to be ready for whatever it was, so she said to Violet and Daisy, "The two of you stay here and keep your heads down. I'll be right back."

"What are you going to do, Sally?" Violet asked.

"I think Monte is planning something. I want to know what it is."

Daisy said, "He's not going to let you take part in it."

Sally smiled. "I'm not so sure about that. Monte knows how stubborn I can be. Not as well as Smoke knows that, of course, but he's certainly aware of it."

Moving in a crouching walk, she started toward the spot where the men had gathered.

Behind her, Violet looked at Daisy, nodded toward the back of the room, and said quietly, "Come on."

"Come on where?" Daisy asked. "We can't go out there, not with all that shooting going on." She lowered her voice even more. "Do you think it's Linc and the other men? Why would they do something like this?"

"I don't think it's Linc." Violet leaned closer to her sister. "I think it's Whisper."

"Whi—" Daisy started to exclaim. She caught herself in time to keep from saying the name out loud. Violet was already hushing her. Quietly, so that only Violet could hear, Daisy said, "It can't be him. He's in prison."

"I didn't say anything about it, but I thought I saw him last night. Remember when I said I heard something behind the shop as we were about to go into the cottage?"

Daisy nodded. "I just figured it was a cat."

"I caught a glimpse of a man ducking into an alley, and I'd swear it was him. You know how big his ears are. It's hard to miss them."

Daisy didn't look convinced. "It just seems impossible—"

"Nothing's impossible where that man is concerned," Violet said. "And if he's holding a grudge against us for taking over the gang, there's no telling what he might do to get back at us."

Daisy groaned softly and said, "I knew it was a bad idea when you came up with it."

Violet reached out and closed her hand around her sister's arm. The fingers dug cruelly into Daisy's flesh as Violet said, "But you didn't mind spending the money we got from it, did you?" She seemed to catch herself as Daisy winced in pain. She let go of the younger woman's arm and muttered, "Sorry. I'm just worried about what Whisper might do. I want to get back to the shop and make sure he doesn't try to burn it down, or anything like that."

"You really think he might?"

"He has a mean streak a mile wide, Daisy, you know that."

"He never hurt us or Ma."

"And how many people did he kill in his robberies? He shot

down plenty of men who didn't do anything to deserve it. They just happened to be there."

Daisy couldn't deny that their stepfather had a reputation for viciousness. But that didn't mean she agreed with what Violet wanted to do, either.

"It's too dangerous to go outside—" she began.

"There haven't been any shots from behind the church since right after Smoke Jensen left," Violet said. "Jensen killed whoever was back there. I'm sure of it." She gathered herself. "Anyway, I'm going whether you do or not."

"I'm coming with you," Daisy responded quickly. That was no surprise to Violet. Daisy might complain, but she always followed her big sister's lead.

Sally Jensen was talking to the sheriff and not paying any attention to them. Nor was anyone else in the church. Carefully, the Caldwell sisters crawled to the end of the pew next to the wall and then started along it toward the door at the side of the platform where the pulpit stood. That door didn't lead outside, but it opened into a rear hall where the church's back door was located. Violet knew that because she had scouted the place before now, just as she scouted every place where she might find herself.

Violet reached the door, lifted a hand to the knob, and eased it open. A glance over her shoulder told her that Sally was still talking to Monte Carson, although it looked like the sheriff and the other men were about to do something. Violet jerked her head at Daisy and slipped through the doorway into the hall. Daisy was right behind her. They stood up and hurried toward the back door just as gunfire began to crash inside the sanctuary.

Chapter 29

"I'm convinced there's only one owlhoot still trying to keep us trapped in here," Monte had said a few minutes earlier to the men gathered around him. At least half of them wore holstered revolvers and looked competent to use them. "I figure Smoke took care of the others. If some of you open fire on the varmint from the windows and distract him, a few of us can go out the front, circle around the building, and get him."

"What if there really is somebody else still covering the front, though?" a man asked. "Whoever goes out that way will be running smack-dab into a faceful of lead."

"It's a risk," Monte admitted, "but we haven't heard any shots from that direction for several minutes now."

The townsman who had asked the question shook his head and said, "That's not enough to get me to risk throwing my life away."

"You're the sheriff, Monte," another man said.

"That's right, I dang sure am," Monte snapped. "And if you're saying it's my job to smoke out that skunk, it sure is. So you fellas just stay in here and keep your heads down."

"Now, Monte, that's not what I meant—"

Sally Jensen stepped up to the group and said, "I have my gun, Monte. I'll come with you."

The lawman looked surprised by that offer, but not overly so. He had known Sally for several years and was well aware of the stubborn, courageous side of her nature.

"I don't reckon Smoke would ever forgive me if I agreed to that and something happened to you, Sally," he said. "But I do appreciate it."

Several of the men shuffled their feet and looked embarrassed. They didn't like the idea of a woman showing them up.

That hadn't been Sally's intention. She had made the offer sincerely. But if being ashamed prodded them into action, that was fine, too.

"I'll come with you, Monte," one of them said.

"So will I," another volunteered.

Monte nodded and said, "Three of us ought to be enough. The rest of you men who are armed throw as much lead as you can at the fella on that side of the church. If you make him keep his head down, that'll give us a chance to get him."

"Maybe one of us will drill the son of a gun and you won't have to."

"You won't hear me complaining if it works out that way," Monte said. He hefted his gun and nodded to the two men who had offered to accompany him on the charge. "Let's go."

At that moment, something made Sally glance over her shoulder. She did so just in time to see Daisy vanish through the door leading to the church's rear area. Sally didn't see Violet, so she could only assume the older Caldwell sister had already slipped out.

Why in the world would they be leaving under these circumstances? Sally asked herself.

There was only one way to answer that question. Sally slid her hand into the bag she carried, closed it around the butt of the little Smith & Wesson, and started after the sisters.

As she stepped into the rear hallway with a storeroom on one side and steps leading up to the baptistry on the other, the armed men who had remained in the church opened fire through the windows.

Sally said a quick prayer for the safety of Monte and the other men, and at the same time, she saw the building's back door standing open.

Violet and Daisy were gone, but they couldn't have gotten far. Sally drew the pistol and went through the door onto a small porch. A couple of steps led down to the ground. She looked around and didn't see the blondes, but she figured they must have hurried off toward Big Rock's downtown area. They wouldn't have had any reason to wander the other way, out of the settlement.

Sally had just started in the direction she figured they had gone when an explosion somewhere in the center of town shook the ground under her feet.

Smoke, Pearlie, Cal, Chuck Dade, and Jasper Hendryx headed back up the alley the four cowboys had followed to Ranney Street. Smoke knew the explosion probably had come from the bank and wanted to find out what had happened there. He worried that the blast might have started a fire. As in all frontier communities, fire represented a huge threat to Big Rock.

They would have to cross the street to reach the bank, so when Smoke judged they had gone far enough, he nodded toward one of the narrow passages between buildings and told the others, "We'll cut through here and then, depending on what we find, make a dash across Main Street."

The buildings pressed in closely on both sides, and despite the brightness of the morning, it was shadowy in these close quarters.

As they trotted along, Pearlie said to Smoke, “We’re mighty close to the dress shop. You reckon we could check on it real quick?”

“The Caldwell sisters are in the church,” Smoke said. “I left them there with Sally. I’m sure she’ll take good care of them. Monte’s there, too.”

“I know, but the way them outlaws are rampagin’ through town, they might’ve busted in at the shop. I’d hate to see those gals lose anything valuable they’ve got in there.”

Smoke didn’t figure there was anything worth much in the dress shop, at least in terms of financial value. Violet and Daisy had some time and effort tied up in the dresses they had made, and of course the fabric they had on hand had cost money, too, but it wasn’t like the shop would have a lot of cash on hand.

Even so, it wouldn’t hurt anything to stop by there and make sure the raiders hadn’t disturbed the place, he supposed.

“Sure, we’ll take a look,” he told Pearlie, who appeared pleased by the decision.

Smoke motioned for the others to stop as they neared the mouth of the little alley. He eased ahead and peered in both directions along the street. He didn’t see any townspeople. All the citizens of Big Rock who had been out and about when the raid started must have scurried for shelter.

He did spot several small groups of roughly dressed, hard-faced men moving here and there. It was obvious the gang had split up to ransack the town.

Smoke had a decent view of the bank on the other side of the street a couple of blocks away. The brick building was still standing, which was good. It looked like the front window had been blown out, but that was the only damage he could see from where he was. One duster-clad man stood looking at the bank as if he were waiting for somebody to come out, but he was the only one close by, and he was looking in the other direction.

“The dress shop’s just a couple o’ doors up,” Pearlie said.

"I'm gonna have a look and make sure everything's all right there, and then maybe we can corral any of those varmints who are in the bank."

Smoke nodded and said, "We'll all head in that direction."

With him and Pearlie in the lead and Cal and the other two cowboys right behind them, Smoke moved quickly but quietly along the boardwalk toward the dress shop. The door appeared to be intact, and the big display window wasn't broken, which was something of a miracle considering how many bullets had been thrown around Big Rock on this violent Sunday morning.

Pearlie hurried a short distance ahead of the others to take a closer look at the shop. He was standing in front of the door when, without warning, a group of gun-toting men emerged from a building at the near corner of the next block.

The man who seemed to be their leader was saying, "Whisper's orders are to find those girls—"

At that moment, he caught sight of the five men on the boardwalk just outside the dress shop and exclaimed in surprise. That didn't stop him from jerking up the gun he held and shouting, "Get those sons o'—"

The rest was drowned out by the roar of gunfire as he and the outlaws with him loosed a deadly volley toward Smoke and his companions.

Pearlie reacted instantly, ramming his shoulder against the door and bursting it open. He yelled, "In here!" as his momentum carried him into the shop.

Smoke and Cal fired back at the outlaws in the next block as Dade and Hendryx darted into the building behind Pearlie. The air around them was thick with the humming sound of bullets, like a deadly swarm of bees.

Cal was unhurt as he followed Dade and Hendryx, then Smoke came last and slammed the door. Pearlie had busted the lock when he knocked it open. Smoke grabbed a chair and jammed it under the knob to hold the door closed.

After the roar of guns outside, the silence that pressed in around them here in the shop was oppressive. The air smelled of fabric and perfume, like a lady's boudoir. Under normal circumstances, these five rugged men would have felt mighty out of place here.

At the moment, however, it was simply a refuge from those outlaw guns, a place to hole up and fight back.

"Now what do we do?" Chuck Dade asked.

"There's a back door," Cal said. "We can go out that way, circle around, and fight our way to the bank."

"Why don't we just stay here?" Hendryx suggested. "We can defend this place just as well as any, and it ain't our job to fight a whole gang and try to save Big Rock."

Dade said, "If I was wearin' my hat, I'd take it off and swat you with it right now! Those sidewinders shot me. I don't figure on lettin' 'em get away with that."

"We don't want to get this shop shot all to pieces, neither," Pearlie said. "I say let's get out while we still can."

"I agree," Smoke said. "If we move fast enough, we can still do considerable damage to that bunch, and maybe stop them from cleaning out the whole town."

Hendryx shrugged and said, "Well, shoot, it was just an idea. I'll do whatever the rest of you boys want."

"Come on," Pearlie snapped. He swept aside the curtain that hung over the opening between the front and back rooms and was heading for the door when gunshots suddenly erupted right behind the shop.

Sally moved fast. She couldn't imagine that Violet and Daisy would be headed anywhere other than their shop or the little cottage behind it where they lived, so she started in that direction.

She was more familiar with the layout of Big Rock's streets and alleys than the Caldwell sisters were, so she was able to take a shortcut through a shed where a couple of mules were stabled. The animals regarded her stolidly and continued chewing hay as she hurried past them.

She came out into the alley behind the business buildings along Main Street just twenty feet behind the two young women, who were still hurrying along without looking back. Violet and Daisy had almost reached the back door of their shop.

Gunfire sounded close by. Sally jerked her head from side to side, searching for the source of the shots, but she didn't see anything. Whoever was blazing away didn't seem to be shooting at her or the Caldwell sisters. She didn't hear any bullets whining through the air.

Violet and Daisy both had their guns out, small revolvers identical to the one Sally carried. Sally didn't call out to them. Under these perilous circumstances, they might be nervous enough to spin around and start shooting at *her*.

The gun blasts stopped abruptly. They had come from the street, Sally decided. She knew Smoke was somewhere out here in the community and hoped fervently that he was all right.

Violet and Daisy reached the back door of their shop, but before they could open it, several rough-looking men trotted around a corner farther up the alley and saw them. Sally didn't recognize any of them and figured they had to be members of the gang attacking the settlement.

"There's the gals!" one of them yelled. "Grab 'em!"

That almost made it sound as if the outlaws were acquainted with Violet and Daisy, but Sally didn't have time to ponder that. She raised her gun and was about to call to the blondes and tell them to get out of the way, but before she could do that, Violet opened fire herself.

The Smith & Wesson cracked wickedly as Violet sprayed bullets toward the outlaws. They yelled in surprise and scattered as the slugs kicked up dust at their feet. Sally ran toward the sisters, intending to help them fight off the owlhoots.

Before she could join the fight, the rear door of the shop flew open and Pearlie lunged through it into the alley, brandishing a revolver.

Cal was right behind him, but he wasn't holding a gun. Instead, he grabbed Daisy and pulled her through the doorway, handling her a little roughly as he almost flung her into the shop. However, Sally knew he was just trying to get her out of the line of fire.

The outlaws hadn't started shooting, but they were likely to, any second now. Sally, hurrying up behind Violet, looped an arm around her waist and urged her toward the door, saying, "Get inside!"

Violet gasped and struggled for a second, then seemed to realize it was Sally who had hold of her. She cooperated after that, possibly because she had emptied the little revolver.

"Go, go!" Pearlie urged both women. As they practically dived through the doorway, the outlaws finally opened fire. Bullets whipped past Pearlie's head as he triggered two swift shots back at the raiders. Then he threw himself into the shop's back room, too, and Cal slammed the door behind him.

Sally felt strong arms go around her and looked up into Smoke's worried face.

"I thought you were going to stay in the church," he said.

"Plans changed," she said simply.

"You're all right?"

"I'm fine," she assured him. "I think Violet and Daisy are, too."

Sally looked around to see Pearlie and Cal hugging the sisters. They all appeared to be unharmed.

"Was that you shooting out front a minute ago?" she went on.

A grim smile tugged at Smoke's mouth as he let go of her with visible reluctance.

"Yeah, we had a little run-in with some fellas who wanted to ventilate us," he said. "Dade's winged, but not too bad."

Sally realized that two other men had crowded into the back room. She recognized Chuck Dade and Jasper Hendryx, the cowboys who had been locked up in Monte's jail along with Pearlie and Cal. Considering the fact that those two from the Sugarloaf were here, she wasn't surprised to see the men from the Three Sevens, as well.

And with outlaws in front of the shop and more raiders behind it, they were all trapped in here.

Chapter 30

Smoke had been surprised to see Sally when she rushed into the shop's back room with Violet, but he wasn't shocked. Nothing she did really shocked him anymore. She had more stubbornness, not to mention more daring, than any woman he had ever met. Her following the Caldwell sisters here was exactly the sort of bold action he would have expected of her.

He indulged his impulses and hugged her again, then said, "I'm mighty glad you're all right, but to tell you the truth, I wish you were still back there in the church, safe from all of this, with Monte looking after you."

"I don't need looking after, Smoke Jensen, and when I do, you'll be the one to do it."

The contradictory nature of that declaration didn't surprise him, either. He knew what Sally meant and was glad she felt that way.

At the same time, they needed to figure out what they were going to do next.

That decision might be taken out of their hands, at least if the gang that had attacked Big Rock had anything to say about it.

Shouts came from the street in front of the shop. Everyone in the back room heard the sound and turned in that direction.

"I can't make out most of the words," Smoke said, "but it sounds like whoever's hollering out there is talking to you two ladies."

He looked meaningfully at Violet and Daisy as he spoke.

Violet sighed and started in that direction. Daisy caught her arm and said, "Wait. If you go and talk to him, they're liable to start shooting again."

"Not unless he tells them to, and he's not going to do that until he's said whatever he has to say," Violet replied. "You know that."

"Hold on a minute," Smoke said. "Who is this you're talking about?"

Violet looked coolly at him. "Our stepfather," she said. "His name is Whisper McReady."

"Violet—" Daisy began in a warning tone.

Violet turned toward her and said, "Oh, what does it matter now? Nothing's going to be the same after this."

Smoke said, "That name's a little familiar to me, but I can't quite place it."

"He's an outlaw," Violet said, her voice hard and flat. "He's been in prison, but he escaped. Attacking Big Rock and looting the town must have been his idea."

"You didn't know anything about it?" Smoke asked sharply. Sally put her hand on his arm, as if cautioning him, but he ignored it. He knew she liked the Caldwell sisters, and he had, too, but if they had anything to do with what was happening this morning, he wanted to know it.

Violet shook her head and said, "I didn't know this was going to happen, and neither did Daisy. I give you my word on that."

"Is McReady's gang the one that's been causing so much trouble around here?"

Violet caught her bottom lip between her teeth for a second and nodded. "I'm afraid so."

"You knew that?"

"We suspected," Daisy said quickly. "We didn't know anything for sure."

Pearlie said, "Of course they didn't know! You heard 'em, Smoke. That fella McReady's been in prison. If he's an outlaw, they probably never even went to visit him."

"That's true," Violet said. "We didn't."

Just then, it came to Smoke where he had heard Whisper McReady's name before. Monte Carson had recognized the dead outlaw they had brought into town as a former member of the McReady gang and had told Smoke about that.

Judging by the information that had just been divulged, however, maybe that hombre hadn't been a *former* member of the gang at all. It seemed that McReady's bunch was still together.

But none of that actually mattered as long as they were pinned down here in the dress shop and the outlaws were still ransacking the town.

"I have to go talk to him," Violet said. "Maybe I can persuade him to ride out without hurting anyone else."

Smoke thought about it for a second and then nodded.

"The rest of you stay here," he told the others. "Violet, I'll go into the front room with you."

For a moment, she looked like she wanted to argue with him, but then she said, "All right. I won't let on that you're there. That way, perhaps they'll hold their fire."

Sally touched Smoke's arm for a second. Then he pulled the curtain aside, and Violet went into the front room. He stayed low behind her so he wouldn't be noticed by anyone peeking in through the big window.

"—getting tired of waiting, Vi," a man called from outside. "You better answer quick, or I don't know what's gonna happen."

"Is that him?" Smoke asked quietly.

Violet shook her head. "My stepfather can't shout. He was shot in the throat when he was a young man and he can't speak above a whisper. That's Linc Pollard, his second-in-command. McReady talks through him. I hope I can reason with him."

Smoke eased over to the door, staying out of the line of sight of the window in it. When he was close enough, he edged one eye out far enough to get a glimpse of the four men standing in the street.

Two of them looked like typical hard cases. They stood back a little, holding rifles. The two in front of them were more striking. One was tall and lean, with a hawklike face, the other older, shorter, stockier, with large ears that stuck straight out from the sides of his head. He had a slight, silvery wisp of beard on his blunt chin.

The tall man said, "Blast it, Vi—"

Smoke nodded to Violet. She moved the chair and opened the door a crack, then called through it, "I'm here, Linc. You can stop shouting."

Pollard took a step forward and asked, "Are you all right? What about Daisy?"

"We're both fine, but we'll be a lot better if you go away and leave us alone."

Pollard glanced over at the other man, who had to be Whisper McReady. He said something to Pollard that Smoke couldn't hear.

Pollard took a deep breath and faced the shop again. "We can't do that, Vi," he said. "The two of you gals need to come on out here, right now."

"Why would we do that?" Violet asked.

"Because you're comin' with us, that's why!"

"That's insane! We won't do it."

"Whisper wants you to come along. He's your pa—"

"He's our stepfather!" Violet interrupted angrily. "And not much of one at that."

Smoke saw McReady's face darken with rage. The boss outlaw spoke swiftly to Pollard. Again, Smoke couldn't make out what McReady said. The man's voice was nothing more than a rasp.

Pollard started to shake his head, but McReady kept on talking. It was obvious he was issuing orders. Smoke wasn't sure what they might be, but he hoped that McReady wouldn't continue the attack on the shop now that he knew his stepdaughters were inside.

A moment later, Smoke realized he had overestimated the importance of family to Whisper McReady. Pollard yelled, "Vi, get down!"

Then all four men in the street opened fire.

Smoke hadn't waited for Violet to follow Pollard's order. He reached out, grabbed her arm, and dragged her off her feet as a roar of gun-thunder filled the air. Bullets shattered the big window and the one in the door as well, spraying millions of glass fragments into the room. Violet put her arms over her head and shuddered on the floor next to Smoke as the bombardment continued.

As well as breaking the windows, the slugs tore through the dress dummies that had been set up for display, causing them to jerk and jump almost as if they were human. In seconds, the dummies split open under the terrific punishment and toppled over.

Packets of money spilled out, some of them broken so that greenbacks scattered across the floor.

Violet saw the piles of cash and let out a surprised gasp. Instinct made her start to get up as she reached toward the closest bills, but Smoke grabbed her shoulder and forced her to stay down. He thought from her reaction that she'd had no idea the money was concealed in the dress dummies.

Finally, the shooting stopped. After waiting a few seconds to let the echoes die away, Pollard called, "Your shop's all shot to pieces, Vi. You don't have any reason to stay here anymore. Get Daisy and come on out. We'll let those fellas who are in there with you live. We're ready to ride away from this town and you're goin' with us."

Violet twisted away from Smoke and snatched up two bundles of greenbacks as she leaped to her feet. She let out a crazed laugh and shouted through the broken window, "Go to the Devil, Linc, and take Whisper with you!" In her fury, she shook the money at the men in the street as if she were brandishing weapons. "We don't need you anymore, not you or Whisper or anybody!"

"My money!" McReady exclaimed, his raspy croak finally loud enough for Smoke to understand what he said. "You little witches have my money!"

An outlaw holding a burning torch ran up behind McReady and Pollard. Pollard waved an arm at the man and said, "Get away from here with that! We can't burn it down now! The girls are still in there!"

"And my money!" McReady said. He jerked up the pistol he held and fired, clearly trying to kill Violet.

Smoke swept her legs out from under her with his leg, and she fell backward from the window. McReady's bullet whistled through the shop's front room and thudded into the wall.

Violet's unthinking rage had just made things worse. McReady would never ride out of Big Rock and leave behind the loot that was hidden in the dummies.

Things had already been hotter than the hinges of Hades, and now they were about to heat up even more.

Chapter 31

Cal had told Daisy to get under one of the tables that the Caldwell sisters used for dressmaking. That would give her some protection if any of the bullets hitting the walls and the door punched through the wood.

Daisy had done as he said, but she looked up at him and suggested, "You get under here with me."

He shook his head. "Can't do it. I've got to be ready to fight in case those varmints bust in here."

Pearlie said, "They're liable to try knockin' down that door any minute now. You boys best fill up them guns while you got the chance."

Hendryx's shotgun already had a load of buckshot in each barrel. Pearlie, Cal, and Chuck Dade thumbed fresh rounds into the expended chambers of their guns' cylinders. Cal heard Violet talking to one of the outlaws through the front door, but he didn't think negotiating was going to do much good, if any. It was hard to reason with bloodthirsty owlhoots.

An idea occurred to him. He turned to Pearlie and said, "If you fellas cover me, I might be able to get out of here, find a horse, and light a shuck for the Sugarloaf."

Hendryx heard that and sneered as he said, "Run away with your tail tucked 'twixt your legs, you mean?"

"No, that ain't what he means, you frog-faced, no-account—" Pearlie got hold of himself before any other colorful epithets could spill out and went on, "The Sugarloaf's got the saltiest, fightin'est crew of any spread from the Milk River to the Rio Grande! And the idea of fetchin' 'em is a good one. Reckon it oughta be me who does it, though."

"I'm a better rider than you and you know it, Pearlie," Cal said.

"I ain't just about to admit that, but that ain't why I said it oughta be me who goes for help. Gettin' outta here will mean goin' through a hail o' lead, and I'm more naturally allergic to bullets than you are, kid."

"How in the world do you figure that?" Cal demanded.

"Well, I'm quite a bit older than you, ain't I, and I've had a heap more shots fired in my direction. I'm still here, ain't I?"

"That's just a matter of luck—"

"Luck ain't got nothin' to do with it!"

While he and Pearlie were squabbling, Cal hadn't noticed that Daisy had eased out from under the table, where she had taken cover. Dade and Hendryx weren't watching her, either, so none of them knew what she was doing until she reached the door and grasped the knob.

That was when Cal saw her and exclaimed, "Daisy, what—"

"They won't shoot at me!" she cried. "I can bring help from the ranch!"

Before any of the men could get to her, she threw the door open and dashed out, shouting, "Don't shoot! It's me! Don't shoot!"

She leaped down from the little porch as the outlaw guns fell silent, but she had taken only a few steps before shots began to crash again.

She stumbled slightly but kept running. Cal couldn't tell if she was hit or had broken stride for some other reason.

He knew he couldn't stop her now, but he might be able to give her a better chance of survival. He leaped out onto the porch and opened up on the men who were firing around corners at her, tripping the trigger of the gun in his hand so swiftly that the shots sounded like one continuous roar.

Still moving fast, Daisy darted around a corner and disappeared.

"Kid, get back in here!" Pearlie yelled as he leaned out and slammed lead toward the outlaws.

Cal felt a bullet pluck at his shirt, and he recognized the wind-rip of a slug as it passed close to his ear. Then he lunged past Pearlie into the back room. Pearlie kicked the door closed behind him.

"That was a durned fool stunt!" the older cowboy told his young friend.

Cal was a little breathless, but he was able to say, "What, trying to save Daisy's life?"

"By throwin' away yours! You reckon it's what the gal would've wanted?"

Cal shook his head. "My life's not thrown away. I'm fine." He dragged in a breath. "I just hope she is. She was moving so fast, I couldn't tell if she was wounded."

Chuck Dade said, "If she was able to run like that, chances are she's all right. That was a mighty brave thing she did." He paused, then added with grudging admiration, "And you, too, Woods, jumpin' out there to give her some cover. You're lucky those varmints didn't shoot you full o' holes."

"Yeah," Hendryx echoed, scowling, "I reckon that was a good thing you done."

"And she probably wouldn't have made it if they hadn't stopped shooting for a second because they were surprised to see her," Cal admitted. "So I guess she was the right choice to go for help. I just hope she makes it out of town all right and can find the Sugarloaf."

Sally said, "She will, I'm sure of it. We just need to hold out until then—"

Another deafening barrage of shots came in front of the shop at that moment. The windows shattered and splintered. Some of the bullets whipped through the curtain in the opening between the rooms, causing it to jump around. Pearlie grabbed Sally and pulled her to the floor. Cal, Dade, and Hendryx dived onto their bellies, as well.

Holding out, as Sally had been urging, had just become more problematic.

On hands and knees, Violet scrambled around the front room gathering up the spilled cash. Smoke didn't try to stop her. He would have had to wrestle with her to hold her back, and she was so crazed that would take more effort than he wanted to spend.

Besides, he heard stealthy footsteps on the boardwalk outside and knew that one of the outlaws was sneaking up to try to get a look into the shop.

He was ready when the barrel of a rifle thrust suddenly through the opening in the upper half of the door, where the window had been. Kneeling to one side, Smoke caught a glimpse of the rifleman's face and recognized him as one of the men who had been with McReady and Pollard.

The next second, those hard-bitten features became a distorted red smear as Smoke fired and the bullet from his Colt smashed into the outlaw's face. The man flipped backward and died without making a sound. He had let go of the Winchester, and it fell through the broken window into the shop.

That brought on a fresh volley of gunshots from outside. Smoke could tell that more of the gang had arrived on the scene and were joining in the assault on the dress shop.

That thought made a grim smile tug at his mouth. Those men were used to robbing banks, holding up trains and stagecoaches, and shooting up saloons. This was probably the first time they had launched an all-out attack on a place full of ladies' dresses, hats, and scarves.

Pearlie pushed the curtain aside and crawled into the front room. He stopped and stared in amazement at Violet and all the greenbacks scattered around, as well as the bundles of cash she clutched to her bosom.

"What in the ever-lovin' Hades is all this?" he asked when he found his voice again.

"I have a hunch it's loot Whisper McReady stashed in those dress dummies," Smoke said. "It spilled out when they got shot to pieces."

Violet's head jerked up. She seemed a little more in control of herself as she said, "My mother must have done it. Whisper gave her the money to hide, and she put it in the dummies. He wouldn't have known how to do that, but she would have."

"She never said nothin' to you about it?" Pearlie asked.

Violet shook her head. "Not a word."

Smoke was convinced she was telling the truth. She had been just as surprised by the sight of the money as he had. McReady had sounded shocked that Violet had it, too. He hadn't known where the loot was. Her speculation had to be correct.

"Daisy made a run for it," Pearlie went on.

"What?" Violet cried as she looked at him. "Did she get away all right?"

"She made it down the alley, around a corner, and out of sight, that's all I know," Pearlie replied. "She said she was gonna hightail it for the Sugarloaf and bring back the crew to help clean up those rats out there."

Smoke said, "That'll take at least an hour. I don't know if we can hold out that long."

"We have to!" Violet said. "Otherwise he'll kill all of us and take this money." She tightened her grip on the bundles of cash she clutched in her arms. "It belongs to Daisy and me. He has no right to it!"

As far as Smoke was concerned, the money belonged to the folks from whom Whisper McReady and his gang had stolen it. But that could be hashed out later, assuming they lived through this ruckus.

"Now that McReady knows the cash is in here, he'll do whatever is necessary to get it," Smoke said. "He'll gather all his men and try to root us out of here."

"I reckon he's got us outnumbered enough to do it, too," Pearlie said.

"Maybe, maybe not. I left Monte and quite a few good fighting men in the church. There's a chance they've busted out of there and will be getting in on the fight any minute now."

Pearlie nodded and said, "Louis is floatin' around somewhere, too, more than likely. Seems to me like them outlaws bit off a bigger chunk than they can chew."

Smoke said to Violet, "Go into the back room and stay there. If they rush us, they'll pour a lot of lead through these windows, and we can't defend them from in here. Pearlie, you and the other boys get one of those tables and turn it over on its side, then put it in front of the door between the rooms. We'll make our stand from there."

"But I don't have all the money—" Violet began.

"You can't spend any of it if you're dead," Smoke interrupted her, setting aside for the moment the question of who the cash actually belonged to.

Violet looked like she wanted to argue more, but then she seemed to realize the futility of it. While Smoke and Pearlie watched the windows, alert for any renewed attack, Violet crawled past the bullet-shredded ruin of the curtain and into the back room.

Pearlie retreated then, and relayed Smoke's order about using one of the sewing tables as a fortification. Cal and Hendryx picked up a table and moved it over to the opening between rooms. Smoke ducked through, and then the two cowboys laid the table over on its side and shoved it into place. Two men could kneel behind it and cover the windows.

"You and I will be posted here, Pearlie," Smoke said as he went down on one knee at the left side of the opening. Pearlie joined him on the right. "Cal, you and Dade and Hendryx be ready to take our places if we go down, and it'll also be up to you to protect our rear if they try to come in through the back door. Sally, you and Violet stay over there in that corner and pull the other table in front of you."

"I can fight, too, Smoke," Sally said.

He smiled at her. "I know you can, and you may get the chance before this is over."

Then he turned back to the front of the building, rested the barrel of his Colt on the edge of the overturned table, and waited for the inevitable assault from the outlaws.

Chapter 32

A few tense minutes later, two men suddenly appeared at the front window and another was at the door. They shoved double-barreled shotguns through the openings and fired.

Smoke and Pearlie saw the guns in time to duck as the blasts filled the room. The roar was so loud, it seemed as if giant fists slammed into their ears. Smoke felt the table shiver as most of six loads of buckshot slammed into it.

But none of the pellets penetrated the thick wood. Smoke and Pearlie rose up swiftly and thrust their guns over the makeshift barricade.

The shotgunners had ducked back as soon as they pulled their triggers. Two men with rifles took their place, jabbing the barrels through the broken window with the intention of sweeping the room with more lead.

Smoke and Pearlie fired before either of the riflemen could get off even a single shot. The slug from Smoke's gun drove deeply into one outlaw's chest and knocked him backward. Pearlie's bullet punched into the guts of the other man. He doubled over, twisted and tried to turn away from the window, and then collapsed, falling out of sight.

Smoke's ears were still ringing a little, which made his voice sound strange to him as he called without looking around, "Everybody all right back there?"

Cal replied, "We're fine. We all stayed out of the line of fire of anything that came through the door between the rooms."

"Any sign of another attack back there?"

"It's gone quiet," Cal said. "Maybe all the hombres who were behind the shop have gone back around front to help on that side."

"Maybe," Smoke said, but he wasn't convinced. He didn't know much about Whisper McReady, but if the man had led an outlaw gang successfully for many years, he had to have some skill when it came to the tactics of battle. McReady had them caught in a cross fire, and he'd be foolish not to try to take advantage of that.

Smoke would gladly take any delay they could get, though, since it gave Monte Carson and Louis Longmont more time to get in on the fight, and also for Daisy Caldwell to reach the Sugarloaf and bring back the rest of the crew. If that quick-trigger bunch of hellions joined the fight, *that* would settle McReady's hash in a hurry.

And if Daisy hadn't been wounded when she made her dash from the dress shop. Smoke hated to consider the chances, but it was possible the brave young woman was lying dead on the side of the trail even now . . .

Daisy leaned forward in the saddle and held on to the horn tightly with her left hand. That side of her body throbbed with pain, and she worried that she would lose all the strength in her left arm and not be able to cling to the saddle.

She needed her right hand to hold the reins, though, and guide the horse as it galloped along the trail leading from Big Rock to the Jensen ranch.

She knew where the Sugarloaf was, even though she had never

been there before. Violet always insisted that they find out as much as they could about every area where they set up in business, and that included learning about the important people in the vicinity. No one in this valley was more important than Smoke Jensen. Without him, it might not even be settled yet.

The hot, sticky wetness on her side worried her. She didn't know how much damage the bullet had done as it ripped her flesh. She hoped it wasn't a mortal wound, but as long as she could make it to the Sugarloaf and send the cowboys there racing to town to help wipe out the gang, that was all that mattered. Even if she died then, she could do so knowing that she'd done everything in her power to help Cal.

She owed him that much, anyway. It would have ruined his life if she and Violet had been able to go through with the plan to swindle the two cowboys. Daisy hadn't liked what they were doing, but she hadn't taken any action to stop Violet, either.

Once Violet had her mind made up, she was pretty much an unstoppable force, anyway.

The pain in Daisy's side got worse with every lunging stride of the horse. The animal had speed and stamina. She had been fortunate in picking a mount to steal from the first hitch rack she had found with horses tied to it. She was prepared to take whatever she could get, but this horse was a good one.

She was fortunate, too, that she had done so much riding in her life. If she hadn't been a skilled horsewoman, she probably wouldn't be able to stay in the saddle, wounded like she was.

Those thoughts whirled madly through her head, but gradually, they were overpowered by the urgent question of how much farther it was to the Jensen ranch. Why wasn't she there yet? Was she ever going to reach the Sugarloaf?

Without warning, her left hand slipped off the saddle horn. She swayed in that direction and tried to grab the horn again. Her fingers had lost their strength and refused to close around it. Daisy felt herself becoming more and more unbalanced. She hauled back on the reins with her other hand in a desperate attempt to slow the horse. If she fell off while the animal was going at top speed, she was liable to break an arm or a leg or, worse, her neck.

The horse fought her as she sawed the bit back and forth, but it did slow down. That was good because, a moment later, Daisy toppled off the animal.

She had the presence of mind to kick her feet free of the stirrups as she fell so she wouldn't be dragged, but she hit the ground with such an impact that all the breath was driven from her body and all she could do was lie there gasping and hurting.

Even with her brain spinning, her vision blurring, and blood spreading on her side from the bullet wound, all Daisy could think about was the fact that she had failed Cal. With their connection to the gang no longer a secret, Violet wouldn't be able to deceive Pearlie and Cal into giving up their life savings, but that wouldn't matter if her stepfather and the other outlaws killed them.

And Whisper McReady had not even a shred of mercy or human decency in him, Daisy was sure of that.

She was sunk so low in the pit of despair that she didn't hear the swift rataplan of hoofbeats coming closer until the riders were almost on top of her. She tried to lift her head as she realized several horses were being pulled to a halt only a few yards away. Boots thudded against the ground, and then strong yet gentle hands gripped her shoulders and eased her onto her back.

Her head rested on a denim-clad thigh, and as she blinked rapidly, her eyesight cleared enough to allow her to see the concern on the rugged face leaning over her.

"Ma'am?" the man said. "Ma'am, you look like you been shot, but you just rest easy. We'll get you to the Sugarloaf and make you comfortable while one of the fellas fetches the doctor from Big Rock—"

Daisy managed to lift her right hand and grip the man's arm, stopping the flow of words from him.

"You . . . you're from the Sugarloaf?" She forced the words from her lips.

"Yes'm, we sure are—"

She interrupted him again, saying, "Smoke . . . needs your help . . . trapped in dress shop . . . outlaws raiding town . . ."

Another man said in a loud, excited voice, "Ben, that's one of the gals who run the dress shop in town!"

"I know, that's what she just said." The man holding Daisy sounded exasperated, but he turned his attention back to her and went on, "You say outlaws have Smoke trapped in your shop, ma'am?"

"And Cal . . . and Pearlie . . . and Sally. My sister . . ."

Everything around Daisy seemed to be fading away. She could make out the figures of several more men standing around her, but they were vague, indistinct shapes that seemed to waver when she tried to focus on them.

"Don't you worry about a thing, miss. We'll help them and help you, too." The cowboy lifted his head and raised his voice. "Get the boys from the ranch and light a shuck for town! Move, you spraddle-legged toad frogs!"

Something about that made Daisy laugh. She was still laughing when darkness closed in around her completely.

Twice more the outlaws charged the front of the dress shop, but Smoke and Pearlie drove them back with fast, deadly accurate shots that drilled hearts and brains and left owlhoot corpses sprawled on the boardwalk.

During one of the lulls in the fighting, Pearlie said, "You know, if it hadn't been for all that loot stashed in them dress dummies, I'll bet those skunks would've tossed some torches in here before now to burn us out."

"No bet," Smoke said as he reloaded his Colt. "McReady doesn't want to burn up all that cash."

Pearlie turned solemn as he said, "It's hard to figure a low-down varmint like that bein' related to Violet and Daisy, even if it is just by marriage and not blood. I wonder what their ma ever saw in him."

"There's no telling about things like that."

Smoke closed the gun's cylinder. He was starting to run low on cartridges and knew that Pearlie must be, too. There was a limit to how long they could hold out. If Whisper McReady was willing to keep throwing his men against the defenders, eventually the gang would prevail.

Smoke went on, "There's an old saying about love being blind. Sometimes it's deaf and dumb, too, I think. I'm sure the woman had a good reason for marrying McReady, even if we can't grasp what it is."

Pearlie nodded slowly as his expression became even more bleak.

"Hard to believe, too, that the gals were workin' with the gang all along. I reckon they had me an' Cal fooled up one way and down the other. But both of us, we ain't been what you'd call lucky in love, so I guess we were a mite desperate for somethin' to work out for a change."

"Don't think about that now," Smoke told him. "We just need to make it through this standoff."

Both men looked up as shots came from outside, but these didn't seem to be directed at the building. They came from somewhere farther away, swift volleys back and forth that indicated a fierce gunfight.

Smoke and Pearlie looked at each other. "Monte?" Pearlie speculated.

"Or Louis," Smoke said. "Or both. That'll give McReady and the rest of his bunch something else to think about. I'm not sure Monte would have enough men to do anything more than harass them, but every outlaw they manage to gun down increases our chances that much more."

"You think Daisy made it to the ranch?"

"No way of knowing. But even if she did, there hasn't been enough time for any of the crew to get here. We're going to have to hold out for a while longer."

Pearlie nodded, checked his gun. The shooting elsewhere in Big Rock had tapered off and now ceased entirely, to be replaced by a tense, waiting silence before guns inevitably began to crash again.

"I hope you don't think I'm going to apologize."

Sally didn't quite grasp at first what Violet had just said to her. Then she looked over at the blonde and asked, "What are you talking about?"

"I'm not going to apologize for anything I've done," Violet stated. She crossed her arms over her chest and scowled defiantly. "I was just trying to make the best life I could for my sister and myself."

They were sitting on the floor behind a table turned on its side. Their backs were pressed against the wall. They were relatively safe here, but only for the moment. If Smoke and the other men weren't able to hold off the outlaws, there was no telling what would happen.

"I don't blame you for that," Sally said in response to Violet's words, "but I can find fault in the way you went about it. Those outlaws you were working with killed people, you know, and ruined others by stealing everything they had."

"Life is a hard, dangerous business. It didn't take me long to learn that once my father died and my mother was left alone with the two of us to raise. She had to work herself half to death just to keep us all alive until Whisper came along and married her."

"Everybody has hardships in their lives," Sally said. "Some

worse than others, of course. And I won't deny that some are luckier than others, too. I've been very fortunate, myself."

Violet just grunted in seeming contempt.

"But I've suffered injuries, too," Sally went on. "I was lucky to find Smoke. He's a good man, and we love each other very much. But every time he rides out from our home, I worry about whether or not he'll come back. Like you said, it's a dangerous world out there. But I've never allowed that to make me bitter or uncaring."

Violet looked away. "Spare me the lectures, Sally. Whatever happens, I suppose I have it coming, and I'll take it. There's nothing I can do to stop it, anyway."

"Did you really plan all the gang's jobs?"

"Oh, I did more than that." A cold smile curved Violet's lips. "I was going to take your precious Pearlie and Cal for every cent they own. Then Daisy and I were going to disappear, and none of you would have ever seen us again." Her voice caught a little, and for the first time, she showed some genuine emotion. "And now . . . and now I don't even know if Daisy is still alive."

"I hope she is," Sally said. "I really do."

She reached over and put a hand on Violet's shoulder. Violet didn't pull away, so Sally squeezed a little and left it there for a moment.

Then something crashed against the shop's back door.

Smoke heard the impact and whirled around. So did Pearlie. But at that same instant, something slammed against the front door, too. The chair propped under the doorknob held, but both men knew it wouldn't stand up to much force.

"They're breakin' in from both directions!" Pearlie said.

Cal, Chuck Dade, and Jasper Hendryx faced the rear door with their guns leveled.

"We'll cover this way, Smoke," Cal said tensely.

Smoke called, "Sally, you and Violet stay down!"

"I love you, Smoke!" Sally responded.

Before Smoke could say anything, the chair holding the front door closed splintered and collapsed under a second battering. The door flew open and men loomed in the opening, firing their guns as fast as they could. Powdersmoke filled the room with muzzle flashes spurting garishly through the billowing, acrid cloud.

Smoke and Pearlie returned the fire, crouched low behind the overturned table. Bullets whipped past their heads. Behind them, the back door crashed open as well, and more gunfire thundered.

But Cal, Dade, and Hendryx were standing to the sides, so the all-out attack by the outlaws backfired to a certain extent. On both sides, a few men were cut down by missed shots from their allies on the other side of the building. More were driven backward by buckshot as Hendryx's shotgun boomed. Smoke, Pearlie, Cal, and Dade kept their wits about them and aimed coolheadedly, even though they all knew that outlaw lead might smash the life out of them at any instant.

McReady's second-in-command, the man who had been beside him in the street, loomed in the front doorway, both hands filled with flame-spouting Colts. Smoke was about to trigger a shot at him when the outlaw suddenly pitched forward. The guns slipped out of his hands and skittered away. A dark bloodstain bloomed on the back of his coat.

More shots roared outside, both in front of and behind the shop. Help had arrived from somewhere, Smoke knew, either Monte, Louis, and men from Big Rock, or the crew from the Sugarloaf. Maybe both forces.

But Sally's scream warned him it might be too late.

Smoke twisted toward the side of the room where the two women were and saw jug-eared Whisper McReady trying to drag Violet over the table where she and Sally had taken cover. The back room was full of struggling figures as Cal, Dade, and Hendryx now fought hand to hand with the outlaws who had made it inside, slugging with empty guns and throwing punches.

Sally stood up, grabbed McReady's arm, and tried to drag him away from Violet. He let go with that hand and used it to backhand her, knocking her against the wall.

Fury welled up inside Smoke. He triggered a shot at McReady, but the hammer fell on an empty chamber. He surged to his feet. Someone crashed into him from behind and knocked him to his knees.

Before he could get up, McReady bulled past him, carrying a writhing, fighting Violet in his arms.

"Steal my money, will you, you witch?" he rasped at her as he lunged past the struggling men and out the rear door.

Smoke surged up and charged after him, leaving his feet in a diving tackle that caught McReady from behind. All three of them went off the small porch and fell heavily to the ground in the alley.

The hard landing jolted loose McCready's grip on Violet. She rolled over and tried to stand up. Her hair had come loose and straggled wildly in front of her face.

McReady came up on his feet and drew his gun. He lifted it toward Violet, clearly intending to kill her for daring to lay her hands on his loot.

That loot proved to be his undoing. She plucked one of the packets of money from inside her dress and flung it in his face. He batted it aside and it broke apart, showering greenbacks around him. That distracted him even more.

"Smoke!"

The cry came from the porch, where Sally had staggered out of the building. Smoke came up on one knee as Sally tossed her Smith & Wesson to him. His hand closed deftly around the gun and swung it toward McReady. Smoke and the boss outlaw pulled trigger at the same time. McReady's Colt boomed and knocked Violet backward with a strangled cry.

The bullet Smoke fired pulped McReady's left eye, bored into his brain, and killed him instantly. His knees buckled and he dropped to the ground in a limp heap.

Sally jumped off the porch and ran to Violet's side. She propped up the blonde, who had a spreading bloodstain on her right shoulder.

"Vi!" a voice croaked

Smoke whipped around toward the porch and saw Linc Pollard standing there. The wounded outlaw swayed and managed to say, "I'm sorry . . . Vi," before he fell face-first in the dirt and didn't move again. The bloodstain on his back was a lot bigger now.

Monte Carson and Louis Longmont, each holding a smoking gun, ran around the corner. Right behind them were several of the ranch hands from the Sugarloaf. Smoke knew as soon as he saw them that Daisy had made it, after all.

Whether she had survived the desperate ride was another question.

"Smoke, are you all right?" Monte asked as he and the others pounded up.

"Yeah," Smoke replied as he straightened to his feet. "I'm fine. What about the fight?"

"It's over," Monte said. "The whole gang is wiped out, unless there are a few survivors in the shop. I've got men in there now, checking on everybody else and mopping up." He looked down at McReady's body, lying face down with a pool of blood spreading around his head. "Is that the boss?"

"Yes, that's Whisper McReady."

Monte grunted. "He might've broke out of prison, but it looks like justice caught up to him, anyway."

"There's always a reckoning," Smoke said.

"And most of the time," Louis said, "when bad men cross your path, Smoke, it's a gun smoke reckoning."

Chapter 33

It was something of a miracle, but among the citizens of Big Rock, Deputy Ollie Nash was the only one killed during the epic battle against the McReady gang. A dozen or so of the townspeople were wounded, but all were expected to survive.

Four members of the gang were locked up in the jail, the only outlaws to survive the ruckus. They were the only prisoners, too. Under the circumstances, the sheriff wasn't going to lock up Pearlie, Cal, Chuck Dade, and Jasper Hendryx again.

"I reckon you boys have paid your debt to society, and plenty more to boot," he told them.

Violet and Daisy Caldwell were both recovering at Dr. Colton Spaulding's house. Their wounds were serious, but Spaulding expected both of them to recover.

"Of course once they do, they'll have to stand trial for their part in all of this," Monte said as he sat with Smoke, Sally, Pearlie, Cal, and Louis at the owner's personal table in Longmont's. "That's why I've got deputies posted there to keep an eye on them." He looked at Pearlie and Cal. "I'm sorry about that, boys, but I don't have any choice."

"Durned right you don't," Pearlie said. "It's a puredee shame, but they turned out to be crooks. They'll have to pay for their crimes."

His voice was flat, but Smoke could tell that his foreman was hurting. Pearlie had been through tragedies before, and Smoke knew he was resilient, but right now, he felt for his old friend, and for Cal, too.

"Daisy helped save everybody's bacon," Cal said. "Maybe that'll count for something."

"It ought to," Smoke said. "I don't know many folks who could have made a ride like that, wounded as badly as she was."

Monte said, "She told us where to find the gang's hideout, too, so we can recover all the loot stashed there. That might go in her favor."

"You know, when I saw that red mud on Daisy's boots and then asked Mr. Patterson about it, I should have figured it all out," Sally said. "It just didn't make sense that she would ride all the way over to the other side of the Flat Rock country without a good reason."

Smoke shook his head. "You didn't have any reason in the world to suspect them," he told her. "Nobody would have figured that out."

"Maybe not. But I wish I had. Maybe I could have talked them out of doing some of the things they did."

Sally looked at Pearlie and Cal with sympathy in her eyes.

Pearlie cleared his throat, shoved his chair back, and stood up.

"Cal and me better be gettin' back out to the ranch," he said. "It may be Sunday, but there are still chores to take care of."

"Somebody else can do them," Smoke said.

"No reason for that. Sure, me and the kid may be a mite jinxed when it comes to womenfolk, but shoot, our day'll come, won't it?"

The two cowboys left Longmont's. Smoke watched them go and

said, “Well, at least they didn’t lose their life savings. They can be thankful for that.”

“Yeah, it could have been a lot worse for them,” Monte agreed, and Louis nodded solemnly.

Sally looked around the table at them, sighed, shook her head, and said, “Men!”

TURN THE PAGE FOR AN EXCITING PREVIEW!

JOHNSTONE COUNTRY.
WHERE BULLETS
KEEP EVERYONE IN LINE.

In a land conquered by blood, sweat, and tears, two men lay down their own laws with any force necessary in this action-packed Western . . .

In Arizona territory, the prosperous town of Copper Canyon owes its existence to Stinnett's Crooked S Ranch and Alistair Duncan's copper mines. The wealth each man has amassed is beyond measure. They have divided the land's resources between them, employing most of the townsfolk as ranchers and miners. They use their power and profit to maintain control over their empires from competing business interests—and to keep the peace between them.

Alistair Duncan's mines aren't his only legacy. His children, including son Brock and daughter Fiona, will one day inherit everything he's built. Stinnett has no heirs. To ensure his ranch's future, he sets his sights on courting Fiona, and considers hiring Brock as a cowboy. But when Stinnett learns that the Duncans plan to expand their operation after discovering coal and gold in a cave, he dynamites it—unaware Alistair and his sons were inside.

Stinnett was also unaware that Brock survived. With his father and brothers dead and his grieving sister finding solace with their family's murderer, Brock loads his six-guns, hell-bent on a quest for revenge . . .

Chapter 1

Copper Canyon, Arizona Territory/Tyler Stinnett kept a tight grip on his stallion's reins as he rode beside the cattle herd. Thunder loved to run, but this was no time for speed.

Stinnett wanted to give his prize bull—Old Ed—plenty of room to roam. He stayed back while the steer led the herd to town, loping along the well-trod cow path toward town at his own pace. Old Ed had been leading Stinnett cows to market for fifteen seasons now. He knew the way as well as any human.

Market Day had long been a grand occasion for the few people who called Copper Canyon home. It was the one day of the year when they turned out in droves to see the fruits of their labor. Stinnett bringing his cows from the Crooked S Ranch through the heart of town to the railhead in Apache Creek drew a bigger crowd each year.

Some had wondered why the railroad had not built an extension to Copper Canyon. It would have saved the copper mine and the cattle ranch the trouble of traveling more than a day to Apache Creek. The two men who ran that part of the territory had refused to allow the railroad to build a station in their town. Copper Canyon was a small town and they meant to keep it that way.

The town had been established more than twenty years before with the sole purpose of serving the two main interests in the area. One was Tyler Stinnett's Crooked S Ranch. The second was Alistair Duncan's copper mine. The town was not meant to be fancy. It provided food, lodging, and supplies for both cattlemen and miners. Aside from those who came on Market Day, the town's few visitors were mostly bankers or representatives from mining and cattle concerns across the country. Except for a few dryland farmers scattered around the area, Copper Canyon was Stinnett and Duncan land. And they would do anything necessary to make sure it stayed that way. A day's trip to the railhead at Apache Creek was worth the effort.

Stinnett heard a rider approaching him from behind and knew it was Kelly. His ranch foreman would give him a report on how his men and beasts were faring through the first stage of their journey.

"Nothing much to report, boss," Kelly said in his clipped Irish brogue. "All present and accounted for and no stragglers to speak of. A few fell behind at first, but our boys got them back in line right quick."

Kelly had shown up on Stinnett's fledgling ranch fifteen years ago with a small herd of horses and a young bull calf who grew to become Old Ed. Kelly kept the ranch running while Stinnett expanded their empire. "Glad to hear it," Stinnett said. "We'll be in town in a few minutes. Warn the men to keep a sharp eye on the herd as we move through. It's still rattlesnake season in these parts. It only takes one shake of a rattle to send them running."

"I've already told them," Kelly said, "but I'll remind them. They've been using them as target practice in the pasture all week. I'll sure be glad when we move the herd back into the old pasture next year."

"The year after is my aim," Stinnett said. "I want to give the land some more time to heal. We've got enough in the other fields to keep their bellies full until then."

"You always know best, Mr. Stinnett." Kelly favored formality, even when no one else was around to hear it. Stinnett did nothing to discourage it. While he never wanted Kelly to keep anything from him, he knew familiarity bred contempt. He had seen what happened when foremen started believing they knew more than their employers. Stinnett demanded a strict hierarchy on his ranch. There was only enough room at the top for one man.

Kelly pointed up the trail. A few young children began to cheer before running back toward town. "Looks like the natives have sent out a scouting party, sir. Guess we're in for quite a welcome."

Stinnett saw it in another way. Old Ed was not as young as he used to be. The bull had grown ornery in the past couple of years. He was easier to startle and slower to react. In some ways, Stinnett knew how he felt. He would be forty-one in a few weeks' time.

He told Kelly, "Ride back and tell the boys to start tightening up. We'll be in town before we know it and there's bound to be some drunks down there hooting and hollering. Tell the boys to keep the herd tight so they don't fan out."

Kelly rode back to spread the word. Stinnett remained up front. He noticed the cows had closed the distance behind Old Ed but remained in good formation. He would cut in front of the bull when they reached the town limits and lead him through there as quickly as possible. If any old drunk staggered in the way, he would deserve whatever happened to him.

Stinnett began to hear the cheers and applause rise from town as they caught sight of Old Ed and the herd.

That was when Stinnett saw a rattlesnake coiled on the side of the trail.

The rancher reached for the Colt on his hip as the snake sprang.

It buried its fangs high on the steer's left flank before dropping away.

The bull cut loose with a yell and bolted toward town. The rest of the herd followed the bull's lead and charged closely behind him.

The trek to town had dissolved into a full-fledged stampede.

Stinnett dug his heels hard into his mount's sides as he tried to catch up to the charging bull. But Thunder bucked as the cows began to break formation. They cut him off, almost knocking Stinnett and Thunder to the ground.

Stinnett worked his way clear of the herd as Kelly and the men did their best to keep the cattle in line.

Stinnett rode away from the cows and stood up in his stirrups. He saw Old Ed careening toward town, his head down as his hooves kicked up a cloud of dust and dirt behind him. The crowd cheered, unaware that countless tons of frightened cattle were hurtling their way.

Stinnett grabbed his lasso from his saddle and dug his heels into Thunder's flanks. They raced toward town. He hoped he could catch up to Old Ed before the bull ran headlong into the first building he saw.

Thunder galloped hard along the packed dirt of Cooper Canyon. Stinnett took a shortcut around the back of The Copper Cup—the only saloon in town—in the hopes of heading off the bull and bringing him under some sort of control.

Up ahead, on the outskirts of town, he saw a large young man of about twenty or so climb on his horse and ride toward Old Ed. Stinnett called out to warn the boy, but his voice was drowned out by the loud rumble of the stampede.

He watched the boy swing his rope and lasso the bull's left horn. He pulled the charging beast forward and to the left, keeping him on the trail the cattle had always followed through town.

Stinnett was surprised the bull followed the rider. But he was not surprised when the rope slacked as Old Ed aimed his bulk at the unfamiliar horse and rider.

As he raced on, Stinnett watched in awe as the young man rode just far enough in front of the steer to keep himself and his horse from being gored by Old Ed's sharp horns. He saw his men ride beside the rest of the herd, keeping them from barreling through buildings or over unsuspecting spectators. Families cheered wildly as the cows dashed by. They were all unaware of how close they had come to disaster.

When Stinnett caught up to the strange rider, there was less slack in the rider's rope as Old Ed began to slow down considerably.

It was only then that Stinnett recognized the rider was Alistair Duncan's boy. His oldest son, Brock. He had known the lad since he was but a toddler all those years ago.

As Stinnett caught up to him, he watched Brock work his lasso off Old Ed's horn and gather the rope back to him as he rode.

"For a miner, you can rope and ride pretty good," Stinnett said to Brock as he fell in beside him at the head of the herd.

"I've seen you do it enough times." Brock beamed. "Been watching you my whole life."

Stinnett laughed. He knew Brock's father had designs on his oldest boy joining him in the family's copper mining business. "Don't let your pa hear you say that. It'd ruin his day."

Stinnett looked behind him. Kelly and his men had gotten the herd to slow down a great deal. The cattle had fallen into a slower rhythm behind Old Ed.

Brock asked him, "How many head you figure you lost just now?"

"Hopefully none," Stinnett said. "I'd best ride back and take a look for myself." He had an idea. "Want to help me?"

"You don't have to ask me twice."

Brock joined Stinnett in bringing his horse around in a wide circle. Stinnett passed by Miller, one of his men, and told him to take point behind Old Ed.

As Miller raced away, Stinnett and Brock continued riding back toward town.

Stinnett said, "That was a mighty brave thing you did just now, Brock. A lot of boys your age wouldn't have known what to do. Hell, even my own men got caught flat-footed."

Brock shrugged. "Just did what needed doing. Didn't think about it. Guess it was kind of foolish. Old Ed could've stuck us good if he'd had a mind to." Brock blushed as they rode. "What set them to running anyway?"

"A rattler jumped up and bit Old Ed. Happened in a blink of an eye. Before we knew it, we had a stampede on our hands. What you did was dangerous, but you didn't hesitate." He patted Brock on the back. The boy had grown up tall and strong. Smart, too. "That shows you've got good instincts. It's tough to teach a man instincts. It's something he either has or doesn't. You're off to a fine start in life, Brock. Your pa must be proud of you."

"He is in his way," Brock said. "You think my instincts are good enough for me to come work for you some day?"

Stinnett slowed Thunder to a walk. He wondered if the boy understood what he was asking. "Alistair's got ideas about you working his copper mine. He wouldn't think too kindly about you working anywhere else. Even for me."

Brock slowed his horse, too. "That's the problem. I'm not much of a miner. I do it, of course. I do anything Pa tells me to do. But Collum's a natural. He's got ore in his veins, just like Pa. I'd be much happier working for you. Breathing clean air. Feeling the sun on my face instead of dirt and dust."

"Plenty of dirt and dust in my line of work," Stinnett told him. "And lots of danger to go along with it. You handled yourself well just now, but there's more to working cattle than stampedes. It's a lot of long days and even longer nights, where nothing much happens until it does. And when it does, you've got to move fast, or you might get yourself killed. Or worse, get one of the men working with you killed."

But Brock's enthusiasm could not be dampened. "I know I don't even know the half of it, but I can't think of a better way to learn except by working for your outfit. Would you talk to my pa about it, Mr. Stinnett? I'd be forever grateful if you'd just think about it."

Stinnett grinned. The young were always in such a hurry to grow up. "I promise I'll think about it. I'll give you my answer when I get back from Apache Creek. That fair enough?"

"More than fair. Thank you."

Stinnett decided Market Day was as good a day as any to have a little fun. "Let's see how good you set a horse. Last one to the saloon owes the winner a dollar."

The two riders raced along the herd back toward town. It did Stinnett good to pretend to be young again.